"Help me! Michael, Kathi, help me..." screamed Molly. She saw her friends laughing. They didn't understand it wasn't a game.

"It's all right," Jared called over to them, struggling to keep his grip on Molly.

"You're trying to kill me!" she wailed, striking him. She felt the salty wind rise mysteriously, blowing fiercely now all around them. The water of the pool — so close — grew choppy, rising in great white peaks of foam.

"You'll be fine. You'll be a regular" — Jared ducked his head as another of her blows hit his ear — "fish!"

Then he held her out over the water and dropped her in.

She sank immediately, as if she had fallen from a great height. The water of the pool surged over her — and it was red, it was blood foaming around her, filling her ears and eyes and nose and mouth, engulfing her. . . .

Other Point paperbacks
you will enjoy:

Please Do Not Touch
by Judith Gorog

Hide and Seek
by Jane McFann

Wolf
by Gillian Cross

The Warnings
by Margaret Buffie

point

Dreadful Sorry

KATHRYN REISS

SCHOLASTIC INC.
New York Toronto London Auckland Sydney

ISBN 0-590-48406-0

12 11 10 9 8 7 6 5 4 3 2 1   6 7 8 9/9 0 1/0

Printed in the U.S.A.   01

First Scholastic printing, August 1996

For my sons,

Nicholas Graham
and
Daniel Geoffrey

Acknowledgments

Special thanks to Karen Grove of Harcourt Brace & Company for outstanding editorial assistance, and to Tom Strychacz for generous proofreading, several very good plot twists, and continued loving support.

Thanks also to Joseph Molnar for information about fishing boats and stories of the sea, and to Bruce Pavlik for research on native Maine grasses.

"O day and night, but this is wondrous strange."
—William Shakespeare
Hamlet, act I, scene 5

Lost . . .

I know it is impossible, but I'm floating down the hall. The emptiness echoes, the walls press close. I'm drifting along like a ghost in the dark, past closed doors on both sides. My feet skim the floor. I know I am heading for the room at the end of the hall, but why? I know someone is waiting. But who?

All around in the air there's a hum. A buzz like the menace of thousands of bees.

And out of the hum comes a man's deep rumble, right through the door at the end of the hall. I'll just stretch out my hand—reach for the knob—but wait, what's that?

A high, keening cry. And a trickle of red seeps under the door.

Then a wind rushes out, and I am cold. I must get away, must get away, but the walls press close and my legs pump air and the buzzing is a cacophony . . .

Somehow I find a staircase. I use the banister to pull my weightless self down. At the bottom of the stairs a

1

mirror shimmers in moonlight. And there's my face in the mirror, but no, not exactly mine. It is someone else, and she is smiling. There is no escape now, after all.

"Molly, breakfast is on the table!"

At the sound of her mother's voice, Molly's eyes flew open. She lay sideways in bed, sheets and pillows all askew. Her muscles were tense from trying to fight her way out of the dream.

"Look, dawdling in bed isn't going to help." Her mother tapped impatiently on Molly's bedroom door and stepped inside. "You've got to pull yourself together." Her frown changed to a look of concern as she saw Molly's face. "Are you sick? What is it?"

Molly unclenched her fists in the sheets and struggled to sit up. "Nightmare city."

"Another bad dream?" Her mother's frown was back.

"Same old, same old." But hadn't something been different this time? Molly pushed her tangled blond hair off her face and glanced at the clock. "Oh, no." She dragged herself out of bed and headed for the bathroom. "I'll be down in a sec."

She turned the cold tap on and bent over the sink. Grabbing a washcloth, she scrubbed her face hard. As usual after the dream, she felt queasy and guilty and soiled.

Then she brushed her hair, peering into the mirror. How was she supposed to go to school looking like such a wreck? She was horribly pale. Maybe some blush?

2

Then it happened. For just a second, the silvery glass seemed fluid, changed, shimmering as it did in the dream. Molly shook her head groggily.

She opened the small tube of red gel, pressed a dab onto her fingertip, and leaned toward the mirror again.

But before she could dot the blush onto her cheekbones, the mirror shimmered—*glimmered*—again, and the girl looking back was not Molly but someone quite other.

Molly froze, fingertip poised at her cheek. *This can't be happening.*

The face in the mirror gazed back with dark eyes. The hair, too, was much darker than Molly's. The cheeks redder

It must be a trick of light.

Molly squeezed her eyes shut and slapped both hands against the mirror. *Wake up, idiot!* She felt cold all over, just as she had in the dream, and it was a full minute before she dared look in the mirror again.

What she saw, of course, was her own pale face, and a thin smear of red across the silvered surface of the glass.

"Hey, you've already missed the van, you know," her mother called. "I can drive you to school if you're ready in two minutes. Are you dressed yet?"

"Almost," Molly called back. She shook her head ruefully at her reflection, reached for her washcloth, and wiped off the gel.

Molly hurried back to her bedroom and pulled on her school uniform. She twisted her long hair automatically into a single braid. She left the bed unmade.

"I've got to leave." Molly's mother climbed the stairs and handed Molly a bran muffin wrapped in a paper napkin. "You can eat in the car."

Molly held the muffin awkwardly while she stuffed her homework papers into her backpack.

Her mother headed down the stairs. "One more minute," she said over her shoulder. "This is your last chance."

Last chance? The words seem to hover on the landing even after her mother had gone.

Molly swung the backpack onto her shoulder and moved reluctantly down the stairs.

1

$\mathcal{P}$inch me so I'll wake up," moaned Molly as she twirled her combination lock and opened the metal door. "This whole week has been a nightmare." She stripped off her school uniform and pulled on the hateful West River Academy regulation swimsuit.

Kathi nodded in sympathy. "It's too bad your mom found out. But, you know, I wish you'd told me you hadn't taken the test. I'd have helped you." She grinned. "I *do* happen to know a little bit about swimming, you know!"

"That's just it. You're such a star, I couldn't tell you." Molly bundled her clothes into the locker and slammed the door. "And now I'm stuck with Coach Bascombe. Listen, can you come in with me? That way, if I start to drown, you'll be on hand to fish me out." She laughed unconvincingly. Kathi didn't know she wasn't really joking.

But Kathi shook her head. "Sorry. Don't you

remember my cousin is coming today? His school is already out for the summer. Mom's picking him up at the bus station and then coming to get me. They should be here any second."

"Oh, right." With the blow-up with her mother, all the fuss about swim lessons, and the nights broken by the dream, Molly had forgotten. And yet Kathi had been excited for weeks that her cousin was coming to town for the summer. "Maybe I can meet him this weekend," Molly told her. "If my mother lets me out of the house."

"She's pissed, huh?" Kathi's dark eyes were sympathetic. She picked up Molly's blue towel from the bench and handed it to her. "Listen, I've got to go now. I'll call you later."

Molly hesitated at the door to the pool. "Wish me luck." As Kathi turned away, Molly hugged her blue canvas backpack against her chest. Inexplicably, the long hallway from the dream flickered in her mind. *I wish this were a dream, too!* The lump of dread in her stomach was as hard as the cement bottom of the pool. Maybe she was coming down with stomach cancer.

Now *that* would make a fine medical excuse.

"Come on, don't be afraid. Just take a big breath and jump in! If you don't just *do* it, you'll never pass!"

Coach Bascombe's voice rang in Molly's ears, but Molly just stood there staring down at the blue water. Finally she scrunched her eyes shut and edged a cautious foot over the side of the pool. The water, cold and infinitely dangerous, closed over her big toe.

"That isn't good enough, Molly! Jump in! Get a move on!" Coach Bascombe's voice grew sharp. They had been standing around like this for twenty minutes already.

Molly opened her eyes and stepped quickly away from the edge of the pool, the lump of panic heavy in her stomach. "I've told you—I can't." The fear made her voice sullen.

The swim coach put her hands on her hips. "Molly Teague, I just don't know what to do with you! If you don't pass your swimming test, you won't be able to graduate with your class next year. It's as simple as that."

"I have another year before I graduate," murmured Molly. This whole mess was so embarrassing. "I can learn over the summer . . ."

"Learn now and get it over with," continued the coach, warming to her pep talk. "You don't have to be a strong swimmer, but you must jump into the water and swim from one end of the pool to the other. Breaststroke, backstroke, the crawl—any way you like. Just do it!"

Molly reached for the blue towel she had dropped by the side of the pool and draped it across her thin shoulders. She fingered a strand of hair that had escaped from her braid and bowed her head under Coach Bascombe's strident voice and reasonable words.

"For goodness sake, Molly, there's not a soul on earth who can't swim. Babies, old people, people with disabilities! And here you are, a junior at West River Academy—which just so happens to have the finest swim team in the whole state—and you've only managed to stand in water up to your thighs." The coach reached up and adjusted her cap with an exasperated snap of rubber. "You're probably the best student in the whole school—academically, that is." Her tone made it sound as if academic ability wasn't worth quite as much as athletic ability. "Think of what people will say if you don't graduate with your class."

Molly remained silent. Last night's bad dream flickered in her memory like ripples across water. The way she moved, nearly floating, down the long hallway. *Almost like swimming.* She took a deep breath and heard the coach's voice again, echoing now off the high, tiled walls.

"West River's reputation was not built by students afraid to try, Molly. Now, come on. Don't be so silly. I'll be right next to you in the water the whole time." Coach Bascombe spoke firmly. "What could possibly happen?"

"I could drown," said Molly, then bit her lip, dropping the loose strand of hair. She turned away.

"Drown?" Coach Bascombe laughed. "With me swimming right next to you? I assure you it won't happen." She glanced at the big clock on the tiled wall and sighed. "Look, we still have twenty minutes left. Your mother is paying extra for these special sessions, you know. Let's not waste her money." She pointed to the water. "In you go. And this time get more than just your legs wet."

Molly glanced at the water and saw her pale face

reflected in the blue surface. She edged toward the locker room. "I told you," she murmured. "I just *can't*."

"You mean you *won't*, Molly. That's quite different."

But Molly slipped through the swinging door and walked through the empty locker room. All the other girls had left school an hour ago. She pulled off her suit with trembling hands, avoiding her reflection in the mirrors on the wall by the showers. The last thing she needed now was to catch sight of the face from the dream. She grabbed her underwear and school uniform—the white blouse and blue cotton skirt and vest—and dressed quickly. She slung her backpack over her shoulder, expecting Coach Bascombe to appear any second to haul her back to the pool. She couldn't believe she had just walked away from a teacher.

Hurrying now, Molly bypassed the regular pool exit and slipped out the door that led into the back hallway behind the gym, passing a row of hair dryers attached to the wall. They were no use to her; not a single drop of the blue pool water had touched her hair.

She intended to keep it that way.

The corridors of West River Academy were empty, and Molly's footsteps echoed as she ran, her sandals slapping the polished wood. She kept glancing back over her shoulder to make sure Coach Bascombe was not in hot pursuit. It would be just her luck, the way things were going, to get suspended the last week of school for running away. After the uproar over the swimming test, Mrs. Higley, West River's headmistress, wouldn't be surprised at any new crime Molly committed. She remembered the headmistress's sorrowful face last Monday when she summoned Molly to her office in the middle of chemistry. Molly's mother, Jen, had come to school for the end-of-year parent-teacher conference, happy and proud at all the praise about Molly's academic performance. She was perplexed, though, when Mrs. Higley said that Molly would be graduating with honors next year—right up at the very top of her class—provided that she fulfilled the swim requirement.

Jen pointed out that Molly had passed the test a year ago. Molly had brought home a note from the headmistress herself attesting to that fact.

Then it was Mrs. Higley's turn to look puzzled, and she sent the school secretary to bring Molly to the office for a little chat. The whole chemistry class was buzzing at her summons to the headmistress. Molly Teague in trouble? It boggled their minds.

The headmistress frowned at Molly and opened the file folder of her record at West River Academy. "I never wrote your mother a note saying you had passed your swim requirement," she said. "Because, as you well know, you have refused to take the test each semester. And when your guidance counselor urged you to sign up for swimming lessons with Coach Bascombe, you signed up for debate instead."

Molly admitted that she had lied. Her mother was

furious. "I just can't understand it!" she said over and over again. "You forged a letter from the head-mistress? Why not just take the stupid test and get it over with?"

Sick with humiliation, Molly clenched her hands in the folds of her uniform skirt. It had seemed so simple, at the time, to write a quick note and get her mother off her back. She had shoved her guilt over this deception right out of her mind, along with the knowledge that someday the swim requirement would rear its ugly head again. *What a fool I am,* she thought. *A real ostrich.* She muttered, "Mom, I can't swim."

"Of course you can swim!"

"Have you ever seen me?"

"For goodness sakes! I don't know! But why not just sign up for a swim class, then?"

Molly hung her head. "I just can't." She glanced at Mrs. Higley. "I know it was wrong to forge your signature. I'm really sorry." In the pit of her stom-ach she felt the awful hollow ache of guilt and shame.

The headmistress and Molly's mother exchanged a glance. They then carried on for a half hour about honor and trust and respect. In the end they ar-ranged that Molly would take swimming lessons after school with Coach Bascombe. She would begin the very next day. The headmistress would have to think for a while about whether any further disciplinary measure would be appropriate. "We've never had a forgery here before," she said sternly. "I'm so sur-prised and ashamed at your duplicity, Molly, I hardly know what to say."

That night, Molly had had the dream. It was the same dream she'd had from time to time, as far back as she could remember. She never got used to it. Each time the horror was fresh—just as if the dream were a new nightmare she'd never encountered before. In the past there were three or four months between dreams, but since the swim lessons began she had dreamed the same dream three times in a row. And, even worse, each night the dream changed a bit. Each night she floated a little farther down the long hallway, closer to the room and whatever waited for her there.

Now Molly hurried down the long corridor of the recreation wing and turned into the lobby. She heard footsteps tapping down the corridor to her right and pushed wildly through the heavy front doors. Coach Bascombe must not catch her!

She flew out onto the wide stone steps and crashed headlong into a man standing there. She reeled backward. Strong hands grabbed her shoulders and steadied her. Her canvas backpack thudded down the steps.

"Whoa!" he said. "That was close."

Flustered, Molly stared for a second at the blur of his blue shirt, then smiled apologetically up at him. With surprise, she saw Kathi standing on the steps next to him.

"I came back to wait for your lesson to end so you and Jared could meet. I *thought* you would like Jared, but I didn't expect you'd totally *fall* for him like this!"

Molly laughed it off. "Head over heels, but you know what a klutz I am." She glanced up at the boy— not a man as she had first thought. She had been misled by his sheer bulk, but she saw now he was probably her own age. He was built like a football player, tall and stocky and solid. His hair was dark and curly like Kathi's, and his face seemed for a moment just as familiar. *Where have I seen him before?*

There was a sudden rush of wind and, oddly, a smell of salt, as if an ocean breeze had somehow traveled far inland, wafting across the Ohio valley. "Hob . . ." She breathed the name softly, holding out her hand to him.

Kathi snorted. "Not *Bob!* I told you, it's *Jared.*" And as the boy reached out and clasped Molly's outstretched hand, Kathi laughed. "You need formal introductions or something? Okay. Molly, this is my cousin Jared Bernstein, from Columbus. Jared, this vision of grace is the best friend I was telling you about, Molly Teague."

Molly removed her hand from his. *What is wrong with me?* Her blue eyes met his brown ones, and her stomach felt hollow. "I'm so sorry," she whispered.

The salt wind receded. Kathi stared at her, incredulous. There was an uncomfortable silence. Then Jared reached down and picked up Molly's backpack. "Here you go."

"Thanks." Molly stood there awkwardly. She slung the pack over her shoulder. "Sorry—I mean, I was just in a hurry." The inexplicable guilty, hollow shame—the same feeling in the pit of her stomach that she'd felt in the headmistress's office—was

13

gone, and now she felt like a complete idiot. *I could die! Wasn't plowing into him bad enough? Do I have to sound like an idiot, too?*

Kathi began chattering about her weekend plans. "I want Jared to meet everybody," she said, "but he'll have to wait till later because our whole family's going to Lake Pymatuning for the weekend. But when we get back, I'm going to have a party. And now that the seniors have had their exams, they'll be giving graduation parties, too. Jared's probably going to be here the whole summer, isn't that great? His parents are archaeologists, and they've gone to Israel for a summer dig. Jared wanted to get a summer job instead. So he'll be with us."

Having regained her composure, Molly gave Jared her most dazzling smile. "I don't know—it seems Israel would be a lot more exciting than Battleboro Heights! What are they digging for?"

"Oh, ancient city foundations. Fragments of broken pots. Old shoes—you name it!" He pushed his dark hair off his forehead and grinned at her. "I've already been there and back again more summers than I can count. So I begged off for this summer. My mom and dad have dragged me around the world with them so many times, I have permanent jet lag."

Molly made her voice casual. "Have you visited Kathi before? I'm *sure* I've met you."

"Now there's a line!" teased Kathi. "I bet you say that to all the guys."

Oddly flustered again, Molly stared down at Jared's feet in large, dirty basketball high-tops. Why was she being such a jerk around this guy? Chalk it up to the overall bad week she'd been having. Well, at least it was Friday.

"Listen, I've got to get home." Now she was eager to be away. "I'll see you guys when you get back from Lake Pymatuning. Bye, Kathi. Bye, Hob."

Oh, God, I've done it again! "I mean Jared." Face flaming, Molly flapped a hand at them and took off at a run across the lawn in front of the school. She could feel Jared's eyes watching her. She didn't slow down till she reached Mill Road, then walked with her long-legged lope down the big hill to Route 21.

Molly didn't notice her mother's red sports car until her mother tooted the horn and pulled up to the curb. Molly looked up, startled. Her pale cheeks flushed as she approached the car.

"I left the office early today," Jen told her daughter in greeting. "So I thought I'd wait at the school till your swim lesson ended and give you a lift. But you're early today, too."

"Coach Bascombe let me out early." The lie slipped out effortlessly. Molly slid into the front seat and snapped her seatbelt. She glanced nervously at Jen, who was dressed immaculately in cool beige linen, her blond hair, just the color of Molly's own, moussed into careful disarray. Jen always looked radiant. "I think Coach Bascombe had a dentist appointment," Molly improvised, then felt a flash of anger at herself for lying. *Why can't I just tell Mom the truth? I'm never going to swim, and that's that.*

Molly's mother was a partner in a downtown law

firm. She was very successful and enjoyed both her high-powered job and the fact that she was one of very few women in her firm who had risen so fast and so far. She used her maiden name, Deming, and was pleased that her secretary was a man. Her hours were usually long, and she brought casework home every night. She often left the house early in the morning, even before Molly finished breakfast, and returned around six in the evening. It was Molly's job to get their dinner started. The two of them would chat over dinner and then do the dishes together.

Molly wedged one foot at the side of the dashboard and glanced over at her mother. "So how come you left early today?"

"I'm going to dinner with a new lawyer at the firm. So I just told my secretary to divert all my calls and decided I'd come home early to get ready."

"Must be a very important new lawyer. Is it a man?"

"Yes." Jen kept her eyes on the road.

Molly looked at her mother and tried to smile naturally. "Rich and handsome?"

Jen raised an eyebrow. "This is strictly a business dinner." Then she glanced over at Molly and grinned. "I know you. You're wondering when I'll run off with Mr. Right, aren't you? Well, I promise I'll let you know when I find him." The grin turned into a smirk. "But don't you think one puppy-dog-eyed parent-in-love at a time is enough?"

Molly ignored this reference to her recently remarried father. Her mother was always laughing at her father.

Jen stopped the car at a light. "So? How was it today?"

"What?" *I made a fool of myself, that's how it was. And not just at the pool.*

"Your lesson, of course. How did it go?"

"Fine, I guess." *Where could I have seen Kathi's cousin before?*

Jen accelerated smoothly. "You got in the water, I hope?"

"Of course, Mom." *He must think I'm a total dork. Why did I call him that bizarre name?*

"Did you even get your hair wet?"

Molly frowned at her mother. "Of course! I even dried my hair afterward, just like a good sensible girl."

"All right." Jen turned off Route 21 and drove around the bend onto Valley. "I'm glad there's some progress. Really, I wish you'd told me years ago that you couldn't swim. I would have sworn you could. I mean, we never went swimming together, but I just assumed . . . Well, we've been all through that. What really gets me is the lie. Forgery, Molly! Really! And you with a mother in criminal law." She pulled the car into their driveway and cut the engine. "If you're worried about something, I wish you'd talk to me about it. That's the way people solve their problems in this world. By talking things over and formulating solutions."

"You make everything into a business meeting." Immediately Molly regretted her sharp tone. Her mother was only trying to help.

"Business meetings get things done," said Jen. "And I think it would be ridiculous if you weren't

17

able to graduate with your class this time next year."
She shook her blond head and fished in her purse for
the house key. "The smartest girl in the school!"

Molly slipped out of the car and followed her
mother slowly up the walk. "The policy stinks, Mom.
Joe Rabinski doesn't have to take the test."

"Well, it's different with him. He has a medical
excuse. Joe's knee is still in a cast after the car accident. You, on the other hand, don't have a valid reason at all." Jen glanced at Molly as she opened the
door. "Hey, are you all right? You look so . . .
shaky."

Molly hugged her backpack to her chest and
pushed past her mother. "I'm fine."

"Well, never mind," Jen said comfortingly.
"Everything's working out all right now. You'll be
swimming in no time. I asked everyone—and they
tell me Coach Bascombe's the best teacher around."
She kicked off her pumps and moved toward the
kitchen. "I have to leave at seven, but I'll cook tonight—something just for you."

Molly escaped to her room and lay on the bed.
She could hear classical music blasting from the
kitchen as Jen began preparing the meal. Jen played
Beethoven and Tchaikovsky at top volume whenever she cooked or did housework. "It takes me beyond the mundane," she'd explained once when
Molly yelled for her to turn the music down.

Now Molly burrowed her head into her pillow.
Thank God it was Friday. No swim lesson tomorrow. Maybe she'd see Michael—go to a film or

something Saturday night, if her mother let her go. She needed to do something fun.

I need to feel Hob's arms around me again . . .

She sat up abruptly. Across the room on her desk lay the most recent letter from her father, still unanswered. *Maybe I should just go to Maine after all.*

The month she spent with her father each summer since the divorce was always peaceful. But this year would probably be different. Her father had remarried on Valentine's Day, after what he'd referred to (none too originally, her mother pointed out) as a "whirlwind courtship." Molly had almost decided to write and tell him she couldn't come; maybe this was the year to get a summer job and stay in Battleboro Heights. Things could never be the same with a stepmother around.

"You'll just love Paulette," Bill Teague had written in his most recent letter. "She's fifteen years younger than me—and only ten years older than you, Molly. You'll be just like sisters—talking about everything." And then Paulette herself had added a little message to the letter, writing that she was sure they'd be on the same wavelength and would enjoy their time together in the summer, exploring each other's worlds. Her handwriting was round and childish, and Molly could just imagine her voice—all breathless and giggly and California-mellow. When she'd shown Jen the letter, her mother rolled her eyes.

"She and your dad are perfectly suited."

The phone on her bedside table jangled now, but even as she rolled over to answer it, the ringing stopped. Downstairs, Beethoven sank to a hum. Molly was surprised Jen could hear the phone over her music. She went to her desk and read over the results of a chemistry experiment. Then she sat at her word processor and typed up the notes effortlessly, enjoying the click of the keys under her long, competent fingers. While working, at least, she could keep her mind off things.

She never had problems with schoolwork, and she loved burying herself in academic projects. Molly's science project—charting genetic tendencies in frog reproduction—had won first place in the state science fair that year. And her research paper for history on ancient maps and the development of cartography had won a state award for excellence. Her teachers praised her for never being afraid of hard work. She glanced up with satisfaction at the prize certificates mounted above her desk, her fingers flying over the keyboard.

Then she heard footsteps running up the stairs. There was a perfunctory tap on the door before Jen threw it open. She stood there, hands on her hips. "You *lied* to me, Molly! *Again!*"

"What do you mean?" But of course she knew.

"That was Coach Bascombe on the phone." Jen came into the room and sank onto Molly's bed. "She said you have refused all week to do anything more than get your feet wet."

"That isn't true—I've gone in up to my thighs." Molly's stomach contracted at the memory.

"Your thighs!" Jen's face was flushed. "And to-day you walked out twenty minutes early. She didn't have a dentist appointment at all."

Molly looked at her chemistry notebook. "That's true," she murmured.

"What's going on? I don't understand this pre-posterous behavior. It isn't like you, Molly."

Molly took a deep breath. She knew this would happen sooner or later. "I *did* get in at the shallow end, but that's all I've been able to manage." She shrugged, glancing up at Jen. "Look, I'm sorry."

"You should be ashamed of such silliness. It's in-fantile. You can't keep on this way."

Molly covered her face with her hands. "I *can't!*" She had to take a stand this time. "You and Coach Bascombe and Mrs. Higley don't understand. You can't make me! I can't even make myself!" Molly dropped her head so her mother wouldn't see she was trying not to cry.

Jen frowned. "Now look, pull yourself together. Stop acting like some hysterical child. I had no idea you had become this—weak."

"I haven't *become* anything, Mom. I've always been this weak. I've always been scared of water. It just hasn't been a big deal. I mean, how often have we gone near water? Not being able to swim never bothered me before, and it wouldn't bother me now if the school would just drop its stupid requirement and you would get off my case."

"But you *do* have to swim," Jen said succinctly. "Or you won't graduate next year. And I won't have that! West River Academy is the best school around.

21

Your father and I have spent a lot to send you there all these years. And you've done superbly. I'm very proud of you, honey. Don't wreck it all over a stupid swimming test."

Molly's cheeks were wet. There was a humming in her ears. "Look," she said very quietly, "I just have this feeling that I'll die if I go into the water. I know I will."

Jen sighed. "A *feeling?* Oh, Molly, I don't understand this melodrama. It's just plain weird. And it's not productive. There's nothing that ever happened to make you afraid. You never fell into a pool or got water up your nose—nothing to account for this overreaction. Nothing at all."

"I know, I know." Molly couldn't explain the dread in her gut, the certainty that while other human beings floated in water, she alone would sink. "But it's no use."

"What's with this defeatist attitude? There's no such word as 'can't'!" This was the successful lawyer speaking now. "Of course you'll do it. I'll help you. Classes end next week, and if you haven't managed to swim across that pool by then, we'll sign you up for lessons at the recreation center. Okay? We'll make it our summer project."

"Mom, I've got a better plan. I can transfer to the public high school for my senior year. They don't have a requirement about swimming—"

"Molly Teague, you haven't gone to West River Academy all these years just to end up with a diploma from Battleboro Heights High!"

"Snob!"

"Molly!"

Molly was really crying now. They never fought like this, and it felt terrible. "I'm sorry, Mom, but it seems to me you care more about the prestigious name of the school I graduate from than what it'll cost me to get in that pool!"

"And it seems to me, young lady, that you are being self-indulgent and cowardly. Not to mention willing to throw away the education your father and I have worked hard to give you, just because you don't like to get your feet wet."

When Jen called her "young lady," things were bad indeed. "I wouldn't be throwing away the education," Molly whispered. "Just the ritzy name of the school on my diploma."

Jen brushed her hair out of her eyes and glanced at her wristwatch. "Look, enough of this. Your dinner will be ready in a minute, and I've got to get going." She stood up. "Come on down to eat."

Molly bit her lip. She took a deep breath and forced the usual calm to come back over her. The tuneless humming in her ears faded away. She was in control again. "Okay, Mom," she said stoically.

Jen stepped into the hall, then turned back. "But Molly?"

"What?"

"No more lies. I don't like you hiding things from me. I want you back to normal."

Molly flopped onto her bed and lay back on the pillows, feeling battered. But as soon as she closed her eyes, Jared Bernstein's face swam before her, his puzzled brown eyes under dark brows watching her. She sat up abruptly, covering her ears to stop the sudden humming.

Back to normal? But how?

2

On Saturday morning when Molly woke up and went down to breakfast, the breeze through the open kitchen windows was already heavily scented with the rosemary from their little garden. The day would be hot.

Jen was standing by the stove flipping pancakes. "Muggy, isn't it?" she greeted Molly, setting a glass of orange juice next to Molly's plate. "How did you sleep, sweetheart?"

Molly groaned. Her night had been broken again by the dream. She had struggled awake at four-thirty, then forced herself to lie awake till dawn. She didn't trust sleep.

Jen frowned, spatula in hand. "Poor baby."

Poor impractical, fanciful baby. That's what she means. Molly hastened to change the subject. "How was your date—I mean, your business meeting—last night?" She had gone to bed long before her mother returned.

Jen brightened. "Imagine two lawyers at a business dinner actually having fun! His name is Ben. It's going to be nice to have somebody working with me who isn't one of the old guard."

"Jen and Ben. Pretty cute," teased Molly. "Sounds like you were made for each other."

"Like father, like daughter," moaned Jen, sitting down across the table from Molly. "Just try to keep such goopy thoughts to yourself. I'm trying to eat."

Molly dribbled syrup over her pancakes, then picked up her fork. *Well,* she decided, *it's nice that one of us is happy.* Her head was aching from lack of sleep. The dream this last time had been even worse than the others. Same house, same long hall, same sense that something awful waited in the room at the end—but this time the awful humming became clearer. It was as if someone hidden out of sight were tuning up to sing that old folk song about the miner, forty-niner, and his daughter. No words, just humming, but Molly couldn't get the tune out of her mind all night. And even now, at the breakfast table, the words were running through her head: *"Oh my darlin', oh my darlin', oh my darlin', Clementine—"*

The telephone rang. Jen answered it, then handed the receiver across the table to Molly. It was Michael, calling to see if Molly would come to a party at his house that night.

"It's a pre-graduation blast," he said. "To celebrate my last week as a high school senior. It's going to be really excellent."

Molly had known Michael since she was in kindergarten. He and the other first graders had taken the new children under their wings and showed them around West River Academy. Michael had saved a place for her on the best apple tree at lunchtime, and they had been buddies ever since. In high school they saw each other often because they were both on the student council and on the school's award-winning debate team. Michael had been so crushed this past November after his longtime girlfriend, Libby, moved to Colorado, that Molly had tried to cheer him up by asking him out to see movies or to share a pizza. And he had asked her to the Winter Festival Dance at school. They'd even gone to the prom together. But Molly had to smile whenever she heard people call Michael her boyfriend. They both knew they were really just old pals. She had never been in love with any of the guys she went out with, but Michael was fine company. His party would be the perfect way to forget the past week's horrors, especially since Kathi would be busy at Lake Pymatuning with her family. Molly didn't think she could handle having to shine socially around Jared Bernstein. Who knew what idiotic things she might do?

"I'd love to come cheer you seniors out of town," Molly told Michael. "But wait a sec while I ask. I'm in disgrace around here—as you may have heard."

"As the whole school has heard," he said cheerfully. "It's the latest gossip. Even the lowliest freshman knows the story: Molly Teague hauled to the office! Molly Teague forced to stay after school all week to be tortured by Beast Bascombe! Molly Teague can't swim as far as you can throw her!"

"Need a job after graduation?" she asked drily.

"Try writing headlines for the *National Enquirer*." She covered the receiver and raised her brows at Jen. "Mom? Michael's having a party at his house tonight and—"

"Go ahead," nodded Jen. "I'm going to be gone myself tonight, as it turns out."

"On business?" Molly asked. Jen took a careful sip of coffee. "Is it Business with Ben? Ben Business in Battleboro Heights?"

"You should write for the *National Enquirer* yourself," Jen said and took her plate to the sink.

Molly hesitated a moment to push down her unease before stepping into the pounding shower and pulling the curtain shut. She had always avoided baths, but lately showers brought on the same sense of danger. Being forced to take swimming lessons was making her water phobia worse. Now even the thought of raindrops on her head made her nervous. She lathered her hair and scrubbed the fragrant suds into thick white foam, then rinsed quickly and turned off the shower in great relief. She hesitated before inspecting her face in the mirror over the sink. Was her hair getting darker? And her eyes? She blinked, and the reflection seemed to correct itself.

She was pleased now, with a closer look, to see her pale face just as sensible and normal as Jen could want. Molly vowed she would become strong. She would be in control again. Enough of these vague feelings of unease, this stupid water phobia, and the childish bad dream. She rubbed some moisturizer into her skin, then toweled her hair dry and combed it out. She carefully pulled it back into a sensible braid down her back.

But as she turned away, it happened again: the mirror flickered—glimmered—like the surface of water. For a second the other face looked back, and Molly ran, gasping, down the hall to her room.

She threw open the closet, pulling her favorite blue-and-lavender flowered sundress off the hanger. *Calm down. Don't be silly. It was nothing.* She reminded herself of her vow to be strong. Minutes after dressing, though, she felt wilted and turned up the air conditioner. The June days were already so humid that even by nightfall the mugginess remained. July would be worse, August the worst of all. Her father had told her that the nights were cool and breezy on the Maine coast. Maine was sounding better all the time.

She drove Jen's little red sports car to Michael's house and parked in the street.

Michael met her at the door and led her into the living room to say hello to his parents, then out to the back garden, where the party was in full swing. The patio was illuminated by flickering lanterns strung above the grass on a clothesline. Music thumped loudly from Michael's sound system. Some people were dancing on the brick patio, some were clustered by the picnic table, and others were lingering in pockets of darkness by the bushes. Michael's two little sisters hung over the bowls of chips, stuffing themselves. The oval swimming pool, lit softly from beneath the water, glowed in the dusk like a topaz.

Molly stood for a moment, surveying the scene,

then took a deep breath and felt her lungs expand with the evening air that was scented by flowers growing along the fence. She spied some kids from the drama club and crossed through the chattering flock of her classmates on the patio to reach them, with Michael following. "Hi, you guys!"

"Molly, are you and Michael coming to the graduation play?" Tina was playing Nancy in West River's production of *Oliver!* next weekend.

"I wouldn't miss it for anything," Molly answered. "It's my vicarious thrill, you know, listening to you sing. I wish *I* could."

Laura, who was the stage manager, shook back her dozens of black braids tied with little silver beads. "Must be the only thing you *can't* do, then, in that case. You're brilliant. I get *my* thrills watching you take on Mr. Marec in psychology!"

Derek chuckled. He had a naturally unpleasant laugh, which Molly felt made him perfectly suited for the part of Bill Sykes in the musical. "Singing's not the *only* thing Moll can't do, or so I hear." He leaned toward her and put a hand on her bare arm. "How're the swim lessons going with old Bascombe, Moll?"

"Oh shut up, Derek," said Michael easily. "I've seen you in swim class struggling to keep your own head above water."

"Yeah, but at least I haven't resorted to forgery to cover it up," he retorted.

There was a moment of silence, broken by laughter from the other side of the patio.

"Want some munchies?" asked Laura, gesturing toward the table. "I'll load you up a plate."

"Thanks. I'll get something myself," Molly told her and filled a plate with potato chips and dip. She pushed past Derek to mingle with her schoolmates on the patio, congratulating the seniors on having only another week to go, commiserating with the members of her own class about the year they still had left. People started dancing fast. She danced with Michael, with Laura's boyfriend, Peter, with Tina's date, Sean—even with Derek.

"Hey, Moll, I didn't mean anything, really," Derek said during a slow song. "It's just the novelty of seeing a top student in trouble that fascinates me. Makes you more human."

"They don't come any more human than me," Molly bantered, but she moved slightly away from his close embrace and scanned the crowd for Michael.

Instead, she saw Kathi waving from the double doors of the house. "Hey, Molly!"

Kathi? Here? What happened to Lake Pymatuning? Molly's heart beat faster as Jared stepped in front of Kathi. She felt her face flush and lowered her head onto Derek's shoulder.

"I like that," he breathed into her hair. He hummed along with the music until the song ended and she broke away. "Hey, Moll! Let me get you something to drink."

Derek followed her over to the tubs full of ice and soft drinks. They stood together at the edge of the patio, sipping Cokes. Molly watched Kathi making the rounds, introducing her cousin to all her school friends. The pulsing music thudded around her, and the crowd on the patio swelled as more people arrived and were drawn outside by the music. Dozens of bodies leapt in the lamplight now, shrieking and laughing and calling out the words to the songs. And she just stood there, sipping her drink, shivering despite the warmth of the summer night. She saw Jared turn from a group of kids by the pool, laughing, and she felt horribly hollow. But what had she ever done to Jared Bernstein?

Molly moved closer to Derek and finished her soda. She breathed deeply to reclaim the control she'd vowed to keep. But then suddenly Jared was in front of her, his dark hair springing around his face as he was jostled by some of the dancers. "Want to dance?"

His brown eyes were level with her own, smiling at her. His voice was deep, deeper than Michael's or Derek's. It sounded somehow so familiar to her.

"Nah," Derek answered for her. "Moll hates to dance. She'd rather go swimming. Right, Moll?"

"Wrong," she said, frowning at him. She glanced up at Jared. "Just ignore whatever Mr. Sykes here tells you. He's nothing but a thug and a murderer."

Jared raised his brows, and Derek, with his evil chuckle, explained about the play. Then Molly and Jared left Derek and moved onto the patio for a slow dance.

"I thought you were going to be away this

weekend," said Molly as they pushed through the dancers to a clear space.

Jared explained that his uncle, Kathi's father, had unexpected work come up at his office. The trip to Lake Pymatuning was off until next weekend. "I don't mind, though. It's nice to meet Kathi's friends." One hand holding hers, the other firm against her bare upper back, he spun her around. His palm was warm, and she could feel the pressure of all five fingers against her skin. Inexplicably, the wave of sadness assailed her again.

"I'm *sorry!*" she murmured.

"What for?" he said. "You didn't step on my feet or anything."

"Oh, I thought I had," she covered her slip quickly. "You're really good at this. I mean, not like the other guys, just stepping back and forth." She looked down. "You actually move your feet. Have you taken lessons?"

Where have I seen him before?

"I've had lessons in everything I think it was my parents' way of keeping me busy while they were in the field on digs. I took ballroom dancing lessons in Germany one summer while they were exploring Roman ruins. I've had piano lessons and karate lessons and even, don't laugh, basket-weaving lessons. That was in Brazil. And I had swimming lessons every summer until I got good enough to give lessons myself. In fact, that's what I do to earn money now—teach kids to swim. I'm on the swim team at my school, too."

"You and Kathi," Molly said. "It must run in the family."

"We're both fish," he agreed.

He tightened his arms around her, and she rested her head on his shoulder, which felt solid and strong beneath the fabric of his shirt. All that swimming. She raised her head when the song ended and smiled at him. He smiled back, his lips full, his teeth white and even.

An old Beatles song started, and they danced together again. She turned her head and rested her ear against his chest. She could hear his heart thudding steadily and felt relieved and comforted by the sound. Jared began humming against her hair. She closed her eyes, breathing in the scented evening air, feeling more peaceful than she'd felt all week. But then, after a moment, she realized he was humming a different tune. Huskily, he gave it words, his breath puffing gently against her ear: *"Oh my darlin', oh my darlin', oh my darlin', Clementine—"*

She pulled away from him. "Don't sing that!" she cried and backed into another dancing couple.

Jared reached out and grabbed her arm. "What's wrong?"

She couldn't look at him. "It's pretty late." She felt raw. The darkening evening pressed around her like the gloom of the hallway in her dream.

Jared looked at her quizzically. "Will you turn into a pumpkin? Or what?" He followed her off the patio onto the lawn. "Please don't go. Did I do something? Whatever it was, I'm really sorry."

"That song you were humming—" She fought

34

back the panic and looked up at him. "I heard it in my dream last night. It was awful—a nightmare." She swallowed. "I'm being a jerk, I know."

He was frowning. "That *is* weird. I mean, I don't know why I sang it. It just came into my head." He tried to make a joke. "I know my voice isn't great, but it never sent anyone running in terror before!"

Before Molly could respond, Kathi called to them. "Hey, Molly and Jared, come on over here!" She had changed into her bathing suit and was standing by the pool with some of the other kids.

"You go ahead," said Molly.

"I don't want you to leave." His dark eyes looked into her blue ones. "Please don't leave yet. Let's just go see what she wants. Then we can dance again—and I promise I won't sing."

"I didn't bring a suit, anyway. I don't like to swim. I guess Kathi told you?"

"She just said you got in trouble for not taking a swim test or something."

"Something."

He reached for her hand and led her across the lawn. "You mean you really can't swim at all? I could teach you easily, you know. We could start tonight." He pointed at the swimming pool.

"No thanks." *No way!*

"This water's heated, so it'll probably be nicer than your school pool. At my school, I mean, the water's always freezing."

The hollow guilt formed in her stomach again. "I'm so sorry," she told him.

He looked at her, puzzled.

"I mean, I'm sorry—sorry that you don't like cold water." The more she tried to make sense, the more idiotic she sounded. *What? Sorry about what?*

Kathi laughed. "No water could be warm enough to tempt Molly!" She nudged Molly.

Molly averted her eyes from Kathi's sparkling ones. Wasn't it enough that Kathi could swim like a dolphin? Did she have to tease her in front of Jared?

Kids were leaping into the water, splashing each other and shrieking. Some of them had brought bathing suits, but others were stripped down to their underwear. One bold girl was trying to get people to skinny-dip. The music from the patio pounded across the grass to the pool.

Jared squeezed Molly's hand. "Look, we'll start easy." He tugged her over to the side of the pool. "First thing we do is, we sit here at the side of the pool—like this."

She shook his hand off hers. "Listen, you don't understand—"

"Come on, just stick your feet in. You don't have to get your dress wet."

She bit her lip, then kicked off her sandals and sat down cautiously, bunching the skirt of her sundress up around her thighs. The warm water closed around her long legs. The sight of them, pale beneath the surface of the water, made her shiver.

"Great! Okay, now just dip your hand in the water. Just one hand. Like this." He stuck his fingers in the water and wiggled them. "See?"

She kept her arms folded stubbornly. Enough was enough.

"We'll have you off the high dive in no time," teased Jared. Or maybe he wasn't teasing.

She felt ridiculous sitting fully clothed at the side of the pool while this boy cheered her on and Kathi watched with an expression of encouragement. The other kids were still clowning around in the deep end, not taking any notice of them.

Jared's voice grew soft, deeper. "Come on, now both hands in. Like this."

She dropped her hands into the water next to his, waved her fingers around under the surface. And under her own surface, the ever-present lump of fear expanded.

"Now down to the elbows." His face was impassive. She leaned forward slightly and lowered her arms. "Good job," he said.

"Way to go, Moll," shouted Derek from the diving board. He held his nose and danced at the end of the board. Michael stepped up behind him and shoved. Derek plunged out of sight, then came up sputtering and laughing. He swam to the shallow end and stood. "See?" he appealed to Molly. "Easy as pie." Then he splashed away to chase one of the girls.

Molly pulled her arms from the water. She held them, dripping, away from her sides. "There. Lesson's over."

Jared crouched beside her. "Hang on a sec." She was very aware of his bulk, his strength. "Listen, I know you're afraid," he whispered. "Lots of kids are at first; you'd be surprised. But I really want to help you."

"I don't think so." She stood, narrowing her eyes as she saw Jared and Kathi exchange a look. The smell of chlorine was very strong. She moved her shoulders up and down and rubbed the tight muscles at the back of her neck.

"How am I going to teach you anything if you won't even get into the water?"

"I admit it's a problem." She smiled, though her heart was pounding. She tried for a joke. "Thousands before you have tried and failed."

He stripped off his shirt and jumped into the pool in his shorts. The water slapped out onto the tiles. Molly shuddered.

"Jump in. You can do it."

"No." Why didn't she just walk away? There was a charge in the air that had only partly to do with her fear. Something about Jared drew her, but something equally strong now warned her away.

He was standing in the water at the four-foot marker, his hair curling wetly over his forehead, his eyes somber. She was at the side of the pool only a foot away from him, her arms folded tightly across her chest.

He splashed some water onto her feet. "Last chance." When she didn't respond, he began the song again. He sang softly, gently, splashing water onto her feet in time to the tune: *"Oh my darlin', Oh my darlin', Oh my darlin', Clementine. You are lost and gone forever, Dreadful sorry, Clementine!"*

She leapt back and screamed at him: "You shut up!"

He vaulted out of the pool in a single motion and towered over her. "Get in the pool," he said in a low voice.

"Way to go!" shouted Derek from the deep end.

"Hooray for Molly!" called someone else. "It's swim time!"

Molly turned to run, but he caught her by the shoulders. His eyes were black pools. "Get in, or I'll throw you in."

"Go to hell."

Then his arms were lifting her—one around her shoulders, one under her knees. He carried her without effort. She screamed and beat him with her fists. He flinched at the blows but stepped closer to the pool's edge.

"Help me! Michael, Kathi, help me! Help!" screamed Molly. She saw her friends laughing. They didn't understand it wasn't a game.

"It's all right," Jared called over to them, struggling to keep his grip on Molly.

"You're trying to kill me!" she wailed, striking him. She felt the salty wind rise mysteriously, blowing fiercely now all around them. The water of the pool—so close—grew choppy, rising in great white peaks of foam.

"You'll be fine. You'll be a regular"—Jared ducked his head as another of her blows hit his ear—"fish!"

Then he held her out over the water and dropped her in.

She sank immediately, as if she had fallen from a great height. The water of the pool surged over her—and it was red, it was blood, it was blood foaming around her, filling her ears and eyes and nose and mouth, engulfing her.

She lay on the bottom of the pool, her ears roaring with the pressure of the water; her eyes were wide open, seeing not the blue-and-white tiles of the pool's floor but, through the dark water, tangles of green. Seaweed in Michael's pool?

Molly breathed deeply and her lungs filled. Just before all the red went black, she looked up at the surface and saw lengths of broken wood and webs of net; she saw crates tumbling in the waves; she saw something like a round, patterned box, floating away.

3

Somehow she knew it was a hatbox. It was floating away and she wanted it back. It contained not a hat but something precious. She reached out desperately, but her fingers grasped cloth rather than water. Molly was spinning, first in water, then in space. Whirling and spinning, whirling and spinning, then settling, coming to rest.

The blood and water stopped roaring in her ears. And at first everything was very quiet.

Then Molly heard her father's voice. "Molly? Darling?"

And then the horrible song began in her head:

> *Oh my darlin',*
> *Oh my darlin',*
> *Oh my darlin', Clementine.*
> *You are lost and gone forever,*
> *Dreadful sorry, Clementine—*

Her mother's voice broke through: "Molly? Wake up, dear. It's okay. You're okay now."

And she opened her eyes. It was hard to see her parents through all the water. Her parents—together? Something must have happened. She blinked, and her vision cleared. "Mom?"

"Yes, I'm right here." Molly felt a gentle pressure on her arm.

"And Dad, too?"

"I flew down as soon as your mom called me last night," her father said. She felt his big hand on her head, stroking her hair. "You've been going in and out of consciousness all day. We've been so worried."

"What happened to me?" But even as she asked, she remembered everything. Coach Bascombe and the swim lessons. The nightmare about the house. Jared Bernstein and the water flowing in her lungs. She moaned.

"Shhh," murmured her father. "It's okay now. You're safe in the hospital, and everything is okay." He reached for the button by her bed to call the nurse. "But I think we'd better have the doctor back in here to check you."

"But I'm fine! I mean, I'm fine—" Molly thrashed on the bed.

"Pull yourself together." Jen touched Molly's hair again. "Everything is all right."

"I drowned—"

"You *nearly* drowned." Her father's voice was tight.

"He threw me in—"

"Kathi told us, Molly. She and her cousin saved your life."

"Mom"—Molly turned her head on the pillow to look at Jen—"the kids wouldn't help! They thought it was funny. They let Jared throw me in. I *said* I couldn't . . . I told them *no,* but they—"

"Shhh," said Jen. "I know, I know."

"I hate Jared!"

"I can believe it," her father growled. "What kind of friends are they who would let some strange guy come to a party and nearly kill a girl?"

"Oh, Bill, no one knew Molly would react so badly. I remember telling Coach Bascombe myself that all Molly needed was to get into the water. I said if she could just get in once, she'd be over her fear. Kathi's cousin is a swim instructor, Bill. No doubt he thought the same thing." Jen faltered under his glare. "Well, it seems *logical,* Bill."

"Well, you were wrong, weren't you?" he snapped. "Both of you."

Molly was lying very still now under the white sheet. Her head ached behind her temples, and her mouth had a horrible, bitter taste, fuzzy at the back of her throat. Her father had said she'd been unconscious, but she knew she had been dreaming about the house. She was wandering through the hallways, opening doors, and someone was humming that hideous Clementine song. Suddenly there was a girl walking along beside her, a girl with hair in two dark braids wound up on top of her head like a coronet.

She wore a long gray skirt that swirled just above her ankles as they walked together toward the room at the end of the hall. Her cheeks were flushed, her dark eyes wild. She raised her hands, palms up, as if to show Molly—what? In the dream, Molly shook her head, not understanding.

But then the girl's hands were suddenly stained with blood, and she was crying, crying for someone to help—and Molly broke away and ran back the way she had come, her legs pumping in slow motion, as if trying to tread water.

Now here she was, safe in the hospital. The girl and the house were only part of the nightmare. And she had not drowned, after all.

"I'm so glad you're safe." Jen reached for Molly's hand where it lay limply on the white sheet.

"Yes. Thank God," echoed Bill. It seemed that about this, at least, her parents were in complete agreement.

Then Bill smiled and stroked Molly's cheek. "Well, honey, you'll be happy about one thing, at least. You've got your medical excuse."

Molly's voice came out a whisper. "You mean— no more lessons?"

"Not even one. The doctor said a reaction like yours means you have a real full-fledged phobia. And that's your medical excuse."

"So I'll graduate next year without even passing the swim test?" She began to tremble.

"So long as you're not flunking any of your courses. And, knowing you, that won't be likely."

"Oh, Dad!" The vastness of her relief could fill a whole ocean bed.

Jen cleared her throat. "I'm not too happy about that diagnosis, actually, Molly. About calling it a phobia—officially, I mean. And if you think about it, you'll agree with me. It's no good being labeled a phobic. And it's not safe to be so helpless around water. It's downright dangerous. So I'm definitely going to sign you up at the rec center this summer and—"

"For crying out loud, Jen, give the girl a chance to recover." Bill groaned. "She nearly died, and now you're telling her she's got to take swimming lessons?"

Jen frowned at him. "Of course she'll have a chance to recover, Bill. But you know the old saying about getting right back up on the horse that throws you, don't you? I just want Molly to be strong about this, and Coach Bascombe agrees with me."

He frowned right back at her. "Well, I say hold off on the swimming lessons and get her to a good therapist instead. Her fear *is* dangerous, as you admit. She needs to talk to a professional."

"Oh, Bill, you know what I think about shrinks! They're all lay-your-gut-out-on-the-rug types. Molly doesn't need to *talk* about this thing, for goodness sake. She needs to get in the water and *deal* with it."

"Well," he said, "we've seen how she deals with getting in the water! Look, the doctor recommended a psychologist right here in Battleboro Heights. But I think it would be even better if I took Molly home with me to Maine and found a psychologist for her up there—"

"I want Molly here. She can come up to Maine to visit you later in the summer. But first things first, Bill."

"You mean she has to learn to swim first? It's always duty before pleasure with you, Jen, isn't it?"

Then the doctor strode in. She hovered above Molly, but Molly hardly noticed. She heard the doctor's words and her parents' words floating over her like a cool mist, settling around her like puffs of cloud off a cold, gray sea. What they said didn't register. What they said didn't matter at all. Only two words that had been spoken had any meaning at all, and these she fastened onto, held tightly in her mind as if in a vise: *"medical excuse."*

They were beautiful, life-giving words. She had a medical excuse! No more blood, no more seaweed, no more boxes floating mysteriously above her. No more pool, no more swimming coaches, no more Jared Bernstein, whose horrible song she could not endure and whose hard, unforgiving arms she could still feel holding her, if she let herself remember. Jared Bernstein, who had tried to kill her. She shook her head on the pillow to banish him, then smiled beatifically up at her quarrelsome parents. She might be an official phobic or a major wimp of the first degree, but she had a medical excuse at last and life was good.

The seniors' graduation exercises were held the weekend after Molly's near-drowning. She did not attend the ceremony or go to any of the graduation festivities, though Michael called and begged her to come. Her accident, as people were calling it, provided an excellent excuse for her to stay away from the school crowd. She wasn't feeling very friendly toward the schoolmates who had stood idly by when Jared tossed her into the water, and the last thing she wanted was to be a celebrity to those people who thrived on near-disaster. There had been a short article about her in the *Battleboro Bulletin,* and although Jen refused to let the reporters have a photograph of Molly for the article, someone had taken one from the yearbook. The headline read:

NEAR-DROWNING AT TEEN PARTY: WEST RIVER
ACADEMY STUDENT REVIVED BY SWIM STARS

The stars had been Kathi and Jared, of course— big-deal swimmers on both their school teams. How gallant of Jared to drag her off the bottom of the pool, Molly thought sarcastically when she read the article. Sweet of him. It had been Kathi who rushed over and pumped out her lungs. But it had been Jared who gave mouth-to-mouth resuscitation.

Oh, God, *that* didn't bear thinking about.

Jared had tried to see her twice in the hospital, but the first time Molly had been sleeping and the second time she had pretended to be. Then he had called the day she went home from the hospital, but Molly signaled Jen to say she couldn't come to the phone. He kept calling. Bill had spoken to him once or twice and told Molly afterward that the poor boy was very upset and really seemed to need to talk. Jen said Molly was being silly. But Jared was the last person in the world she wanted to hear from.

Bill Teague stayed for two weeks after Molly left the hospital, spending the days with her while Jen was at work, sleeping at night in their little guest bedroom. Jen canceled all her evening dates with her new colleague, Ben, and came home to cook dinner for Bill and Molly. Having her parents in the house together made Molly uncomfortable, though they tried to be on their best behavior and avoid quarreling with each other. During the day, Molly slept a lot on the couch while Bill read books about how to run an inn. He and Paulette, he told her enthusiastically, were planning to turn the big house in Maine into a bed-and-breakfast place. When she came up to Maine, she could help them with renovations. Paulette called every evening to talk to Bill, and always asked to speak to Molly, too. But Molly never had much to say. Paulette sounded so *frisky*. The sound of her voice sapped what little energy Molly had.

Bill rented videos and they watched movies every afternoon, eating popcorn. It was the perfect way to pass the time. Molly felt too tired to talk or do much of anything but sit around. The pool water that had filled her lungs now seemed to flow through her veins, cold and numbing. At the end of the second week, Bill flew back to Maine, urging Molly to come up for her visit soon.

The day after her father left, Molly stayed home alone. She napped, read, watched a soap opera, and napped again. Whenever the phone rang, she let the answering machine take the call. Each time it was Jared: "Please talk to me, Molly. I'm very, very sorry—and I really need to see you. Something very weird is going on."

Tell me about it, she thought, rewinding the tape. She left the air-conditioned house and braved the heat and humidity to sit out on the back patio, where she couldn't hear the phone. She stayed there drowsing in the sun over the newspaper until Jen's car pulled into the driveway, then helped carry in bags of groceries.

Molly set the bags on the kitchen counter and saw that the answering machine light was flashing again. She was just reaching out to erase the messages, when Jen pushed the play button.

"Let's hear them first," she said and frowned at Molly. "You're not the only one who gets phone calls, you know. I'm expecting a call from Ben."

The first call was from Bill, saying he had arrived home safely and he and Paulette couldn't wait for Molly to come up.

"Call him back tonight," Jen said, unpacking cans of soup. She stowed them in the pantry. "Tell him you'll be there once you've learned to swim and not a moment before."

Molly pressed her lips together. She wasn't especially looking forward to meeting her new stepmother, but Jen was making it awfully difficult to want to stay home.

The second call was from Ben, inviting Jen out for dinner Saturday night.

The third message was from Jared. Molly's heart beat loudly in her ears when she heard his voice. Jen was watching her, the frown still in place.

"You'll have to see him sooner or later," she said. "It's been two weeks. And after all, he's Kathi's cousin."

"I'm finished with Kathi, too," said Molly. "She knew he was going to throw me in. I don't want to see either one of them." Her best friend's betrayal sat like a stone in Molly's heart.

"I don't think you're being fair," Jen said. "Why are you doing this to your dearest friend? Kathi's the one who saved your life, for goodness sake! She and Jared both worked like crazy to get you breathing again."

"You don't understand, Mom!" Molly stamped into the family room.

She had missed the school play during graduation weekend but could still see the musical on video. And maybe Lionel Bart's songs would chase that spine-chilling Clementine tune out of her head for good. She pushed the video cassette into the player and turned the volume up loud to drown out the sounds of Jen in the kitchen making dinner. Soon she was lost in Oliver's story.

The door to the family room opened. "Can we eat in here?" Molly asked Jen, not taking her eyes from the screen. "This is one of the best parts."

But it wasn't Jen. Jared Bernstein stood just inside the door, his big hands clenched at his sides.

"What are you doing here?" she demanded,

jumping up. "Mom! Did you let him in? I told you not to!"

Jared raised his hands. "Please, wait a minute. Molly, I need to talk to you. Your mother said it was okay." He pushed his dark curls off his forehead. "Just give me a few minutes."

"I have nothing to say to you."

"Then just listen. *Please*." He shut the door and leaned against it. "I just have to ask you one thing . . ."

"What?" She crossed her arms.

"About what happened—at Michael's pool. I don't know what happened. I never *meant* to throw you in. I still can't believe I did it. It was just, suddenly, well . . . I don't know."

She stared at the television, where Fagin's boys were teaching Oliver how to steal.

Jared touched her arm tentatively with one finger. She flinched as if his finger burned her skin. "Molly, that's not all. I mean, there's something else. It's driving me crazy, and it's got me so scared—I need to know. About the seaweed and—Molly, what was that stuff in the water? Blood?"

There was a roar of wind in her ears. She could not hear the television. She could hear only Jared's insistent voice.

"And what was that box? That round box?"

She couldn't believe what she was hearing. It was impossible that he had shared her hallucination. She shoved him aside, wrenched open the door, and careened through the kitchen, past Jen at the stove and up the stairs to her room. She lay on her bed, clutching her pillow, dazed and numb. Through the pounding in her head she could hear the humming again.

The knocking on the door roused her. "I am not going to talk to you," she yelled. "Get it through your head, asshole!"

"Molly, it's me." Jen's voice was low. "I'm alone. Jared went home."

"I don't believe you, Mom. You tricked me. I told you I didn't want to see him."

"Honey, I thought it was best if you saw him. Now, please come down—"

"No way. Just leave me alone." Molly hugged her pillow.

There was a long silence. When Jen spoke again, there was a tremble in her voice. "Dinner's ready."

"I'm not eating." Molly walked across the room and turned off the air conditioner. She was trembling so hard, she needed a warm blanket. After another long minute, she heard Jen go downstairs. She undressed swiftly, thinking how very fragile her body felt. How very delicate. She burrowed in the back of her closet, then pulled out her winter bathrobe and wrapped herself up in it. She was all at once conscious of being the guardian of her body. It was up to her to make sure her body lasted well into advanced old age. And that meant staying away from Jared Bernstein, whatever it took.

"I'm sorry I let him upset you, honey, but I think it's only fair to give him a chance to say what he wants to say to you." Jen faced her daughter over the breakfast table the next morning. Her usually well-groomed hair was lank and her face was without a trace of makeup—unusual even on a Saturday. "I hardly slept a wink all night, worrying about you. I'm starting to think your dad is right. Maybe you do need a psychologist to talk to. You have to admit, the way you were acting last night—the way you've been acting for weeks—well, it just isn't normal." She paused. "It scares me, Molly."

When Molly didn't answer, Jen continued. "Kathi called again and begged you to call back. And Michael called. He wants you to go out for pizza."

Molly reached for the pitcher of orange juice and poured herself a glass without answering. Jen sighed. "Come on, honey," she coaxed. "Don't you want to see your friends before they go off and get summer jobs or go on vacation? All the seniors will be leaving for college in August. You don't want to miss everyone while you're hiding out in your room, do you?"

Molly shrugged. She drained her glass of juice and smacked it down on the tabletop.

Jen sighed. "I want to help you, honey. It's like falling off a horse, you know? You get back on. That's the only sensible thing to do. First we'll get you seeing your friends again. Then we'll tackle the swimming. It'll be easy with me here to help you."

"What do you mean, Mom?" Molly's tone was ominous. She shoved back her chair to leave the room.

"Well . . ." Jen hesitated. "I've reserved a place

for you at the rec center pool. You start lessons on Monday." Jen frowned at Molly's gasp and went on quickly: "Look, I know you're scared, but facing your fear is the only way to get over it. Trust me on this, honey."

Molly spent the day up in her room reading old copies of *National Geographic*. In one issue there was an article about wildlife along the Maine coast. She studied the photographs with interest. She didn't wander downstairs until late in the afternoon, when her stomach was growling with hunger. Jen was on the phone in the kitchen. She hung up when Molly came in and smiled uncertainly.

"Ben just called and asked me to go see the Rodin exhibit at the art museum before dinner. He's invited you, too. How about it? I want you to meet him. He can pick us up in about twenty minutes." When Molly didn't answer, she walked over and gave her daughter an awkward hug. "Honey, are you all right?"

"I'm okay," Molly answered faintly.

Jen looked doubtful. "Maybe I'd better stay home. You look funny."

"No, it's fine. Really, Mom. You go right ahead. I'm just so tired, you wouldn't believe. I'm going to eat something and just hang out."

"But wouldn't you like to come with us? You like sculpture."

Molly took a box of crackers from the cupboard and carried it into the family room. She flopped down on the couch. "Some other time, Mom."

Jen followed her. "Do you want a pillow? Should I turn up the air conditioner?"

"No thanks," Molly murmured. She felt she was behind a glass wall. Her mother's voice came to her only faintly. "I'm really fine. You have a good time." She flicked on the TV. Within seconds, it seemed, she was asleep. Or half asleep—for she heard the sound of the doorbell over the laugh track from the sitcom, heard her mother's voice in the kitchen and Ben's deeper rumble. The door to the family room creaked open and she knew Jen was looking in on her just the way she did when Molly was sick. *And maybe I am sick,* she thought. *Maybe that's why everything seems so weird.* She heard them leave the house, heard Ben's car in the driveway. And then nothing more. Eyes closed, she was floating. After a while she fell straight into the dream.

This time I can see that the walls of the hallway are paneled and the floor is covered with a thick Oriental carpet—all deep reds and browns. There are doors on both sides of the hallway, dark wood, with gleaming brass handles. I hover at the top of a wide staircase, looking down the hall. This time another girl floats beside me. She is wearing a long dress. Dark braids are wrapped around her head.

There's a man's deep voice rumbling through the thick wooden door at the end of the hall. Then there's a shriek, high and keening, full of pain. Driven by a desperate urgency, I float down the hall and reach out for the doorknob. The girl, right behind me, grabs my arm. "No!" she cries.

*But I shake her off as I know I must, and I push the
door slowly open. The next cry I hear I recognize as my
own.*

*Oh, there is blood everywhere. On the bed sheets. On
the woman who lies so still atop the coverlet. On the man
who bends over the bed. He hears my scream and whirls
around. His face above his dark beard is white. Teeth bared
in a grimace, he spits the words at me: "Now we've lost
her. Damn you!"*

Behind me, the girl is crying.

*I try to run, but my legs pump air. I must get away,
must get away, must get away. And somehow I reach the
stairs. At the bottom I catch sight of the ornate wall mirror
and stop. The room spins dizzily around me and my
stomach lurches with sick dread, for the face in the mirror
is not my own but that of the rosy-cheeked girl in the hall.*

"Molly! Come on, Molly! Let us in!"

She opened her mouth in a cry that wrenched
her, finally, fully awake.

"Molly, we just want to talk to you for a few
minutes."

She sat up on the couch and saw Kathi and Jared
tapping on the glass of the sliding door to the patio.
She stared at them, twisting her hands together, trying
to separate reality from the dream.

Kathi's wry smile was clear through the glass
door. "It isn't every evening I make such an effort
to talk to a friend," she called. "But I figure you're
worth it."

Dazed, Molly walked slowly over to the door,
reached out a hand as if to open it, then instead

grabbed the tie that released the blinds. She tugged hard. They clattered down from the ceiling, covering the glass, obscuring the trespassers from view.

"Hey!" cried Kathi.

Molly ran to the kitchen and grabbed her mother's car keys off the counter. Then, heart racing, she slipped out the kitchen door and ran out to Jen's car. Thank God she and Ben had driven off in his. Kathi's blue car was parked behind Jen's in the driveway, but Molly turned the key in the ignition, gunned the engine, and spun the wheel hard enough to make a tight turn onto the grass. In seconds she would be away from them.

Then she saw Jared running toward her across the grass. "Molly! Molly, wait!"

In blind panic, she wrenched the wheel to the right and careened across the lawn, narrowly missing him. She spun down Valley Road toward Route 21. "It's nothing to do with me!" she yelled at the top of her lungs.

She slowed to a safer speed as she neared the shopping center. *Calm down, calm down,* she told herself. She would be absolutely fine just as long as Jared stayed away from her. Just as long as no one mentioned water or blood, just as long as she stayed awake and on guard and didn't let herself dream even for a second about old houses and long hallways. Or hatboxes. She was one hundred percent fine as long as she pushed from her mind the memory of the face she saw in the mirror—the face that was not her own.

How much finer could anyone get?

When she was stopped at the traffic light back near the shopping center again, she saw Kathi's blue car turn the corner. Kathi was driving with Jared beside her. At the sight of him, Molly's stomach felt hollow again. But *he* should be the one feeling guilty—after what he'd done to her!

She heard the whisper in her mind: *And after what you did to him!*

She accelerated with a lurch and zoomed down Route 21, past antique stores and housing developments, right on into the next town. After twenty more minutes of driving aimlessly through unfamiliar neighborhoods, she felt considerably calmer, and headed home. When she let herself in the kitchen door, the house was quiet. But the flashing red light on the answering machine didn't have to be loud to get her attention. It made no sound, but flashed there, on and off, with the impact of an emergency siren at top volume.

Molly threw the keys onto the counter. She rewound the tape on the answering machine without listening to the message and ran upstairs. She flopped across her bed and stared up at the ceiling, willing the calm of her room to quiet her pounding head. Was she really cracking up? Jen would be so ashamed.

Downstairs, the doorbell rang. And rang. And rang.

She pulled her pillow over her head and waited until Jared and Kathi went away again.

Finally, all was quiet. She started to cry. She had to get away from here. Dragging herself out of bed, she crossed the room to her desk and picked up her address book. She sat on the edge of her bed and reached for her phone on the bedside table. She dialed numbly, staring out the window. Dusk had fallen.

Bill answered on the first ring.

"Hello, Dad?"

"Molly! What a surprise!"

"Dad—listen, I've changed my mind. I do want to come see you and Paulette. Right away."

"Hey, that's great. Why the sudden change of heart?"

She clutched the receiver tightly, winding the cord around her hand. Her line to safety.

"I just decided I'd rather be with you."

"I'll admit I'm flattered. And relieved. But what does your mom say?"

"Oh, you know Mom." Molly hesitated. Then she tried to make her voice light. "She'd rather I stayed here, actually. She's got me all signed up for swimming lessons at the rec center."

There was a silence. Then Bill cleared his throat. "I see," he said. "Yes, I think I'll make those plane reservations right away. Don't worry, honey. You're on your way to nice, peaceful Hibben, Maine. There's not a rec center for a hundred miles."

They talked another few minutes. In the background Molly could hear Paulette's giggle of excitement. By the time Jen returned from her date, Molly and Bill had settled all the details of their arrangements: Molly would leave on Monday, the day after tomorrow. Her tickets would be waiting at the airport.

That night Molly slept dreamlessly.

4

Molly pressed her forehead to the window and stared down at the Cleveland area as it disappeared beneath a fluffy layer of clouds. As the plane whisked her to Boston on the first leg of her journey, she closed her eyes, and the muted hubbub from all the other passengers receded. She felt the vibration of the aircraft through her body. Taking a few deep breaths and rubbing the back of her neck, she resolved not to think about anything but the restful vacation that lay ahead. She would forget all about Michael's surprise at her sudden change in plans when she called to tell him her new summer address. She would forget about Jen's annoyance and the fact that she had not called Kathi to say good-bye. She resolved especially not to think about Jared Bernstein.

Her mother had not been pleased when she'd learned of Molly's plan to leave. She seemed angry that Bill had made the flight arrangements, but Molly

suspected the anger was really more at her for having arranged her escape.

"You're running scared," Jen told her, shaking
her head. "It's weak, Molly." She was sitting on the
edge of Molly's bed while Molly threw her clothes
into two suitcases, and she reached out a hand and
smoothed one of the rumpled T-shirts. "Honey, I'd
really rather you stayed here for another month. Take
swimming lessons during the day, go out with your
friends at night—then fly up to see your dad when
you've gotten yourself back together. That's Dr. Jen's
prescription for a happy summer. Running away
won't help anything."

But her mother didn't understand about Jared
Bernstein. She didn't understand about the dreams.
Molly wondered whether her mother was afraid of
anything. Didn't she have even passing knowledge of
the sick clutch to the stomach that fear could bring?
Evidently not—or she would know that turning tail
and running was the most natural response in the
world.

Molly had taken a deep breath and replied firmly,
"Look, Mom. I miss Dad like anything, and I want
to see his new house. I want to meet Paulette—and
I'll write you all the details so you can have a good
laugh. Okay?"

Jen shrugged. "What can I say? You don't fool
me for a second, and you're taking the coward's way
out. I want you to promise me one thing. Promise
me you'll learn to swim while you're there."

"I promise." She'd promise anything for the

chance to be hundreds of miles away from Jared Bernstein.

In Boston she caught her connecting flight to Bangor, Maine. The plane was uncrowded, and this time Molly had two seats to herself. She sat by the window and leafed through the magazines provided by the airline. Shortly after take-off, an elderly man lurched down the aisle toward the toilets in the back of the plane. He was shaking, and the woman directly behind him kept a firm grip on his shoulders. She was wearing a gray skirt and white blouse but had the official air of someone in uniform. *Maybe a daughter,* thought Molly idly. *But probably a nurse. Was the old guy going to be sick?* Molly watched them pass. Ten minutes later they made their slow way up the aisle again and came to a halt next to Molly's seat, their passage blocked by a woman reaching for her sweater in the overhead compartment. The man peered down at Molly and said hello.

"Hello," she responded with a smile.

"A plane's no proper place for man nor beast," he told her. "I prefer to travel by boat myself. Don't you?"

"I like solid ground best of all," she answered with a smile. He reminded her of somebody, somebody she liked, but she couldn't think who. The old man nodded, then hesitated as if he'd like to settle in next to her for a good chat, but as the woman in the aisle put on her sweater and sat down again, his companion directed him to their seats just in front of Molly's. Molly wondered fleetingly whether he lived in Maine or was just going to visit, then dismissed him from her thoughts. She turned back to the window. There wasn't much to see—just a steadily darkening sky.

The plane circled over Bangor, then touched down smoothly and taxied to a stop at the terminal. Molly reached up into the overhead compartment for her blue backpack. The old man asked her to hand down his carry-on bag, as well. She glanced down at the top of his head with a smile. "Don't get up," she said. "Just tell me which one it is."

"Black leather satchel," he said. He coughed; it sounded like a bark. Molly carefully lifted the black bag down and set it on his lap. "It's got all my medicine inside. I won't make it home without it."

"He'll be fine," said the woman, speaking for the first time. "Likes to make a bit of a fuss, that's all."

The old man winked at Molly. "Somebody meeting you here, my girl?"

"Yes," she told him. "My dad."

The man nodded. She said good-bye and moved down the aisle. It was funny, she thought, how many people you come into contact with in a lifetime—or even a day—who don't matter to you at all. You'll never see them again. They don't have any impact on your life, nor you on theirs. And yet sometimes a random encounter turns out to be one of the most important moments of your life.

It had happened like that for Bill and Paulette— a chance encounter on a plane when Bill was flying home from a business trip to California and Paulette was traveling from her home in California to New York to attend a friend's wedding. Fate had seated them next to each other. Paulette inadvertently splashed her apple juice in Bill's lap when the plane hit turbulence, and he dumped a forkful of chicken Kiev onto her sleeve. They apparently had a marvelous time mopping up and apologizing—and were married a few months later. Molly hoped he'd be happier with Paulette than he'd been with Jen.

She remembered the tension in their house before the divorce. Bill Teague was a peaceful man, "laid back" he liked to call himself. Jen's efficiency, among other things, annoyed him. He hated the crashing classical music she played. He liked soft rock. He liked soft mattresses, too. Once Jen threw away the old mattress on their bed and bought a new, extra-extra firm one, and Bill hit the roof—actually, he hit the mattress—when he came home and discovered the change. He punched the unyielding bulk with his fist. "You see? Doesn't even make a dent. How am I supposed to sleep on this board?"

"It's good for your back," said Jen in a tight voice. "It's healthy."

"Hard mattresses aren't *cozy*, Jen! They don't feel good!"

"That's one of the problems with you," Jen said. "You want everything cozy! You want everything to feel good!"

Even at ten, Molly had known they weren't only talking about beds. She'd heard all their arguments, and they were always about the same sorts of things: that Jen wanted order, but Bill didn't mind a bit of mess. That Bill wanted to watch a fantasy movie, but Jen preferred documentaries. That Jen liked security and worked hard, but Bill was always thinking of quitting his job for something more fun.

Molly's parents had been divorced for seven years when Bill met Paulette. In all that time he had rarely dated. They had married out in California on Valentine's Day, almost on the spur of the moment, without telling their families until afterward. "It was all so romantic," Paulette had gushed to Molly on the phone when Bill called to tell her of their impetuous wedding. They moved back to New York and toured New England on their honeymoon, where Paulette fell in love with the enchanting coastal towns. In a little fishing village on the Maine coast, they saw a big old house for sale. And both of them, Bill told Molly, knew right away that they were just *meant* to buy that house. (It was just like Bill, Jen scoffed when she'd heard the news, to marry a flaky California bunny and then buy a run-down old house— all on a whim!) Bill and Paulette quit their jobs and moved up to Hibben, Maine, determined to live off their savings until they could turn the old Victorian house into an inn.

Could that be Paulette now? A short, slim woman wearing jeans and a green T-shirt was waving frantically as Molly walked down the ramp to the gate. The woman was small-boned, with carrot-colored hair cut very short, almost in a crew cut. Yes, it had to be Paulette—Molly recognized the hair from the wedding pictures Bill had sent. But where was *he?*

"Molly? Molly!" Paulette ran forward and embraced her, squeezing tightly. She was a full head shorter than Molly, and the carrot-red hair tickled Molly's chin. "At last!"

Molly stepped back, smiling politely. "Hello, Paulette. Where's my dad?"

"Oh, dear, I don't want you to panic, but there's been an accident!" Her voice was high and breathless, and Molly had a sudden image of her father dead from some terrible car crash.

"Oh no—"

"He fell off a ladder this afternoon while we were pulling down the old wallpaper in the dining room and broke his left ankle. Poor baby." She looked up at Molly with round green eyes while passengers moved around them toward the baggage claim. "God, you're tall! Billy said you were, of course, but I didn't know he meant *really* tall." She giggled. "And such blue eyes. I love your long hair. Do you ever do French braids? I'll fix your hair for you tomorrow, if you like."

Relieved that Bill was still alive, Molly ignored the comments about her appearance. Jen always said people shouldn't make personal remarks. Maybe people in California didn't worry about such old-fashioned things as manners. "So is Dad in a cast?" she asked.

"You can be the very first person to sign it. We

were at the hospital for *ages* today. I'm telling you, they know how to give lessons in patience there. But now Billy's lying home in bed, waiting to see you. We'd no sooner got back from the hospital than it was time for me to leave for the airport."

"But is Dad all right?" Molly asked. "Can he walk with crutches?" They started moving along with the crowd, heading toward the baggage claim to pick up Molly's suitcases.

"Oh, he'll be able to hobble around, my poor Billy. But probably not tonight. The doctor gave him some sort of really strong painkiller, and it has kind of knocked him out. I mean, he wasn't in any condition to drive all the way down to Bangor, and he might be asleep by the time we get home. But he's *ecstatic* that you're coming to stay." She reached over and squeezed Molly's arm. "And so am I."

"Poor Dad," said Molly. She realized she'd never seen Bill sick or injured. "Well, I'll help take down the rest of the wallpaper," she told Paulette. "That's something I can do."

"That'll be *super,*" said Paulette. "You'll be able to reach almost as high as Billy. But we don't want you to work too much while you're here. After your horrible accident, you probably need some R and R. That's rest and relaxation. We want you to have fun."

"Thanks." Molly saw her blue suitcases drop from the conveyor belt onto the baggage carousel and moved forward to pick them up. She noticed the old man standing with the dour woman and waved to them. The man looked confused. The woman moved closer to the conveyor belt, searching for their bags.

"Here, let me help you," said Paulette, reaching for one of Molly's suitcases.

"No, I'm fine."

"Well, give me the backpack, then," she said and giggled. "I may be tiny compared to you, but I'm strong as a packhorse. At least that's what Billy says, and he knows *everything* about me!"

Spare me the details, please. Molly followed Paulette out to the parking lot. Paulette took her keys out of her back pocket and unlocked the side door of a blue van.

"Here we are," she said, shoving aside rolls of wallpaper. Molly lifted her suitcases inside next to several gallon-size cans of paint. "Let's hit the road." Paulette dropped Molly's backpack inside and slammed the door. "It's a long drive, and I know you want to see your dad as soon as you can."

Molly sat in front next to Paulette. They drove away from the Bangor airport and headed northeast, up toward the coast. "Did you look Hibben up on a map?" asked Paulette. "You probably couldn't find it! We're way out on the edge of *nowhere*."

"Dad said it was pretty remote."

"Well, there's a new tourist trade just getting started, and we're hoping that our inn will get going just in time to take advantage of it. You know, all the rich people down east—that's what they call the south of Maine and New England, too—they've pretty well taken over places like Kennebunkport.

It's getting crowded down there. That is, crowded for Maine. So tourists are starting to build summer homes up in the little fishing villages, and lots of guest houses and hotels are springing up. We're hoping to be part of this trend. If our timing is right, we'll do really well. The villagers have mixed feelings, I think. They don't like the peace disturbed, but they're sure happy enough about all the money tourism brings in. A few of them are opening bed-and-breakfasts in their own homes, but mostly it's people like us—*outsiders*—who are setting up the tourist places. You wouldn't believe how much the locals value their privacy!" Paulette laughed. "Up here, unless your family has been here a hundred years, forget it! You're a foreigner. It takes some getting used to. In California you're practically an old-timer if you've lived there two years."

Molly murmured something in response. The fatigue that had pressed down on her so heavily at home assailed her again as they left the highway and drove along a narrow road through what seemed to be miles of dense forest.

"Would you just look at these trees?" Paulette said brightly. "I still can't get over how much of Maine is mostly forest. Two minutes out of a city and you're in the wilderness, practically. There's bears in the woods. And, would you believe, moose?"

Molly yawned, then covered her mouth. "Sorry. I'm just so sleepy."

"Go ahead and have a nap, then. We'll be on Route 9 till we get to Machias. Then we have to go further over to the coast, to Starboard. Even then, it'll be a drive. Hibben is tucked between Bucks Harbor and Benson. I mean, barely on the map. You'll see. Way north, and then so far east, we're just about the first people in all of America to see the sunrise each morning."

Molly retreated gratefully behind closed eyelids. She didn't want to talk to Paulette. She was feeling unaccustomedly awkward and ungainly next to this slender, small-boned woman with a haircut like a little boy's. She wanted only to see her dad and then go to sleep for a week or two.

"It's dark, anyway," chattered Paulette. "But you'll just love the scenery in the daytime. Especially since Ohio is so flat. The mountains and trees weren't such a shock for me, since I'm from San Francisco, you know. Not that there are very many trees in the city, of course, but it's only a short drive to the mountains. And of course there are hills all around. This is different, though. It's like the cities up here in Maine are just little patches of paint on this big, wild dark green canvas of a state. There's miles and miles of farmland, too. People grow crops of potatoes and corn, mostly. Wait till you see our own crop of wild blueberries! I can't wait to show you around. Billy and I have driven all *over* the place buying supplies for the house. Not that it's in terrible shape or anything. The house, I mean. Nothing structural, really, although one of the porches had dry rot and we had to replace it. It's mostly just an old, musty place. We want to freshen it up with new

70

paper and paint and trim and all that. We want it to have a *cozy* feeling—you know? Billy likes things cozy." She giggled again. "You know?"

Molly feigned sleep while Paulette rabbited on and on. The young woman's high, breathless voice rose and fell in a quick cadence almost like a song. Soon Molly really did sleep, or figured she must have, because in no time at all, it seemed, she opened her eyes and found they were on a winding road. She could smell the sharp salt smell of the ocean even through the closed windows. Paulette's voice was still going strong:

"You can't see it very well in the dark, of course, but the ocean's churning down there like you wouldn't believe! You can see it from the cliff by our house if you walk out on the headland. When there's no fog, that is. The fog just seems to pile up around our house. I know you don't like water much, or is that just in pools? You can't swim in the water around Hibben, really, anyway, because the waves are too rough and there's no real access to the water. Well, there's the wharf, with a little pebbly beach, but the villagers keep their fishing boats there, and the ferry docks there, too. So it's kind of not the *best* place to swim . . . But you won't be wanting to swim anyway, right? I hope you won't feel afraid with so much water nearby."

Molly couldn't see well in the dark van, but she sensed Paulette was peering over at her with worry. "No, as long as I don't have to go swimming in it, water's fine," she reassured her stepmother. She smiled in the dark van and felt herself relax for the first time, it seemed, in weeks. Her father wouldn't pressure her at all. She wouldn't mind the sea as long as she didn't have to go near it. She breathed deeply, listening to her stepmother's chatter. She looked contentedly out at the dark road and the dark shapes of trees, smelling the salt in the night breeze through the open window. Paulette was friendly and seemed happy Molly had come. Things would be all right now.

Suddenly the van lurched to the left and started up a rutted road. "We've got to do something about this," said Paulette. "Maybe gravel? Or should we pave it? What do you think?"

"Is this the road to your house?" asked Molly. "I didn't even see the town."

"Hibben's just farther along that road, but we turned off to go along the headland. We'll be home in a sec. Watch now—you'll see the house."

Molly straightened up in her seat. They had left the coast road and were jerking along a dirt road lined with evergreen trees. Molly could see them outside the van window, black shapes whipping back and forth in the sea wind that reached all the way up here on the headland. Ahead of them the trees gave way to a tangle of overgrown grasses. And rising out of the dark grass was the house.

It was a massive shadow with stone steps leading up to a wide porch in front. Lights burned in several windows like lighthouse beacons through the night.

Molly's contentment vanished.

"We've got to buy a tractor mower to deal with all this grass," Paulette was saying. "Another thing to put on my list!"

Molly watched the blowing grass and pressed her hands to her mouth to contain her sudden cry of— of something. Fear? Not exactly. But as they stopped in front of the porch and Paulette cut the engine, Molly felt her body trembling slightly and thought: *I've been here before!*

But that was impossible.

"Home sweet home," trilled Paulette. "Let's run in and see if my wonderful, sweet Billy has been knocked out by his painkillers yet. We can bring your stuff in later."

She jumped out of the van and ran lightly up the steps of the porch, then stopped and waited for Molly. Molly unlatched her seatbelt slowly and opened her door. *What's wrong with you?* she asked herself.

"What is it, Molly?" asked Paulette.

"Nothing." She stepped up onto the porch after Paulette, fighting down her growing unease. Paulette led the way into a big, paneled hallway with a staircase leading straight up ahead of them to a landing with windows. There was a narrow table against one wall, with a lamp on it sending out a welcoming glow. Several closed doors led off the hallway into other rooms. A drop cloth and buckets of paint sat on the floor next to the stairs. The house smelled old and musty, overlaid with the sharp freshness of new paint.

"I'll show you around after we say hi to your

dad," said Paulette, flicking on the light at the foot of the stairs. "Watch out for the mess." She stepped over a wallpaper roll on the first step and headed up. "There are eight bedrooms, can you believe it? We'll use five or six for guests and keep the rest for ourselves."

Molly followed, her stomach tense. Somehow she knew it was coming, sensed it, but didn't know what to do to stop it. The fear, along with the exhaustion, had not been left behind in Battleboro Heights after all. Both had followed her here. At the top of the landing the stairs curved to the left, and she climbed them after Paulette's light step with heavy dread.

She clenched her teeth so hard that her gasp sounded only in her head. Straight ahead of her stretched the oak-paneled hallway. There were four doors along either side. Their brass doorknobs gleamed in the soft light from the overhead chandeliers. And at the end of the hall was a door standing open. Molly stopped.

She closed her eyes, then opened them, but the hallway looked the same. It *was* the same. She pressed her hands over her eyes to blot out the sight of the hallway before her.

"What, Molly?" Paulette put her hand on Molly's arm. "What's wrong?"

"It's the hallway from my dream," Molly whispered, eyes closed.

"Oh, *wow!*" said Paulette worriedly. "*What* dream?"

Bill's voice boomed from the end of the hall. "Molly? Paulette? Is that you?"

"We're home, my love!" called Paulette. "Be right there!"

At the sound of Bill's familiar voice, Molly uncovered her eyes. She clenched her hands into fists at her sides—they were shaking as badly as the old man's on the plane. She took a heaving breath to calm herself.

"Hey, save the tour for later! Just get in here and let me kiss my daughter," bellowed Bill from the end of the hall. "Or I swear I'll drag myself out of this confounded bed and—"

"We're coming, Dad!" called Molly. She hurried ahead of Paulette down the hallway to the door at the end, steeling herself as she stepped into the room. She fully expected to see the same bed where the woman had lain covered in blood, where the man had turned to her, angry and accusing. But no, the bed was against the wall opposite the windows. And it was a different bed, of course, and the person lying in it wasn't a woman at all but her own father, his ankle encased in a white cast and lying raised on a pillow. There was no blood anywhere.

"Dad!" Molly ran to him with a glad cry.

"It's great to see you, honey," he said, hugging her. "I could just kick myself for falling off that damn ladder. What bad timing!"

"I'm just glad you're okay."

"Oh, I'm fine. But my paper-stripping days are over for a while. Six weeks, looks like." He pulled her down on the bed and reached out a hand to draw Paulette over. Paulette took his hand and stood at the side of the bed, smoothing his hair.

"My two ladies," he said, grinning. "Together at last. Well, Molly? Was I right? Isn't Paulette a wonder?"

"Yes," said Molly, surreptitiously peering all around the room. She was still trembling.

"And Molly is everything you said she was," said Paulette.

"Well, I'm glad to have us all together, that's all I can say." Bill lay back on his pillows. "How was the trip, Molly? Are you hungry?" He yawned through his smile. "I ate what Paulette fixed me before she went to get you, or I'd join you. All I want to do now, I'm afraid, is go to sleep."

"Me, too," Molly said sympathetically. "And don't worry about me. I ate on the flight to Boston."

Paulette stroked Bill's face. "Poor Lamb Chop, you look totally shattered. How about if I take Molly on a house tour and then get her settled for the night? You just go to sleep now, and we can all talk in the morning."

He closed his eyes. "It's just this pain medication they gave me. It knocks you out."

"Molly's going to be here a long time," Paulette said reassuringly. She headed for the door. "Coming, Molly? Let's get you something to drink, at least." She turned back to Bill. "Can I get you anything, my poor, battered beloved?"

Even through her daze, Molly had to wince at Paulette's goo-goo voice. Jen would be on the floor laughing.

Bill kept his eyes closed. "Nothing for me, Puppy. Just take good care of Molly."

"Good night, Dad," Molly said softly, and followed Paulette back into the hallway. They didn't go back down the main stairs but instead headed down a steep, uncarpeted flight at the back of the house, ending up in a big, old kitchen with stained red linoleum on the floor.

Paulette closed the door to the back stairs firmly, then gestured to a chair at the round kitchen table. "Here, sit down and make yourself cozy. What do you want? How about lemonade? I'm afraid I don't have any Coke. That stuff isn't good for you."

"No, really, I'm fine."

"I'm having a cup of herbal tea. Join me?"

"Sure."

Paulette bustled around the big kitchen, chattering as she assembled her tea things and put the water on to boil. "Can you believe the size of this kitchen? Of course, there must have been servants once. It's a challenge to make a meal here, with the fridge over in one corner and this big old stove over here, and the sink over there by the windows! They sure didn't know about efficient meal-making then, did they? Then again, you had to keep the servants busy, I guess. After we finish papering the downstairs, we're going to start remodeling this kitchen. I like old things, if they're usable. But I don't really go for vintage just *because*. You know?"

Molly nodded, hardly listening. She was looking around the kitchen, shivering a little despite the warm night air breezing in through the screened window over the sink.

The children hung their coats on hooks by the back door.

This knowledge came to her, unbidden. But—what in the world? *What* children?

Paulette held up a china mug patterned with roses. "Like this? I found it in one of the cupboards. It was probably there for years. This house was empty for a long time before we moved in."

Molly sat still, feeling lumpish and numb while Paulette flitted on fairy feet around the big room. She tried to force some of the tension out of her muscles by taking slow breaths. She thought of Jen, at home now, probably watching a video. Maybe Ben was there, too. For an instant she longed to be with them.

She'd been desperate to get away from home, desperate to come to this safe haven. And yet, one glance down that hallway had told her this was no haven at all.

Finally the tea was brewed to Paulette's satisfaction. She carried the small teapot to the table. Then she opened a tin canister and arranged some cookies on a plate. She set it in front of Molly. "There. Mint tea from the mint growing right in our own garden. And homemade oatmeal raisin cookies—specially made with love for my only stepdaughter in the world!"

Paulette pulled out a chair and sat at the table across from Molly. She poured them cups of tea and watched intently until Molly took a cookie and bit into it. "It's good? You like it?" Her voice was eager, her green eyes sparkling.

Molly nodded.

"And do you like the house?" She frowned. "What did you mean about a dream you had?"

Molly hesitated. No sense letting this nice woman decide on the very first night that she had a neurotic stepdaughter. "I like the house," she said. "It's just that it was a shock, at first, because I've had dreams about a long hallway—sort of like the one upstairs." She reached for another cookie, half-convinced now that the hallway was only similar to the one in the dreams. Not identical. A lot of big houses have long hallways.

"Were they good dreams?" Paulette studied her. "Or bad?"

Molly finished her cookie. "How about that house tour now?"

Paulette hesitated, then stood and carried their cups to the sink without another word. Molly suspected it cost the chatty woman quite a lot to hold back the zillions of questions she probably wanted to fire at Molly, and Molly liked her all the more.

She followed Paulette out of the kitchen, pressing back the flash of—something—that assailed her as they moved into the front hallway and she saw the staircase again. Recognition? The stairs looked like the ones she had run down in the dream when she saw the other girl's face in the ornate mirror. Surreptitiously she glanced at the wall, then gasped when she saw the brighter square on the faded old wallpaper. Something had hung there once.

Probably only an old picture.

"Are you okay?" asked Paulette anxiously.

"Of course!"

They walked past the stairs into a large, high-ceilinged room with long-windowed French doors at both ends and a fireplace with a carved oak mantel in the center of the far wall. "The living room," announced Paulette. "Or should I say the parlor?"

Molly could imagine it had been a gracious room once, but now, uncarpeted and empty of furniture, it seemed to be waiting for someone to bring it back to life. Paulette bubbled with excitement as she told Molly her plans for the house.

"We want to furnish it with antiques from the period when the house was first built. Mid-nineteenth century. Billy and I have been combing the flea markets and auctions around here. Now that he's hurt his ankle, maybe you'll come with me?"

"Sure." If she threw herself into the renovations, she wouldn't think about hallways or patches of wallpaper where maybe a mirror had hung.

From the living room they moved to a large, formal dining room, also empty of furniture. A stepladder lay on its side on a plastic ground cloth speckled with wallpaper paste. An overturned bucket of paste had spilled onto the cloth and spattered on the floorboards as well. "The scene of the accident!" proclaimed Paulette. "This is where your daddy was working when he fell—my poor darling. I didn't even have a chance to clean up."

"I'll help you." Molly stepped carefully around the mess. "He's lucky he didn't break *both* ankles."

"We'll clean up tomorrow." Paulette sighed. "I'm afraid I blame myself. I was holding the ladder, but then the phone rang and I went to get it—and that's when he fell."

"It wasn't your fault," Molly said comfortingly.

Paulette led Molly into a glass-walled room with five sides. "This is what they called the conservatory," she said, flicking on the lights. "Can you imagine how *gorgeous* it will be once we get some big plants in it? I want it really lush. It will be a great place to serve our guests their breakfasts."

In the daytime, Molly supposed, there would be a panoramic view from this room over the entire headland. But now, in the dark, it was just an odd-shaped, empty room with dirty glass walls.

Paulette led her through the butler's pantry ("Too bad it didn't come equipped with a butler," Paulette giggled) and into a small, bare room with wide wooden floorboards and built-in corner cupboards. "This is the servants' dining room. Can you imagine having so many maids that they had their *own* dining room? We'll probably turn this into a playroom for the baby. The guests' kids could use it, too. We want to cater to families, you know. Make them feel right at home—or even better than at home."

"Did you say 'baby'?" asked Molly.

"*Ooh!*" Paulette clapped her hands over her

mouth, her eyes twinkling. "I'm not supposed to say *anything!* Billy wants to tell you himself."

"You and Dad are having a baby?" A thrill of excitement banished the lingering fear.

"Yes! Isn't it super? But don't tell Billy I told you. He'll tell you tomorrow. You've *got* to act surprised! I shouldn't have let it slip, and I'm not going to tell you another thing until we're with Billy."

They circled back through the kitchen into the front hallway, Molly's thoughts on the new sister or brother she'd be having. How soon would it be born? She scrutinized her skinny stepmother and thought maybe there was the slightest swell to her belly under the T-shirt. *What great news!*

Another door off the main hallway led to a dark-paneled room much like the parlor, with French doors leading out to a side porch. Built-in bookshelves lined all four walls, extending even around the fireplace. The shelves weren't completely empty—there were moving boxes pushed into the lower ones. Paint flaked off the high ceiling. Bits of it lay on the floorboards. "The library," announced Paulette. "Won't it be *beautiful* once we unpack our books? Not that we have enough to fill all these shelves, but we'll order some, or join a book club or something. Billy says there's a place in New York City near his old apartment where you can buy books by the *yard*— isn't that funny? They're used books, of course, and people buy them just to fill up space and look good, I guess. We'll let our guests use this as a sort of family room."

"Get a big library table for that alcove at the other

end," suggested Molly. She knew exactly the sort of table it should be: rectangular, made of oak, with carved legs. People could sit there and do puzzles in the evening. With a fire going and the window seat piled with cushions, the room would be really cozy. The cushions on the window seat would be covered with a woven tapestry pattern of flowers and vines in pinks and blues and grays. There would be a leather easy chair pulled up to the fire, with a little ottoman to prop your feet on. She could just see it all right now, as if—she sucked in her breath—as if she remembered it from somewhere.

The children did their lessons by the window.

Paulette glanced at her curiously but crossed to a door in the wall next to the fireplace. She flung open the door. "And here's where we've been living these past eight months since we moved in," she said, gesturing Molly inside with a flourish. "The study. This room will be off limits to guests. We're going to keep it as our private living room. What do you think?"

Molly bit back a scream.

She backed away, tripping over Paulette, and ran through the library out into the hallway. The staircase loomed above her, and she moaned, turning wildly this way and that, not knowing which way to run. Then she saw the front door and reached for the handle. She flung the door open and ran out into the cool evening air. She sucked great mouthfuls of it into her lungs. Paulette was right behind her, arms outstretched, crying her name.

"Oh, *Molly!*" She wrapped her arms around

Molly when they reached the van. Molly didn't have the will to resist. She stood in the circle of Paulette's arms and sobbed.

She found herself crying: "I know that room! I've been there before!" She didn't know how it could be so, but she'd seen the same warm red of the Oriental carpet, the same polished surface of the big desk before. She knew the gray stone fireplace, knew that same acrid smell of smoke.

She was babbling aloud, almost without knowing it, to Paulette, who stood holding her close. "It's the same room, all the same furniture—*everything* the same," she kept repeating, as Paulette rubbed her back soothingly.

Finally Molly pulled away, exhausted and trembling. Paulette kept one hand on Molly's arm. "Listen," Paulette said. "Come back in with me, Molly. Come look at that room again. It's *nothing* like what you've described. There *is* no desk. There *is* no fireplace. I *wish* we had an Oriental carpet—but we *don't*. Come look!"

Molly hung back. "No, no, I can't go in there."

Paulette opened the van and reached for Molly's suitcases. "You can just stand in the doorway, okay? Just take one look. It's the only room in the house besides the kitchen and the two bedrooms that has any furniture in it at all. But it's not what you say, Molly." Her voice was breathless and bewildered. "I don't know what you saw, but it wasn't *our* room."

The dark shapes of trees on the headland offered no sense of sanctuary. Molly could hear the sound of the ocean hurling itself against rocks. Where could she go, if not back to the house? She reached for one of the big suitcases, but Paulette shrugged her off and struggled with both of them herself. Molly followed, holding her backpack in one trembling hand.

Paulette set the suitcases down at the foot of the big staircase. Then she and Molly walked back into the library and through the room to the door at the back. "Just one peek," urged Paulette. "You'll recognize the furniture all right, but it's not anything like what you described. It's the stuff from Billy's old New York apartment. Look—on the wall, there's the picture of him that you drew when you were a little girl. He's had it framed. I think the ears stick out a little too much, don't you? But it's so *cute!*"

Molly forced herself to look around the study. Sure enough, it was just as Paulette had said and just, in fact, as she remembered from her father's New York living room. The same old plaid couch, covered with the green afghan. The sagging green armchairs. The leaning bookshelves crammed to overflowing. A coffee table, cleared and polished in Molly's honor, no doubt, held a single vase with summer wildflowers. There was a television with a VCR in one corner and a shelf above the television holding stacks of videotapes. And there was, as Paulette had said, no fireplace at all.

"You're right," Molly said, embarrassment flooding her where only minutes before there had been pure terror. "You must think I'm really bizarre. I probably woke up Dad, too, when I yelled."

"I doubt it," said Paulette. "Those painkillers are pretty strong." She hesitated, then spoke again, her voice cautious. "Molly, I don't understand. You seem afraid here. Want to talk about it—whatever it is?" She regarded Molly with wide eyes.

"No," Molly whispered. "I'll be all right."

Paulette nodded. "Well, let's go upstairs now." Molly followed Paulette out of the study, through the library, and back into the hall. "Can you carry your small bag? I'll take the suitcases."

Molly slung the carry-on bag over her shoulder and followed Paulette, who struggled under the weight of Molly's heavy suitcases, up the stairs to the long hallway. *She's pregnant,* remembered Molly. *I shouldn't let her carry heavy things.*

But she felt too weak to help, to speak, to do anything. *I'm becoming a zombie,* she thought. It sounded pathetic but seemed right on the mark. She kept her eyes down so she wouldn't see the long hall stretching before her.

Paulette opened the first door along the hallway and flicked on the light. "Here you go, Molly. It's pretty small, but this is the only bedroom besides ours that we've fixed up. I hope you like it."

Molly stumbled in and dropped her carry-on bag on the floor. She saw through bleary eyes that, though not large, the room was high-ceilinged and freshly papered in white with sprigs of daisies. The double bed had an ornate brass headboard, which gleamed in the soft overhead glow. There was a mahogany dresser with a vase of the same wildflowers Molly had seen down in the study. A small rolltop desk stood by the window. The floor was covered by a braided rag rug in many deep colors. "It's great," murmured Molly. "Thanks."

"The bathroom is right next door," continued Paulette. "But the shower doesn't work yet, so just use the bath." She hesitated. "Do you need anything else? Are you all right now?"

Molly sank onto the bed. "I'm fine. I'll be fine." She fingered the end of her braid and looked up at Paulette. Something more seemed to need saying. "I'm not always so weird," she offered. "Really."

Paulette smiled unconvincingly. "Well, sleep tight," she said. Then she closed the door. Molly heard her footsteps darting down the hall to the room she shared with Bill. Molly was so tired she couldn't even drag herself to the bathroom. She curled up right on top of the soft bedcover and fell immediately asleep.

Sometime in the middle of the night she awoke with a pressing need and left the room to use the toilet next door. Groggily she made her way back into her bedroom and climbed into the bed. She pulled the cover over her this time and settled her head on the soft pillows. As she drifted again into sleep, she thought she heard the sound of children's voices somewhere. The singing was soft and distant but all too clear: *"Oh my darlin', Oh my darlin', Oh my darlin', Clementine—*

She sat bolt upright in bed, clutching the covers,

straining to hear. But there was only silence. She waited another few minutes, listening, hardly daring to breathe, then at last lay down and pulled the pillow over her head. She must have been dreaming again.

5

$\mathcal{M}$olly slept heavily until a hand shook her shoulder. Paulette stood at the side of her bed, wearing an oversized T-shirt with a picture of a panda on it. Her uncombed carrot-colored hair was spiky.

"Good morning!" Paulette crossed to the window and pulled back the long curtains. Sunlight flooded the room. "Rise and shine! I'm indulging our favorite invalid with breakfast in bed, and I've set up trays for you and me, too. How do you want your egg?"

Molly sat up groggily and pushed her hair out of her face. It had fallen out of its braid. Her face was unwashed and her mouth felt fuzzy and horrible.

"Your dad's having a poached egg, but I'm having scrambled."

"I'll have scrambled, too." She yawned widely, then tossed back the covers. "Is it all right if I shower first?"

"The showers aren't installed yet, remember? You can have a bath, but it takes a while for the water to warm up, I'm afraid."

Molly followed Paulette out into the hall. In daylight the hallway seemed less forbidding, less like the one in her dreams. Sunlight from the tall window over the stairs made diamond patterns on the carpet.

In the bathroom Molly shed her clothes, then started water flowing into the funny old tub. The tub stood high on curved iron legs, its porcelain chipped in places, revealing rusted patches. When the water was warm enough, she stepped in gingerly and knelt on the bottom. She left the rubber plug for the drain hanging from its little chain so the water would rush out almost as fast as it poured in. Leaning forward, she splashed water over herself with cupped hands. She grabbed a washcloth from the pile on the windowsill and washed her face. She ducked her head under the flow from the faucet and shampooed quickly, then turned off the water, expelling her pent-up breath in a gasp of relief. In less than five minutes total she was out of the tub, toweled dry, and dressed in jeans and a red West River Academy T-shirt. She'd managed it—almost a bath. But she eyed the tub warily and wondered whether they sold shower attachments for the faucet in such a little town.

Outside the window the June morning sparkled. The sun beat down on the headland, the gentle sea breeze stirred the long grasses around the house, and through the open bathroom window Molly could smell salt. The ocean must be very close.

She toweled her wet hair, bending from the waist to shake out the tangles. Then she braided her hair into her customary long tail and walked barefoot down the hall to the master bedroom. The door was open. Molly gave her father a hug. "How's your ankle?"

He was sitting up against several pillows, his blond hair tousled, blond stubble of a beard scratching her face when he squeezed back. "Oh, it's there. I didn't sleep very well." He patted the bed and she sat on the edge.

"I didn't either, with this great lummox flailing around next to me," said Paulette, reaching over to ruffle Bill's thinning hair. He grabbed her fingers and kissed them.

Paulette set their breakfast on tray tables near the bed. There was a stack of toast, little jars of jam, an egg each, orange juice, and three small bowls of blueberries. "The blueberries grow right here on the headland," she told Molly. "I picked these this morning. They're great with milk and a little sugar."

"Thanks." Molly drank her juice. Paulette poured them each a cup of mint tea. Bill stretched, shifting his ankle with a groan, then settled back on his pillows.

"So, Molly, how did *you* sleep?" he asked. From the significant look he exchanged with Paulette, Molly knew her stepmother had told him all about Molly's unusual reaction to the house the night before.

She pleated the bedspread between her fingers. "I just don't know what's going on with me, Dad.

But it's not only here. Things were weird at home, but I thought coming here would help. Looks like it hasn't."

"Since when have things been . . . *weird* at home, honey?" asked her father. "Since your accident?"

"I'm not so sure it was an accident," she muttered.

"But what kind of weird?"

"Well, you know the bad dream I've always had? It used to come just once in a while, but not anymore. Now I'm having bad dreams all the time. They're making me crazy."

Bill Teague looked concerned. "What brings on the dreams, Molly? Stress? I know Jen keeps your nose to the grindstone—"

"No, it isn't really anything to do with Mom." Molly hated it when her parents criticized each other. "Things started getting worse a few weeks ago, you know—when I got caught lying about passing the swim test, I think." The humiliation still felt fresh. "That night I had the dream again. First time in a long time. And then every night. It was hellish, Dad. Swim lessons by day, nightmares by night." She forked up some egg. "Look, let's not talk about it. I'm trying to forget."

Paulette had been sitting quietly, sipping her tea. Now she spoke up. "Recurring dreams come to us for a reason, you know. And I bet there's some connection between the swimming lessons and the dreams. If we were in San Francisco, I could take you to this great therapist who does dreamwork,

Molly. I don't know about Maine—they might not have that sort of thing here."

Molly buttered a piece of toast. *Dreamwork!* Jen would get a kick out of the word. It was so very Californian.

Bill saw her expression and put his hand on hers. "Let's drop it," he said. "You're here now and under no stress at all." He tried for a joke. "You just relax and strip wallpaper. What could make for a better summer?" Then he looked serious. "You should explore the village. Maybe you'll make some new friends."

"Oh!" exclaimed Paulette. "Bill, that reminds me—the phone call!" She turned to Molly. "I forgot to tell you last night that your friend called."

"My friend? What friend?" *Kathi sure didn't give up easily.*

"It was a boy. Nice, deep voice. Jonathan or Jason or something." Paulette giggled nervously at Molly's anxious face. "He sounded very nice. Said he was a friend of yours and planned to do some traveling up here this summer. He was hoping we needed somebody to work on the house."

"Oh, my God, was it *Jared?* Was his name Jared Bernstein?"

"That boy!" exclaimed Bill.

Paulette hesitated. "I think that was the name . . ."

"When did he call?" Molly wailed. "How could he have known I was here?"

Paulette sank into a green armchair, looking

drained, as if having Molly as a guest was proving to be more exhausting than she'd anticipated. "Well, let's see," she began, running her hands through her hair. "We were papering the dining room and the phone rang in the study. I went in to answer, and it was this boy. He sounded . . . well, *nice*. He said to say hello to you when you got in."

"You didn't hire him," said Molly, fearing the worst.

"Well, no," Paulette assured her. "I said we couldn't afford to hire anyone, and we were doing fine ourselves. And then just as we were hanging up, I heard this awful crash. I ran back to the dining room to find Billy had fallen off the ladder—my poor lamb! Then we had to rush to the hospital, and everything else has been happening since." She looked at Molly anxiously over the rim of her teacup. "I would have told you about your friend's call sooner, but it completely slipped my mind."

"Don't call him my friend, whatever you do," said Molly. "I came here to get away from him!" She closed her eyes, then added in a softer voice; "And to see you and Dad, of course." She didn't want to offend Paulette on top of everything else. *But, my God! My life is becoming something right out of the Twilight Zone.*

She fought for calm, invoked her mother's reasonable nature, and opened her eyes. "Jared is the boy who threw me into the pool."

"I didn't know that, Molly." Paulette set her cup down on the tray with a clatter. "Bill, why didn't you tell me?"

"I thought I had," answered Bill. He put his hand on Molly's arm. "Look, honey, don't worry about it. There's no way I'd let that guy near the place now, knowing how he upsets you." His voice was reassuring. "I don't doubt he's sorry about what happened, but the way to atone is to leave you in peace, not to pester you."

"Thinking about him makes me feel sick." She drained her juice and set the glass on her tray table.

Bill shifted his ankle and grimaced. "Well, then, let's move on to a happier subject. Paulette tells me she has already spilled the beans about our big news."

Molly mustered a grin. "I think it's great about the baby, Dad."

Paulette snuggled next to Bill and rested her head on his shoulder. Bill reached up one hand and stroked her face. "I always wanted lots of kids," Bill beamed. "But your mom didn't think it was practical to have more than one. Just think—now you'll be a big sister. Won't you love helping to take care of a new little Teague?"

"I can't wait!"

Paulette nuzzled Bill's neck. "You sure made a beautiful baby the first time, Billy Boy. Do you think our own little Christmas angel will look like Molly?"

"I hope so," said Bill, smiling at both of them. "What's on the agenda today? I'd intended to show you around Hibben, Molly, but it looks like I'm stuck here for a while."

"Don't worry, I'll do the honors," said Paulette. "We'll go this morning."

After washing up the breakfast dishes, Molly and Paulette left the house for the breezy headland. Molly went straight over to the van, but Paulette shook her head. "We can walk," she said. "It isn't far. Just back down the drive and turn left. It's maybe a mile."

They walked side by side, though Paulette had to skip occasionally to keep up with Molly's long stride. Molly tried politely to adjust to her stepmother's speed but inadvertently took the lead again as the road dipped downhill, and Paulette had to scurry to catch up.

She caught Molly's hand and swung it. "Isn't it a gorgeous day?" she cried, then sang it to the tune of "Twinkle, Twinkle, Little Star":

"Isn't it a gorgeous day, isn't it a gorgeous day?
Now that Molly's here to stay
And we're walking on our way—
Isn't it a gorgeous day, now that Molly's come to play!"

Molly laughed. Paulette was acting like a little kid. Molly could imagine Jen's smirk if she could see Bill's pregnant wife singing and dancing along the road. Molly was glad Jen *wasn't* there to see. She liked Paulette and knew she wouldn't be making fun of her with Jen anymore.

The road from the headland wound through the trees and ended at a narrow, paved road. Paulette led them to the left, down a hill to the town. Paulette broke off her song to point to the sign that read: Hibben, Maine, pop. 812. "Soon to be 813," Paulette giggled, patting her belly.

Massive chunks of gray granite lined the road on one side. The first building they came to was a picturesque white clapboard church with a graceful steeple. It was surrounded by a low wall built of the gray stone. Behind the church was a cemetery, the old headstones dotting the grass.

"A lot of houses in the town are built of this rock," said Paulette. "See there? Unusual along the coast, where most houses are made of wood. That's the old schoolhouse—it's an antique shop now. We'll have a look around on our way home. And that's the post office—it used to be the general store. Isn't it quaint?"

Molly stood on the narrow sidewalk and looked down the street. A street sign informed her this was Main Street. It led down a hill lined with buildings of gray stone and white clapboard and ended, it seemed, right in the sea. Molly could just make out the masts of dozens of small fishing vessels and pleasure boats where the street stopped and the water began. That must be the wharf. There were only a few streets leading off Main Street. Molly paused at the bottom of one marked Cotton Lane. It led up the cliff sharply to the right and was unpaved. Dust blew across the rutted dirt lane. She blinked the dust out of her eyes—and saw she'd been mistaken. Cotton Lane *was* paved, after all.

Then she felt it—the curious sense of recognition. She stood for a long moment, wrapped in thought, trying to remember. *Where have I seen this before?*

"Look there," Paulette was saying. She pointed to a group of camera-laden men and women carrying shopping bags, who trudged past them up the hill. "Hibben is changing from a little old fishing village, and there's nothing the old-timers can do about it. But that's good news for us. Tourists need a place to stay, and what better place than a romantic old Victorian on a cliff? I bet they'll flock to us once the inn is open. Hibben's history is full of the stuff tourists love to hear about: ships wrecked in the cove in the fog, huge storms the villagers call 'northeasters' whipping in from the ocean in winter, ancient Indian sacred grounds just over the hills . . ." Then she paused. "Molly? What's wrong?"

"This little street," began Molly. "Where does it go?"

"Cotton Lane? It just goes up the hill. Ends at the cliff. There are a few old cottages left, and some new condos. And the public library, such as it is."

Molly started up the steep lane without a word.

"Hey, wait up!" cried Paulette, scrambling along behind.

As Molly climbed on, she clenched her fingers into fists. She climbed steadily, all the way to the end of the row of whitewashed cottages, and stopped abruptly at the last cottage. It, unlike the others, was of gray stone, and it had a bright blue gate set into the fence in front of it and a painted blue door to match the wooden addition built onto the side of the house. The sign on the gate announced: Hibben Free Library, est. 1941.

She put her hand on the gate and flung it open, then hurried along the path up to the blue door. The humming began in her head, insistent.

She gripped her hatbox and basket tightly.

Box? Basket? What's going on?

She approached the plump, fair-haired woman sweeping the stoop. "Mrs. Wilkins?" she asked, untying her shawl (*shawl?*) and settling it loosely over her shoulders. She put up a hand to check that her braids were still neatly pinned across her head.

"Yes, dear?" The woman stopped sweeping and leaned on her broom. "Oh, you're one of the Holloway girls! How are you this morning?"

"Clementine Horn," she corrected. "And I'm fine, thank you."

"Molly! *Molly!*" Paulette cried, her small hand gripping Molly's arm like pincers. "What are you doing? The library's *closed*. Nobody's here at all!"

Molly collapsed on the stone step of the house and stared up at Paulette, dazed. Then she glanced down at herself—she *wasn't* wearing a shawl, wasn't carrying a wicker basket or a round hatbox. *But she had been.* She put her hands to her head. Her hair was in a single braid hanging over her shoulder—not in two braids wrapped around her head like a coronet. *But it had been.*

"Oh, Paulette," she whispered. Tears welled in her eyes. "What in the world is happening to me?"

Without a word, Paulette pulled her to her feet and back along the path, away from the library and down Cotton Lane. She glanced left and right as Molly stumbled along beside her, and no longer looked like a schoolgirl at play. Her eyes were serious and her mouth was set in a firm line. She hurried Molly back onto Main Street and down the hill to the pier, not meeting the curious eyes of the tourists and townspeople who watched their progress. She stopped at last in front of a small café by the wharf. Vendors near the ferry dock sold hot dogs and soft drinks and little whittled sailing ships. The smell of fish was everywhere.

They went inside and Paulette asked for a table in the far corner. She pushed Molly gently into a chair. "Get something to drink. How about some juice?"

How about a shot of vodka? That might bring me to my senses. "A Coke," she mumbled.

"A Coke," Paulette told the waiter, her voice firm. "And some orange juice, please." When the waiter left, she leaned across the table. "All right," she said. "Will you please tell me what that was all about?"

Molly stared at the tabletop and twisted a paper napkin between her fingers. "I thought I saw a woman in front of that cottage—the library, I mean. I knew her. I had come because . . ." She hesitated, trying to recall just how she'd felt on Cotton Lane. There were strands of memory, but nothing she could weave into anything meaningful. "I had a *plan,* I think. I wanted to talk to somebody inside that house." She shook her head. "Nothing is making any sense."

Paulette ruffled her hair into spikes, then gestured at the restaurant around them. "Have you ever heard of *déjà vu?* It's French for 'already seen.' It's the feeling when you think you've seen something already."

"I know what it means," said Molly.

The waiter brought the drinks, and Molly seized her Coke gratefully. When he moved away, Paulette leaned forward. "I heard you say a name. Clementine Horn. Who is that?"

"I don't know. I never heard that name before in my life." She hesitated. "Only—here's something else weird, Paulette—that Clementine song has been in my head for weeks now. I hear it in my dreams, too."

"The Clementine song?" asked Paulette, puzzled. "Oh, you mean the one about the miner?" And then, as uninhibited as she'd been walking down the road, Paulette burst into song right there in the café: *"Oh my darlin', Oh my darlin'—"*

Molly froze. "Stop it!" she cried. "It's horrible."

Paulette broke off, aghast. They sat in silence a long, tense moment. Paulette's next question seemed to come out of the blue. "Have you read Shakespeare, Molly? Do you know *Hamlet?*"

Molly blinked. "I took an honors course in Shakespeare just this last year. We read everything."

"Well then you certainly must know the part when Hamlet says to Horatio: 'There are more things in Heaven and Earth, Horatio, than are dreamt of in your philosophy.' "

Molly shrugged. "Yeah."

"And do you agree, Molly? Do you believe that Hamlet was right, that our philosophies are limited? That people don't really understand all there is to understand in the world?"

"Of course. Scientists are always discovering new things."

"But was Hamlet talking about science?" Paulette shifted in her plastic chair. "Or was he talking about something more than science?"

"Who knows, Paulette? What are *you* talking about?" Paulette had the tenacity of a moth buzzing at a light. Molly wanted only to go back to the house and fall asleep. She stood up.

"Let's go home, Paulette."

Paulette stood as well, picking up the bill the waiter had left on the edge of their table. "It's not irrelevant, you know," she said. "The weird things that are happening to you have to be one of two things, don't you see? Either it's just as bad as you think, and you are having some sort of breakdown—or else it's something else, something we can barely conceive of, something that might even make a sort of sense, if we only had the right philosophy. Get it?" She paid the bill, and they walked outside onto Main Street.

Hibben was sleepy in the warm sunshine. A few tourists were on the pier snapping the colorful fishing boats out in the cove with their zoom lenses, but otherwise the streets were all but empty. Molly's head was aching fiercely now, and that same lethargy that had plagued her back in Battleboro Heights weakened her limbs now. She trailed behind Paulette up the hill to the house.

After lunch Molly threw herself into stripping wallpaper in the dining room. The work was tiring her out, but that was good. If she were tired enough, she would be able to forget. The thought of what had happened that morning in town made her break out in a sweat of panic. Better not to think. Work and sleep, that was the way to handle things.

They ate dinner together in the master bedroom upstairs—Paulette's lentil soup and homemade croutons and a salad. When they finished, Bill and Paulette exchanged a look. Molly braced herself.

Bill wasted no time getting to the point. "Molly, honey, Paulette told me about what happened this morning in town. I admit I'm worried."

"Maybe a doctor—a psychologist—could help," suggested Paulette. "After all, your unconscious may be trying to tell you something through all these dreams and now these . . . well, *visions* in town."

"I don't need a shrink," said Molly. "I'm just tired. What I need is sleep, that's all." She left them looking after her as she hurried down the hall to her bedroom and shut the door.

The next morning she and Paulette helped Bill hobble down the back stairs to the kitchen. At breakfast Bill and Paulette were careful not to mention anything out of the ordinary, and Molly was grateful. After breakfast two carpenters and a plumber arrived on the headland to consult with Bill and Paulette about renovating the existing bathroom and adding several more for the guest rooms. Molly went back to work in the dining room. She found it peaceful there, standing on the stepladder pulling strips of faded, flowered paper off the wall. The old glue was yellow and brittle. It tore away easily, sending a fine dust onto the scuffed wooden floor.

By noon the workmen had gone. Paulette served lunch in the study, and while they ate, Molly quizzed Paulette and her father on names for the new baby. "It'll be born near Christmas, right?" she asked. "How about something festive? Noelle? Carol?"

"What about Star?" suggested Paulette.

"Too New Age," objected Molly.

"Hey, we could name her Holly. To rhyme with Molly. Perfect for sisters."

Molly wrinkled her nose. "That's too cutesy."

"Well, how about Wreath?" asked Bill. He grinned at them. "What makes you so sure the baby will be a girl, anyway?"

"Okay, then, what about Rudolf? Or Santa?" teased Molly. "Saint Nick."

"Nick's not bad, actually," said Bill. "Nicholas Teague. It has a nice ring to it."

When they finished their sandwiches, Bill and Paulette started looking at paint samples for the guest bedrooms. Molly moved to the couch and turned on the television. The soap opera actors were sobbing about someone's nervous breakdown. Molly watched with interest. Was this how people would react when she was carted off?

A crash from the other side of the room made her look up, and she saw that the big book of paint samples had fallen off the table as Paulette leaned across to kiss Bill on the tip of his nose. Molly smiled indulgently. They were like a pair of little kids. Then she looked beyond them to the wall. Something made her smile stiffen. That was the wall where she had imagined a fireplace the first night she arrived. Was it Molly's imagination, or was the old floral wallpaper buckling where the wall met the ceiling? She felt compelled to get up and check.

"Hey, what are you doing?" Bill asked in surprise as she dragged the ottoman over to the wall and climbed on it, stretching to reach the edge of the strip that was loose.

"Hey, *Molly!* We'd decided to leave this paper alone," protested Paulette. "Don't rip it!"

But Molly tugged harder and the old paper ripped away from the wall, revealing brick. She pulled more off, lower down, shouldering aside the small bookcase. Next to the brick, a section of plywood came into view. She stopped. Unaccountably, she was shaking.

Paulette jumped off the couch and rushed over. "Now, who would put wallpaper over brick? Look at this, Bill—oh! It's a fireplace, I think. Boarded over." She stared at Molly with wide eyes.

Bill hobbled over to inspect the board. "Well, well! This is great. Maybe the last owners didn't use the room much or didn't want drafts. But I'll get somebody to come out and inspect it. We'll enjoy toasting our toes in here by a fire come winter." Then he looked at Molly. "How in the world did you know this would be here?"

She hugged herself, shivering. "I don't know." She tried to press the patterned paper back into place. Softly, very softly, the humming was starting in her head again. *I've got to get out of here,* she thought desperately. *I have to get away!*

"I'm going out for a walk," she said hoarsely. A walk on the headland might make her feel better. Fresh air.

"Good idea," said Bill, looking at her oddly.

And Paulette added: "Check out the harbor seals. Sometimes you can see them sunning themselves on rocks down in the cove."

Molly crossed the yard surrounding the house and moved through the trees along a path leading toward the cliff. Tall strong grasses waved gracefully in the breeze, beckoning her. When she turned and looked back at the house, the many windows winked at her like eyes.

Ahead of her the cliff jutted out over the cove. Molly stopped and listened to the surge of waves crashing against the rock. She kept carefully away from the cliff's edge, not wanting to see the water. The sun beat warmly on her head, and the sea breeze stirred her braid. Overhead gulls wheeled in the sky, then plunged out of sight over the edge of the cliff. When she was in sight of the house again, Molly sank down in a soft clearing at the edge of the trees.

She lay back and crossed her arms under her head, staring up at the sky. As she watched, gray clouds blew across and blotted out the sun. Should she see a psychologist, as Paulette suggested? Jen would never approve. And Molly didn't feel crazy—but on the other hand, maybe part of being crazy was not knowing you were. *Use your famous brain,* she ordered herself. *Why is this happening to you?* She closed her eyes to think.

She must have been dozing, one arm flung up over her eyes, when she heard a rustling in the tall grass and knew she was not alone. She heard the whispers of children. She held her breath. The rustling and whispers stopped. A cool, damp wind began to blow. It smelled like rain.

She then opened her eyes and saw Jared Bernstein standing over her. She shot to her feet. "You!"

Now I know I'm dreaming.

He stepped across the grass to stand next to her, but she backed away. "Molly, please," he said, and his voice sounded real enough. "I've come all this way."

He was standing there in dark blue shorts and a white T-shirt. His dark, wavy hair looked freshly trimmed.

"Are you kidding? How dare you track me all the way to Maine!"

"I didn't exactly *track* you," he said slowly. He didn't move any closer, sensing she would run back to the house if he did. He sat down in the grass, instead, and looked up at her. "Come on. Sit down and I'll tell you all about it."

She remained standing, hands on hips. "How the

hell did you get here?" He was real. He was as real as she was.

"I flew, same as you. Then took the bus from Bangor. It's a hellish trip on that coast road, let me tell you. Stopping at every little podunk town along the way. I thought I'd never get here."

"What I want to know is how you knew where to find me in the first place!"

"I just asked your mom where you were. That's all."

"And Mom *told* you?"

"Sure. Obviously." He held out one hand toward her. "Oh, Molly—I've been going absolutely crazy, and it's your fault because you won't talk to me. I called here the other day to see if your dad would hire me since they're doing a lot of work on their house, but—"

"My mom told you that, too?"

"Yeah. But the woman who answered said they didn't need anyone, and then the connection broke. When I called back later to talk to you, no one was home. So I told my aunt and uncle I had to make a little trip to visit a friend, and I booked my flight, and here I am. I got here this afternoon, and I'm staying until you'll talk to me."

She couldn't believe any of this. What was she supposed to say to this person who had nearly killed her and now felt drawn to seek her out, wherever she might travel? It occurred to her that *he* might be crazy. Like one of those weirdos who stalk their favorite movie stars, always phoning and harassing them. You had to be careful with people like that. You couldn't trust them at all.

She glanced around, hoping to see her father or Paulette coming toward them, but they were alone. She frowned. "Where are you staying?"

"There's a campground about two miles around the cove—toward the next little town. I've got a tent." He patted the ground in front of him. "Come on. Please. Sit down. Just for a few minutes. If you'll just answer a few questions, I promise I won't bother you again."

She sat down in the grass and wrapped her arms around her knees. The wind picked up and sea gulls screamed, circling overhead. A sprinkle of raindrops scattered down, then stopped. "All right, you get five minutes. Then I'm going in, and I won't see you again."

Jared rubbed his hands through his thick hair. "Fair enough. Okay." He studied her face a long moment, silent.

When he did not begin, she looked pointedly at her watch. "Four minutes—and the clock's ticking."

Then came a rush of words. His voice grew choked: "I don't know what it is, Molly, but it's something to do with you. And it started at Michael's party that night. We danced—and it was like I'd held you before. You seemed so familiar to me. And then when we were at the pool and you wouldn't get in—well, something just happened. It was like something snapped in me." He held up his hand to stop her from saying anything. "Look, I told you already. I don't know why I did it. It was scary. I knew it was wrong, and I did it anyway. I sort of *had* to."

Had to? Molly edged further away from him.

"I'm really sorry, Molly. But—about the things I saw under the water? That's what we have to talk about. There was a round box. And there was *sea-weed*—and I saw blood in the water. I know, I know—it had to be a hallucination. But right after that I started having dreams. Bad ones. I had the first one that very night, after we'd revived you and taken you to the hospital. It was about you, I know it was—but the girl didn't look like you. She looked like some old-fashioned girl, wearing a long skirt, with her hair pinned up. You know, how they wore it, like, a hundred years ago?" Jared's eyes burned into hers. She could not look away, though the panic was welling inside her. "She was you, somehow, Molly, in my dream. And I was singing that song to her, you know the one—" And he began to sing in a husky voice:

"Oh my darlin', Oh my darlin', Oh my darlin', Clementine. You are lost and gone forever—"

Molly jumped up. This was beyond crazy. She began running for the house.

"Molly! Molly, wait!" He rushed behind, heedless of the raindrops that now spattered down from the gray sky.

She reached the back door, but it was locked. She hammered on it with her fist, blind panic overtaking her now. "Get away from me!" she howled as the door opened and she tumbled into the kitchen.

Paulette stood there, astonished. "What in the world is going on?" she cried.

"Close the door! I don't want to talk to him!" Molly tried to push it shut, but Jared was there, frantic that she shouldn't get away from him again.

"Please, Molly—"

"Five minutes are up!" she yelled.

"But I haven't finished!"

"You have for now, I think," said Paulette, pushing Molly aside and standing in front of Jared. "She *said* she doesn't want to talk to you. Whoever you are."

"But—I need to see her!" Jared was much taller than Paulette and looked over her head to where Molly stood near the kitchen table. "Molly, come on. We have to talk about what these visions mean. Why do you run away when I sing 'Clementine' to you?"

Paulette's eyes widened. She glanced over her shoulder at Molly, who was edging toward the pantry. Then she frowned at Jared. "Listen, maybe we'd better talk about this."

"I'm trying to, can't you tell?"

On the counter in the pantry was a basket of red tomatoes. Molly reached for one. Her arm ached with wanting to lob it across the kitchen to splatter smack in the middle of Jared Bernstein's forehead. The force of wanting this made her clench her hand, and the tomato split. Juice ran down her fingers.

Blood on her hands? She stared down at them, her head pounding.

"Are you the boy who called about a job here?" asked Paulette. She studied him with her green eyes.

When he nodded, she shook her head. "Well, who can blame Molly for not wanting to see you? But you know our phone number. Maybe you can discuss this better over the phone."

Jared's shoulders sagged. "Believe me, I've tried." The rain dripped off his hair and ran into his eyes. He wiped his face as he turned away from the door. Then he looked back once and shouted: "I'm calling tomorrow, Molly. And you'd better talk to me!"

"Oh yeah?" she called from the safety of the pantry, wiping her hands on her shorts. "Or else *what,* Jared Bernstein?"

Their eyes caught and held across the room. The look was angry, challenging—but full of something else, too. The silence stretched out between them, electric. Molly couldn't look away.

"Or else . . . or else I'll call again, I guess," Jared finally said, simply. "And again."

Then he walked away in the rain, and Paulette closed the door. She turned to Molly. "We need to get to the bottom of this," she said.

Molly bowed her head. She could hear Jared's husky voice singing to her on Michael's patio. And again on the headland. *"You are lost and gone forever—"* She could hear the soft laughter of children echoing through the house. Her head was aching fiercely.

"I need aspirin," she gulped.

Paulette walked over and placed a small, cool hand on the back of Molly's neck. "Come on upstairs," she said, "and I'll give you a head rub. A good massage will help more than aspirin. And I want to try a meditation technique I know."

"Sounds very New Age, very California," said Molly, but she was too upset to argue. They went upstairs. Molly lay on her bed, her head cradled by a pillow. She closed her eyes.

She felt Paulette tug the elastic off the end of her braid and unravel the long strands. Then she felt Paulette's hands on the top of her head. At first she tensed, uncomfortable. But then, despite herself, she yielded to the touch of her stepmother's fingers against her scalp. For such small hands, Paulette's were surprisingly strong. The softness of the pillow under her neck and Paulette's firm pressure on her head made her relax. She felt she was in a cozy nest. Her eyes fluttered, and Paulette smiled at her reassuringly. Molly closed her eyes again, embarrassed to be this close to her stepmother, touching like this. Jen gave her a hug now and then, but they didn't really touch very often. Nor for very long.

After a few moments of silent massage, Paulette's voice came softly. "Are you relaxed?"

"Yes." Molly's voice was a sigh.

"Good. Now, do this for me. Imagine you can see a candle. Picture the flame. Can you see it?"

Molly had no will to resist. She gave in to the hands rubbing her scalp and face. Behind her closed eyes a flame leapt high. "Yes."

"Watch the flame. Concentrate on the flame."

Paulette's voice was soft. After a long pause, she continued. "Now in that flame you can see a long tunnel. It's a tunnel you can walk down, a long, long tunnel. Imagine yourself walking down that tunnel." Paulette paused again. "Do you see it? Are you walking down the tunnel?"

"Yes."

She smoothed Molly's temples. "And along the sides of the tunnel are doors, Molly. Behind these doors are memories of all the things you have experienced in your long, long life. In your many lives. I want you to go to the door that has the girl in your dream behind it. The girl with the name you heard people call you. Clementine Horn. You will open the door and see Clementine Horn, whoever Clementine is. When you open the door, you will know her story, and you will be able to tell it. You will not be frightened, Molly. You will see scenes almost as if they were a film." Paulette paused again, but her hands kept rubbing Molly's head. "You will not be frightened," she repeated.

Now Molly could see the tunnel in the candle flame behind her closed eyes. But when she tried to visualize the doors, she saw instead a large round box, with her hand holding down the pulsing lid. She knew this box. When she heard Paulette's voice telling her to open the door, Molly imagined herself lifting the lid off this box. Was it the hatbox? Was it Pandora's box, from which all the evils of the world would escape? She listened to Paulette's reassurances: "You will not be frightened." Then softly, slowly, as if only background music, the humming began. It merged with Paulette's voice and expanded in Molly's mind until her head pulsed relentlessly with the tune.

And Molly knew suddenly that, frightened or not, what she had to do now was open that box. It seemed she had been waiting all her life to release its contents. And so she did.

6 Clementine

After her chores were done Clementine left the big house by the kitchen door and hurried across the headland toward the sea. She tried to keep well hidden by the double line of washing flapping in the brisk wind, holding up her long skirts and running between the twin walls of sheets, then walking swiftly through the scrub and tall reed grass toward the cliff.

She had cut the children's lessons short and taken them down to the kitchen, where Janie would give them a snack. They'd be eating it now, giving her perhaps a half hour of privacy. Nonetheless, she glanced back over her shoulder to make sure Abner, the one who clung to her like a barnacle, was not following. She saw the many windows of the house winking in the sunlight. They watched her, she felt, like the watchful eyes of her uncle and aunt.

She hurried through the thick screen of reed grass to her favorite spot right at the edge of the cliff. From there she liked to watch the water roll into the cove. The semicircle formed by the walls of the cliff made the cove into a churning caldron. Sometimes seals sunned themselves atop the rocks, and she never stopped marveling that they could swim in water that always looked at the boil.

When she was younger and had first come to her uncle and aunt's house, Clementine used to take her doll out to the cliff and pretend she was a giant, cooking soup for supper. She'd pull up fists full of pebbles and fling them down into the pot, then twist off stalks of the reed grass and hurl them down, too. "Now just a little pinch of salt," she'd bellow in a giant's huge voice, and kick dirt over the cliff wall into the boiling broth. "Time to eat, dear Mollydolly," she would shout, staring down into the froth of foam against the rocks.

At the cliff's edge she would set up a rock table for Mollydolly. The doll could drink her soup from a curved leaf. But Clementine could just lean forward and suck her soup right out of the cove. Giants were powerful. They didn't need to bother with table manners. They didn't even need a table.

Once Clementine had carelessly knocked Mollydolly over the cliff. She had feared there would be no chance of recovering her beloved doll, one of the few links left to her home and parents. She had lain on her stomach to peer over the edge down into the spray. And luck was with her. There was Mollydolly, resting only six or seven feet down the side of the cliff on a wide shelf of rock.

Clementine had taken off her shiny button shoes and black woolen stockings. Then, scooting backward over the edge, grasping great handfuls of the tufted grass that grew from the cracks between the rocks, she eased herself over the cliff. The rock face bulged out slightly so the drop wasn't sheer, and there were footholds enough so that she was able to drop safely onto the rock shelf. She grabbed up the little doll and hugged her. She then saw to her surprise that the shelf she stood on was actually a little natural front porch to a cave house. She crept inside and found herself in a low-ceilinged room just big enough for one or two children to sit in. She sat down, holding Mollydolly in her lap.

What a perfect hiding place. Her aunt and uncle would never find her here. She could have all the privacy she needed. If only climbing back up were as easy as climbing down had been, she could come as often as she liked, and no one would ever be the wiser.

She stuffed the little doll down the front of her dress. Feeling for footholds and reaching up to grab the cliff plants, she then shimmied back up the rock face. She reached the top, exhilarated. The deadly drop into the cove should her feet slip didn't worry her at all. Her need for a place where the children couldn't find her made her brave.

But games of giants and secret caves belonged to childhood. Now when Clementine came to the cliff's edge, she came alone, and not to play. There were no hiding places anymore. Even the little cave offered no sanctuary ever since little Abner trailed her to the cliff a few months back and hid in the grass. He had watched her lower herself down to the ledge, then peered over the edge and called to her, exultant that he'd found her, demanding she let him come down and see. He scurried over the cliff's edge so fast she had to reach up and catch him. Then there was nothing she could do but show him the safe handholds of tufted grass, the best footholds in the rock. She made him promise it would be their secret, but since then the cave held no magic for her.

Still, she came out to the cliff whenever she could to escape from the many children who were her responsibility every afternoon. Soon—if Aunt Ethel and Uncle Wallace had their way—the children would be her responsibility every morning as well. Morning, afternoon, and evening, Clementine was to be in charge of all her cousins. She had had her seventeenth birthday a month ago, in May, and the very day after, Uncle Wallace gave notice to the children's governess. When the school term finished, he said, they would no longer need her because Clementine would be stepping into her place. Now Miss Finch was upstairs packing her trunks, readying herself to move out in a few days' time.

A terrible anger had come over Clementine the day after her seventeenth birthday and settled in her bones like a sickness. She hated to be leaving the little school in the village. She wasn't ready! She was thirsty for more knowledge and longed to go on to college. More and more girls were continuing their education these days. Clementine was sure her own mother and father would have encouraged her to learn as much as she could. But Aunt Ethel and Uncle Wallace were adamant: her place was home with her family.

Clementine stared rebelliously down at the water in the cove, her resentment surging with the waves. Into the cove, then out again, then in again to be dashed against the rocks. There was no escape for the water. Its function was to fill the cove and slap the cliff walls, then recede in a froth of white, then rush back in again. But for her?

She must get away from here! There were several colleges and ladies' seminaries of higher learning down east. Why shouldn't she be allowed to go? She had tried again the other day to make Uncle Wallace see reason, but he had just laughed.

Clementine hurled a rock over the side of the cliff and watched it disappear into the water, as completely and quietly as she herself would disappear. She had come up with a strategy. A plan. She would run away after school was out for the summer. She had no money and wasn't sure yet where she would go, but those were mere details. They would be worked out. College would cost a lot, she knew, and her uncle wouldn't be giving her a penny of his considerable wealth if she ran away. But she could work, certainly she could—and hard, too. If she could be an unpaid governess for her many young cousins, surely she could be a governess for someone else's children for a tidy salary. Not in Hibben, of course, but somewhere where her uncle wouldn't be able to find her. And if she saved her money, why shouldn't that cover the cost of her tuition at an academy of higher learning? She would talk to Miss Kent at school tomorrow and ask her advice about which school to apply to, and where she might advertise her services as a governess.

School had always been a source of joy and a place of refuge for Clementine. When she'd first come to live with her aunt and uncle, a tragic little ten-year-old still numb with grief over the loss of her parents, the school had comforted her where her uncle's family could not. Her uncle's children took their lessons in the nursery schoolroom with Miss Finch until they were ten years old. Then they went off to boarding school in Bangor or Boston. But Uncle Wallace and Aunt Ethel had felt that boarding school wasn't necessary for Clementine. The village school would be good enough for her.

Aunt Ethel and Uncle Wallace were very proud of their station in life. They lived in the biggest house in Hibben, built high on the headland above the village a generation earlier by Uncle Wallace's father. The Holloway family owned the fishing fleet that sailed out every day, manned by village fishermen. They kept themselves separate from the villagers. It wouldn't do for their children to mix with village children, but Clementine, after all, wasn't really their own. She wasn't a Holloway but a Horn. She settled in at the village school, mixing easily enough with the rough fishermen's children. Blood will tell, thought Uncle Wallace.

Clementine had become a model student at the

village school, outshining even the older pupils with her accomplishments. Her favorite subject was geography, and she took pride in knowing the names and locations of all the states and territories. She had enjoyed the daily walk down into the town, right along Main Street to the stone schoolhouse next to the whitewashed wooden church. She loved the smell of powdery chalk, the smooth black surface of the slates, the crisp pages of books, the pads of lined writing paper, the ink pots, and sharp pens. She loved catching whiffs of Miss Kent's faint perfume whenever her teacher walked by her desk. The heady exhilaration of coming in first in the math contest, of being the top student in geography, of writing the best essay or performing flawlessly in recitation—all these triumphs made life without her parents bearable.

Clementine had a mind like a trap. It captured and retained all information that came her way. She was much smarter than her cousins, she knew, but when she had asked Uncle Wallace to please let her join the older girls at the boarding school in Bangor, Uncle Wallace said boarding school was out of the question for Clementine. They needed her at home to help with all the babies.

There had been two children away at boarding school when Clementine first came to live with them, and three younger ones at home. Now there were three away at boarding school or college—Arnold, Avery, and Alex. Anastasia had married last year and lived in Boston. There were seven still at home—

Anne, Andrew, Amity, Aaron, Abner, Alice, and Augustus. They slept two to a room, with Clementine sharing the nursery with baby Augustus so that she might answer his cries in the night. She had assisted at most of their births and helped her aunt through labor and delivery more than once when the doctor didn't arrive in time. And Clementine was very good with the children—"a natural," Miss Finch once said approvingly. She had the knack.

But having a *knack*, Clementine often fumed, was not the same as having a *calling*. And now there was only one week of school left, and the six senior students would be leaving forever.

Clementine stared down over the cliff now, brooding. The only other senior girl, Jilly Peters, was eager for babies. She and Richard Wallings planned to marry at Christmastime, and Jilly wanted a baby by the end of summer. Richard had left the school a year earlier and was working on his father's fishing schooner. That was what most of the boys in the village did when they finished school—many left school at sixteen to get a head start working on the vessels that would provide their livelihood. Three of the four boys in the senior class—Hob Wilkins, Sam Sawyer, and Gilbert Hanks—all planned to work with their fathers on the boats. The fourth boy, Earl Wallings, Richard's younger brother, had decided he would go south to work in a papermaking factory in Lewiston. The end of school was a dream come true for the other seniors. Only for Clementine was it a nightmare, for it meant she would become full-time nursemaid to all her young cousins. Her spirit rebelled against a life taken over by babies with sticky fingers, games of hide-and-seek, and rhymes from Mother Goose.

It was a nightmare she intended to escape. She watched the churning water another few minutes, her resolution firm. Then she turned to walk back to the house, sighing as she heard the laughter of the children and saw them running toward her across the lawn.

"There you are, Clemmy!" they cried. "We were looking all over!"

Little Alice took her hand. Abner grabbed her other hand. Aaron and Amity and Andrew jostled each other and made sighing, fainting sounds. "You look like you're about to swoon, Clementine!" Amity said. "Have you started wearing stays?"

"You'd better start soon," said Anne, "or else you'll end up fat and no man will want you." Anne, who was ten, would be the next Holloway girl to leave home for boarding school in Bangor. She was eager to put her hair up, lower her skirts, and take her place in a world that didn't include babies and toddlers. Clementine was horribly jealous.

Abner tugged her arm till she bent down to his height. "Can we go down to the you-know-where, Clemmy?" he whispered, his sweet breath hot in her ear.

"Not now," she said. Abner was the most persistent of the children, always dogging her footsteps. She took him to the cave only when the other children were napping or busy elsewhere, and she was driven to distraction by his begging. He was always needing kisses and hugs and reassurances of her love. He needed mothering more than all the other children put together, thought Clementine. Even more than baby Augustus.

Clementine let the children pull her around the glass conservatory full of ferns and potted aspidistras, and up onto the back porch. In the kitchen Janie was washing the children's snack plates. "The baby's with his mother for a bit. Do go up, Clem, and make sure he hasn't tired her."

Clementine climbed the stairs, trying to shake off her small cousins. The hallway stretched before them, doors on either side. The room at the end was Aunt Ethel's. Officially, Uncle Wallace slept there, too, but Clementine knew he spent most nights in the small room next door, or down in his study.

She stopped outside her aunt's door and knocked. "Come in," came the soft, weak voice.

Clementine opened the door and peeked inside. "Excuse me, Aunt Ethel, but I've come to get Augustus. Is he ready?"

Clearly he was. He held out his arms to Clementine as soon as he saw her. The other children crowded in at the door, and Aunt Ethel seemed to shrink back into her pillows. They were always eager to see their mother, although their visits with her never lasted more than a few minutes—just long enough for her to hear about their day and to hold the baby for a kiss or two. They then were sent back to their playroom, which doubled as a schoolroom.

"Go on now, dears," murmured Aunt Ethel. "I'll

see you again tomorrow." They moved away reluctantly. But Clementine, holding the baby, lingered in the doorway. She didn't miss the look of annoyance on her aunt's face but asked boldly, "May I stay a moment, Aunt Ethel, and talk to you?"

"I'm very tired, dear."

"Oh, I'll only take a moment. It's about school again, Aunt Ethel."

The Eternal Invalid closed her eyes and leaned back on her white eyelet pillows, looking alarmingly weak. "You aren't going to start in about going away to study, are you? I can't bear any more discussion, Clementine."

"I don't want to go against Uncle Wallace, Aunt Ethel," begged Clementine, "but I know my own parents would want me to go on to college!" Her father as well as her mother, who had been Aunt Ethel's own sister, had valued education for girls as well as boys, and for women as well as men.

"Your father was a bad influence on my sister, I always thought," Aunt Ethel said. "Poor Bess married beneath herself."

Clementine, standing at the side of her aunt's bed, bit back her angry retort. "I just wanted you to talk to Uncle Wallace." It would be far more pleasant to leave with her uncle's blessing than to be forced to sneak away like some common criminal.

"Oh, Clementine," sighed Aunt Ethel, "you know we've always tried to do our best for you."

"Yes, I know. And you have. But now—"

"Now you're a young girl nearing maturity, my

dear, and there is a lot you need to learn about running a household and managing a family before you get married."

"But Aunt Ethel, don't you understand? I don't want to learn about housekeeping. There's so much else to learn! I was thinking about—well, geography. It's fascinating, Aunt Ethel. I want to travel, to learn different languages, to know all about other places on earth! And college will help me do that! I don't think I'll ever want to get married."

Aunt Ethel pressed her lips together. "Such unseemly notions you have, young lady! I'm sure your mother would be appalled."

"She wouldn't, Aunt Ethel!" Clementine's eyes filled with tears. She blinked them back, then wondered if they might help her after all. She let them well in her eyes again and drip onto her cheeks. One tear plopped onto Augustus's head and he gurgled up at her, intrigued.

Aunt Ethel tried to reach a handkerchief on the bedside table, but her arm fell weakly back onto the coverlet. "Please compose yourself, my dear," she murmured. "I wish I could help you, but I do feel you are striving for something entirely inappropriate for a young lady."

Clementine sighed.

Her aunt lay back and closed her eyes. "You're a good girl, Clementine. You'll do what's right. We've brought you up to know your duty to your family and your duty as a woman."

"Yes, I hope I do know my duty. But—"

"Please don't bring this up with your uncle again, dear. It only upsets him."

"Yes, Aunt Ethel."

"Then I trust there will be no further argument." Her aunt reached up a thin arm and adjusted the pillows. "Please take the baby away now. He tires me so."

Hoisting chunky Augustus up against her shoulder, Clementine dragged her feet down the hallway. She peeked into the playroom and saw Aaron pretending to be a pirate, chasing Amity and Alice around the room. Andrew was pulling Abner around the perimeter of the room in a small wooden wagon, even though Janie, the hired girl, said the wheels made marks on the floor. Anne, who disdained childish play these days, had no doubt retreated to her bedroom to read. Clementine listened to the laughing and shrieking and decided no one was coming to any particular harm. Miss Finch was nowhere to be seen. She was firm about her hours and was "on duty" only during the school day. It was then up to Clementine to take charge, settle the children down, read some stories, play some games, and get them ready for their baths and dinners.

But until that minute came she would try again to make Uncle Wallace see reason. She stopped the wagon and settled Augustus in with Abner, cautioning the boys not to treat the baby roughly. Then she slipped back down the stairs. She crossed the library and stood for a moment outside the door to her uncle's inner sanctum. Then she knocked, hard.

Uncle Wallace, a large man with a black beard, frowned when he saw her. "Aren't you supposed to be looking after the children, Clementine?"

"Yes, but I wanted to ask you to reconsider, Uncle. I am determined not to stop my education. I want to ask whether, since you are so convinced I must remain here as a governess, I might be paid for my work. That way, you see, I could save up the money, and when the children are older, I could leave for college."

Uncle Wallace stood and came around the side of his desk to face her. "Pay you! My dear, you are not a servant. You are a member of this family. Your place is here with us. You will stay with us and help your aunt with the children, and then in the future, when you marry, you will have children and a house of your own."

"But—," she objected, clenching her hands tightly in the folds of her ankle-length skirt.

He scowled at her, eyes fierce under bushy black brows. "My dear Clementine, surely you don't object to helping out the family that has sheltered you and cared for you all these years?"

She lowered her eyes. "No, sir." But she *did* object! She did! She had never asked to come live with them in the first place.

"All right then." He smiled at her. "Perhaps you don't realize we have already given you far more comforts and luxuries than your own parents ever could have—no disrespect to the dead, of course." Clementine gritted her teeth. She knew Uncle

Wallace and Aunt Ethel always enjoyed the notion that their niece had risen to new heights since coming to live with them. Their high opinion of themselves had long annoyed Clementine, but she never let on.

Now, sure of her obedience, Uncle Wallace smiled broadly, teeth gleaming white in his black beard. "In any case, dear Clementine, let us hear no more of this nonsense. Ladies' seminaries, indeed! We don't want you becoming one of those ridiculous suffragettes! Now, please go back up to the children. I do not want them pestering their mother."

Clementine slipped into the bedroom she shared with Augustus. She could hear the children laughing and shrieking in the playroom, but she couldn't face them, not just yet. She knelt by her narrow bed and pulled out from underneath it a large hatbox patterned with roses. She sank onto the mattress and lifted the lid, lost in memory.

Her father, Jacob Horn, had been the manager of the coal mine. He left early every morning for work after kissing Clementine and her mother good-bye. He carried his lunch in a wicker basket and walked with a spring in his step that Clementine said made him look like a wind-up toy. He would come home at night tired and often blackened with the coal dust that could ruin the lungs of miners who breathed it in, though Jacob himself worked most of the time in the office at the head of the shaft.

One day was different. Bess had packed his lunch as neatly as always and covered it with a clean white napkin. As always, she left it for him on the bench by the front door. But when Jacob left for work, he forgot to take it with him.

That morning Clementine was high up in the fork of the apple tree with her doll, Mollydolly. She was eyeing a branch higher up than she'd climbed before. The doll was delicately crafted and only ten inches tall. In its painted eyes was a look of mischief almost exactly like the expression in Clementine's own eyes. The doll had a pink-and-white china face and brown yarn hair tied back in braids. Jacob had bought the doll on a trip to Philadelphia, and Bess had sewn a blue gingham dress just like Clementine's own. For Christmas, Bess had outfitted the doll with a complete wardrobe—hat and coat, tiny knitted sweaters, little shoes made of felt, a long white cotton nightgown, and, best of all, a party dress of lush green velvet. Clementine took her doll everywhere.

Clementine waved good-bye to her father as he walked out the gate. She didn't notice he had left his lunch behind.

Later, Bess ran out of the house carrying the wicker basket. She stopped at the white gate and smiled at her daughter.

"I'll be back as soon as I take your dad his meal," she told her, holding up the basket covered with a crisp white cloth. "Be a good girl."

"Bye!" called Clementine, bracing herself to climb higher up onto the next branch.

"Climb down now, Clementine." Bess opened the white gate and stepped out into the road. "You can play just as nicely on the ground as up in trees, I should think."

And then her mother's famous last words as she looked up at her little girl: "Or will you come along, too, Clementine?"

What if she had answered yes and scrambled along at her mother's side? Clementine often wondered if anything would be different now, if maybe she could somehow have kept her mother from arriving at the mine. After all, Clementine walked more slowly than her mother. Wouldn't her shorter legs have kept them out of danger in the end?

But that day Clementine had only just reached her perch on the higher branch and didn't want to climb back down right away. "No, I'll wait here," she said.

She watched through the leaves as Bess walked away down the street.

It seemed only minutes later that she heard a strange booming thud and felt the earth rumble from way down deep. The leaves of the apple tree rustled around her face, and Mollydolly fell from the tree into a pile of leaves. Clementine slid off the branch, back into the fork, then lowered herself carefully until she could jump down into the pile of leaves, too. She stood with her arms out for balance. The apple tree bowed and waved its branches beguilingly, as if inviting her to dance. After a few seconds everything seemed oddly silent. Even the birds in the apple tree were mute. But soon they started chirping again, and people came streaming out of their houses, shouting and running toward the mine, and Clementine pushed open the gate and was swept along in their tide.

She could smell the burning and knew intuitively the explosion had come from the mine. Nearing the shafts, she tried to run and began calling "Mama! Dad!" at the top of her voice. But she was hemmed in on all sides by the townspeople. She felt she couldn't breathe. Then someone lifted her high and turned swiftly, walking back toward town. She recognized him vaguely as a man who worked at the general store. "Wait—my mama!"

"I'm sorry, sweetheart." The man's voice was low against her ear. "There's nothing you want to see back there." She had protested, even tried to kick, but he held her firmly and carried her away from the scene of the explosion, back to his home, where his wife made her a cup of cocoa in the kitchen. The man and his wife held a conversation with their eyes— exactly in the same astonishing way her own parents were able to—and then the man left again and the woman sat at the table with Clementine. "There's been a terrible accident, my dear," she said finally and bowed her head. "You're going to have to be mighty strong."

After the funerals, Clementine was sent to Hibben to live with her mother's sister. Aunt Ethel seemed a shadowy copy of Bess—the shape of her face was the same, and the soft brown hair pulled back in a bun at the nape of her neck—but while Bess's blue eyes shone, Aunt Ethel's clouded over.

And while Bess sang as she went about her house-work, telling her little girl stories of fairies and giants and magical spells, or stopping to sit at the table and help with a puzzle, Aunt Ethel, heavy with preg-nancy, sighed on her chaise longue and sipped a ti-sane. Jacob Horn had been warm and indulgent with his daughter, but Uncle Wallace, though kind, was a stern presence in the big house and always distant from his many children.

Clementine often lay in bed at night and remem-bered her other life. She thought of her parents, how Bess taught her to cook, showing her how to be careful with the hot stove. How Jacob, home from the mine in the evening, took her on his lap to tell her tales from all over the world by the fire until bedtime. His beard tickled the top of her head as he talked about children in places called Russia and Ger-many and China and Iceland and Peru. Bess sewed in the lamplight, listening. Sometimes Jacob would get out his special *Atlas of the World,* with its beauti-ful red leather cover. They would gather around the table while he turned the pages and showed them the maps of far-off places. Maybe someday they could all take a trip together, he had said. Wouldn't that be fun?

But Jacob and Bess had gone on a terrible trip of their own. And the only trip Clementine had ever taken was on the train to Bangor, Maine, and then by wagon over to the rocky coast, to Hibben. Along with the trunk containing her clothing, she brought with her a hatbox that once contained Bess's elaborately trimmed Sunday hat. But now it held Clementine's treasures. There was Bess's gold necklace with a locket. The locket opened, containing minute curls of soft hair Bess had clipped from Clementine's head when she was a baby. There was Jacob's red-bound *Atlas of the World.* And there was, of course, Mollydolly and her wardrobe. These few things were all Clementine had left of the family she had loved so much.

She placed the lid of the hatbox gently on the bed now and took out the atlas. She held it on her lap a long moment, smoothing her fingers over the leather cover. Then she opened it. So many places in the world—and here she was, stuck in Hibben, Maine! But not for long. Surely there was more to life than this.

After all, it was 1912. It was the twentieth century, though the villagers didn't seem to know it. Hibben might be the sleepiest town on earth, but out in other places the world was bursting with people and motion and new ideas. Automobiles raced along city roads without horses to pull them. Streetcars drove shoppers to busy marketplaces. Huge, glittering passenger ships traversed the oceans. Some lucky people had even ridden aloft in aeroplanes. Yet here in Hibben only the Holloways owned an automobile. Everyone else walked or traveled by carriage. Hibben's general store was a poor cousin to the big city department stores. Clementine had read about how, at Christmastime, the shops in New York City were decorated with thousands of lights. Here in

Hibben only the Holloways had electric lights in their house. And only a few villagers saw any use in such newfangled contraptions as the telephone. They were rooted in old ways and resisted every change. There was nothing for her here.

She leafed through the pages of maps and charts, her resolve to escape this town and this family growing even stronger. When she replaced the book in the hatbox, she fingered the locket before laying it in the box. She stroked the yarn braids on the little doll and adjusted its dress. "Something will work out for us, Mollydolly," she whispered. "Don't worry."

Then she put the round lid on the hatbox and pushed it back under her bed. She went down the hall to the playroom and dutifully took charge of her cousins. They led her straight into their game, romping and playing until bath time. But even while she stood on the window seat holding the baby competently on her hip with one arm, the other arm outstretched, clutching a wooden sword to do battle with Abner and Alice—pirates guarding the buried treasure—her mind was busy making plans. It was time to move on, and she would not be thwarted. It was time for a brand-new life.

7

"A brand-new life," Molly murmured. She turned her head on the pillows and opened her eyes. She blinked.

Jacob Horn sat next to her bed, his chair pulled close—but no, no, of course it couldn't be Jacob! It was her dad, it was *Bill*. Bill was stroking her arm. "It's all right, Molly. You're here with us."

"You're just fine," said a soft voice on her other side, and Molly turned her head.

"Aunt Ethel!" But as soon as she said the name, she knew it was absurd.

Paulette reached out and patted Molly's arm.

Molly struggled to sit up. Her headache was gone, but she was not at all refreshed from her nap. Drugged with the weight of the incredible dream of Clementine's story and the whole essence of how it felt to *be* Clementine, she rubbed her eyes.

"Oh, Molly," whispered Paulette. "That was amazing! Just hearing you talking—it was like being transported right back in time. I had to rush out and drag Billy in to listen!"

"Listen? What do you mean? What happened?"

Bill continued stroking her arm. "I'm not sure, Molly. I never saw anything like this in my life. When I came in you were wide-eyed and talking a mile a minute like you were this Clementine."

"You never left the bed," added Paulette. "But you made us feel we were right there with you—with Clementine—out on the headland, then inside talking to Aunt Ethel and Uncle Wallace. And all those children! *Very* bizarre."

Molly just stared at her. "You were giving me a head rub. What happened?"

"Just a little relaxation technique," said Paulette, her eyes bright with excitement.

"It was a trick!" Molly glared at her. "What did you do? Hypnotize me?"

"Molly, that's unfair. All I did was massage your head and shoulders. I could feel the tightness—all the things you bottle up inside don't just disappear, you know. They're in there festering. Making you tense, making your head pound. All I did was relax you, and when you were relaxed I suggested you open your mind to let out what was worrying you."

Molly flushed at the thought of being so completely out of control—and being *seen* so out of control. "Very New Age and touchy-feely. But you should have asked me first."

Paulette looked distressed. "You would have said no. I thought you'd rather try to deal with this on your own rather than see a psychologist."

"That's right. *On my own!*"

"Honey," said Bill. "Paulette didn't tell the story of Clementine, *you* did. We just sat here and listened. Paulette didn't put the words in your mouth."

Paulette put her hand on Molly's arm. "Don't be angry. Please. You wanted to remember."

"How can it have been a memory? That doesn't make sense."

"How did it feel, Molly?" asked Bill.

"It felt so real," Molly admitted, lying back with a great sigh. "That girl—Clementine—was the same girl from my dreams."

The pillows were very soft. She felt she could sink right down into them and fall deeply asleep in an instant. Despite the presence of Bill and Paulette at her bedside, the sight of the bedside table with her paperbacks and travel alarm clock on it and her clothes draped on the wooden chair across the room, Molly was still full of other impressions. Paulette was right; the memories were Molly's own: the faces of all the children, the drag of Clementine's long skirts, the weight of the wooden pirate sword in her hand as she played with the laughing children, the clean, warm smell of baby Augustus's head on her shoulder, the happy memories of playing with the doll.

"That name," she said slowly. "Mollydolly."

Bill cleared his throat. "That part kind of threw me, Molly. I'll admit it."

"I think it's thrilling! It proves even more that there's a connection between Molly and this . . . this other girl." Paulette was looking across the bed at Bill, her face eager. "I feel we should be able to make

139

something out of all this—all that Molly told us. But what?"

"It's fascinating," agreed Bill.

"It's not fascinating, it's crazy!" wailed Molly. She had a sudden, desperate longing to talk to Jen. She needed to hear her mother's calm, reassuring voice. She leapt out of the high bed, and in one corner of her mind registered surprise at the sight of her shorts and long bare legs. But what had she expected to see—Clementine's long skirts? "I'm going to call Mom."

"Of all people!" Bill exclaimed as Molly went out into the hall and down the stairs.

She headed directly for the study but stopped abruptly in the doorway. Was that acrid odor from Uncle Wallace's pipe?

She took a deep breath and went to the phone. She pressed the numbers, then sat down on the couch, the receiver at her ear as she listened to the ringing in her own kitchen back in Battleboro Heights.

On the fourth ring, the answering machine clicked in, announcing that no one was at home, but if the caller wished to leave a message he or she should wait for the beep. Molly sighed and announced that she was fine and had called to say hi. She just wanted to hear Jen's voice.

Jen's sensible, no-nonsense voice.

As she replaced the receiver, the study door creaked. Molly turned, expecting Paulette or Bill. Then she froze. She heard whispers on the other side of the door, and a little boy's worried voice: "What's he going to do to Clemmy?"

Molly backed away and bumped against the table. She recognized that voice. Her heart hammered. The whispers vanished into thick silence. After a long moment Molly forced herself to walk over to the door. She took a deep breath before putting her hand on the knob. "Abner?" Her voice rang in the silence. Loud and absurd. She opened the door. The library beyond was empty.

Molly walked out into the hallway. She could hear the teakettle whistling in the kitchen. Bill and Paulette turned when she appeared in the doorway. "How is Jen?" asked Bill. "Did she explain the whole thing to you? Got everything clear now, all concise and reasonable?"

"Don't be snide, sweetie. Molly's had a rough day." Paulette wiped her hands on a dish towel. "Come on and sit down, Molly." She giggled. "I'm just so excited, I don't think I can eat! We've got to figure out what it all means."

"I'm hoping for a ghost, myself," said Bill. "No kidding—as long as it isn't out looking for revenge. A ghost would certainly attract tourists, wouldn't it, darling?"

"I have another theory, Billy. Come on, I'll tell you while we eat."

Molly sat down. As they ate the meal of salad and marinated tofu ("California food," Jen would call it), she listened to Bill and Paulette discuss their ideas of what could be happening to her. Bill wanted a ghost for the inn, while Paulette thought the strange occurrences might have to do with reincarnation. In a past life, she surmised, Molly had actually *been*

Clementine. And now she was remembering things from that past life. "That's why it all seemed so real," she said. "It *was*."

"But *why* is she remembering?" asked Bill with interest. "What's the point?"

But Paulette didn't have a theory about that. Not yet. "Just give me time, I'll come up with something," she said, and winked across the table at Molly.

Molly threw down her napkin, near tears. "You two are acting like this is just some new game," she cried. "But it isn't. I'm hearing things and seeing things, and I want to know why. How would you like to be haunted? Or maybe going crazy?"

Paulette reached over to put her hand on Molly's arm, but Molly pulled back. "You're not crazy," Paulette said. "No one thinks that."

Bill put down his fork. "Don't get angry at us. We're not trying to make this into a game—really we're not."

"It's just so fascinating," added Paulette. "And hard to believe when none of it's happening to us. I can understand that you're frightened. I would be, too."

Molly started eating again, her temper spent. After another minute she spoke up. "I feel like all this is a giant wave or something, sucking me down. Just like the water in the pool. If I'm not wacko and a ghost is really appearing to me in dreams and visions and stuff, then why? What am I supposed to do? It's not like this Clementine person's giving me a message or anything."

"In ghost stories," said Paulette, "you need to bury their bones properly so they can rest. That sort of thing."

"Well, I wish Clementine would tell me where her bones are now and where she wants me to put them," said Molly with some asperity. "I'd rush out and bury them, and then we could all rest in peace."

After the meal she excused herself and hurried up to her bedroom—the bedroom that had been Clementine's. She checked under the bed to make sure no hatbox lurked there, then sat on the bed and wrote lighthearted letters to her mother and Michael. She mentioned nothing of what had been happening to her since her arrival. She did not say that Jared Bernstein had come to Hibben. The effort to put it all out of her head while she wrote exhausted her, and when she finished she set aside the papers and lay back on the bed to think.

She needed to figure this out.

Just say for a moment that Clementine was real. What could she want? Why in the world was she haunting, of all people, Molly Teague from Battleboro Heights, Ohio?

And then there was the house. This house, and the one with the long hallway in the dream. Who were the children whose voices and laughter whispered behind closed doors?

And how did Jared Bernstein fit in?

It was time to stop running scared and use her brain, Molly told herself. She could start tomorrow,

143

utilizing all the tools reason had given her. Rather than just sit and let things happen to her, she would do something her mother would approve of. She would make a scientific inquiry. Do some research. She would begin first thing tomorrow at the Hibben Free Library.

Molly awoke to cheerful sounds of breakfast being made downstairs. Bill laughed. Water ran into the old porcelain sink. The electric coffee grinder whirred scratchily. Molly threw on her clothes and ran to the kitchen. Bill and Paulette were making pancakes and coffee.

"You're up early," she greeted them.

Paulette was wearing Bill's plaid bathrobe and her hair was ruffled. "We're going to the hospital. It's baby checkup time. I just love hearing that little heartbeat." She rested her hand on Bill's shoulder. "*Dup-dup-dup*. It's the sweetest thing."

"Come with us if you like, Molly," added Bill. "The closest hospital is over in Benson. We're taking the ferry because it's a lot faster than driving. The coast road is single-lane traffic the whole way and winds all over the place."

Molly sat down at the table and lifted her plate for the two pancakes that Paulette slid off the spatula. "I think I'll stay here," she said, reaching for the maple syrup, "if you don't mind."

"Listen, Molly," said Bill. "You're going great guns on the dining room walls, but we want you to have fun, too."

"I thought I might walk into town. Maybe go to the library or something."

Paulette looked at her sharply. "What if—?"

"I'll deal with it if it happens," said Molly firmly. "I want to look for history books about Hibben. Find out who lived here, find out . . . you know."

"Good for you," said Bill. "Try the church, too. There's a graveyard behind it."

Molly shivered.

"We can drop you off on our way to the wharf," said Paulette.

"Thanks." Molly forked up a mouthful of pancake. "Leave the dishes, you guys. I'll wash up." When everyone had finished eating and Paulette and Bill went upstairs to get ready, Molly cleared the table. She rubbed the dishes in soapy water and gazed out the window over the sink at the long grasses blowing in the sea breeze. Reed grass, it was called. She knew the name now, she realized, because Clementine had known.

The town was quiet; the only bustle of activity was down by the wharf where tourists waited to board the ferry. Paulette stopped the van at the bottom of Cotton Lane. Bill slipped his house key off his key ring and handed it to Molly. "We'll have lunch in Benson," he told her as she climbed out of the back seat. "Expect us when you see us."

"Okay. Good luck. Good-bye!" The van pulled away from the curb. Molly started up Cotton Lane. After a few minutes she heard the sharp, low hoot of the ferry's horn. She hesitated outside the blue gate of the library's garden. What if she had another vision? This time Paulette wouldn't be there to pull her out of it. Maybe it would be best to go home.

Get a grip! She reminded herself sternly of her resolution of the night before. Knowledge was power, after all; that's what Jen always told her. After a moment she opened the gate and walked toward the door.

A bell tinkled as Molly stepped inside. The library was small. There were two rooms, one facing the front garden, one looking out onto the back, where the rock wall rose steeply only a few feet from the house. There was a staircase leading up, and the sign at the foot said Reference Books and Children's Books, with an arrow angled upward. Molly thought the back room might once have been a kitchen. She could see from the doorway a large brick fireplace filled in with bookshelves and hooks hanging down from the beams where dried herbs or smoked fish once might have hung.

An old woman, presumably the librarian, sat at a table in the back room reading the newspaper and drinking a cup of coffee. She was small-boned, with a hooked nose that was an excellent perch for her thick glasses. A shock of white hair framed her face.

She looked up when she saw Molly. "Well, a library patron at this hour of the morning? I don't get many people in here these days. Nobody reads anymore. Sit in front of the box all the time." She adjusted her glasses. "A real shame. Now, young lady, you shall have a cup of coffee."

"Oh, thanks," murmured Molly, though she didn't particularly like coffee. She walked through the front room, glancing at the framed photographs of old fishing boats that lined the walls above the bookcases. "Most librarians don't let people have food around books."

"First patron always gets a cup," the woman said. "After that, all food and drink is off limits." She poured Molly a cup of coffee from a blue spotted pot. "You don't look like the sort of girl who would spill it. Are you?"

"I'll be very careful." Molly took the cup with both hands.

The old woman peered up at Molly. "Don't live here, do you? One of our new tourists, is that it?"

"Actually, I am living here, but just for the summer," she said. "My father and stepmother bought the big house on the headland. I'm helping them renovate it. The rest of the year I live in Ohio with my mother." Molly took a sip of the bitter black brew. "I'm Molly Tcaguc."

"Well, welcome to Hibben, Molly Teague," the woman said. "If you like books, I'm glad to know you. My name's Miss Wilkins, Grace Wilkins. I've been the librarian here ever since the town's had a library. Some folks might say I *am* the library! Your father must be that tall man with the little red-headed wife. I haven't met them myself yet—but the talk is that they're a very nice couple and aim to bring us some more tourists when they get their inn going, isn't that right? I've seen them around town. Heard your dad has a trussed-up ankle now. Poor fellow.

He won't be getting up on any more ladders for a while, I suppose. But it's good you've come to help out. About time someone fixed up the old Holloway House." She lifted her glasses to peer at Molly through clouded eyes, then settled them back on the bridge of her beaked nose.

Molly stood as though frozen, two names the old woman had spoken echoing in her ears: Wilkins. And Holloway. Names from the past. Not *her* past but Clementine's.

"I've come to do some research," she began. "Do you have any books on local history?"

"All there are, probably." Grace Wilkins gave her a curious look. "Not too many folks are interested in Hibben's history unless they live up here. Now, which period of Hibben's history? We go back all the way to the Abnáki Indians. 'People of the dawn land,' that's what their name meant. Their descendants still live around these parts—the Penobscot and Passamaquoddy tribes. Or did you want something later? Did you know that originally Maine was part of Massachusetts? Before the Revolutionary War, that is. It was separated from Massachusetts by New Hampshire—still is, of course—and was almost entirely virgin forest. The coast wasn't settled until the 1770s, and even then there weren't any big towns, just little fishing outposts. We're pretty far north up here, you know. The southern end was settled first. We didn't become a state until 1820."

Molly interrupted this history lesson with a smile. "I was really hoping to learn more about the Holloway House."

"Now, let's see." Miss Wilkins slowly set down her cup and moved from the table toward the front room. "We have a nice little collection of Civil War narratives from Hibben boys who fought and lived to tell of it. Abelard Holloway fought and died. He lived in your house. Maine was always a free state, did you know that? We never did hold with slavery up here."

"Abelard Holloway?" asked Molly, following her to the shelves. "Was he the one who built it? Is there a book of family history or something I could take out?"

"You are eager, aren't you?" Miss Wilkins laughed. She turned back to sit at the table. "You don't need books when you've got Grace Wilkins still with a tongue in her old head." Somehow her tone sounded wistful to Molly. Miss Wilkins leaned toward Molly. "I once knew that old house quite well. Go on. Sit down and ask away."

What could she ask Miss Wilkins without revealing the confusing visions and dreams? She'd start with something simple, basic: "Who built the house? And when?"

"It was a man named Aloysius Holloway," Miss Wilkins said promptly. "Funny name, but there you go. He built it back in the fifties—the *eighteen*-fifties, that is. He was the son of a village fishing family who took himself off to New York and got a job in the shipping industry before the Civil War." Her voice lost its wistful tone as she warmed to her subject. "Aloysius came back to Hibben a rich man and built himself that big house. People didn't like it—they thought he wanted to build up there to have farther to look down his nose at them here in the village. And probably it was true. The Holloways always did think highly of themselves, I can tell you that. Too good for the villagers." Now the sadness in her tone was back again. She paused. Molly was just about to ask another question, when Miss Wilkins continued briskly.

"Aloysius had magic fingers, though, when it came to making money. He soon owned most of the fishing vessels in the village and had the men, who had previously worked independently, working for him. They didn't like him much, but he was fair, and he offered them more money working for him than they made running their own little boats. Half of Hibben's income came from lobsters, even then. He sure did know how to run a business, and he groomed his son to follow in his footsteps."

"So there was only one son!" exclaimed Molly, relieved but at the same time sorry to hear there had not been nearly a dozen little ones with names all starting with the letter A. She wasn't sure whether she wanted to find proof that her visions were accurate—or proof that she'd made them up. Which would be more comforting?

"No, there were two sons—Abelard and Wallace. But Abelard, as I said, died in the Civil War. Somewhere in Virginia, I think. And poor Aloysius never got over the grief. He hadn't been particularly fond of his second son, thought the boy was stupid. But in the end he brought that young man into the fishing business in Abelard's place. And Wallace tried, I'll grant you that, to be all that his father wanted. But he never really had the knack."

"Wallace!" exclaimed Molly.

"That's right. Not such an odd name this time, eh?" When Molly shook her head, Miss Wilkins continued, "After old Aloysius died, Wallace took over the fishing fleets. He had his father's gift for making money but none of his sense of fairness. He sneered at the villagers and didn't bother to hide it. Nor did his wife. She alienated a lot of the folks down here in the village with all her high-and-mighty airs. Between them they had everybody mad at them, one way or another, and yet many of the families worked for the fishing fleet. My own pa did, in fact."

Molly heard her heart pounding in her ears and wondered whether Miss Wilkins could hear it, too. "And—his wife? Do you happen to know what Wallace's wife was called?"

"Ethel, it was. Ethel Holloway," nodded Miss Wilkins. "Had a huge passel of kids. Almost a dozen of them there were, and all with names beginning with A—maybe it was Wallace's weak attempt to honor his father's name without actually saddling them with the name Aloysius. People had bigger families in those days, you know. Ethel Holloway was always very weak, though, and the twelfth pregnancy killed her."

Miss Wilkins paused and removed her glasses to peer at Molly. "What's the matter, dear?"

"*Uh* . . . I'm okay. Just—well, nothing," Molly

stuttered. She held her hands tightly together in her lap so Miss Wilkins would not notice their tremble.

This is incredible. It's impossible. She wanted to leave but felt glued to her chair. She wished desperately that her mother would storm in and drag her out, away from all the illogical, incomprehensible, unbearably bizarre facts spilling from the librarian's lips. But she urged Miss Wilkins on. "What more do you know about the family?"

"Well, let's see. What *don't* I know?" Miss Wilkins shrugged. "Wallace's children were older than I was. I didn't know any of them well when I was a child, though later—well, never mind." She hesitated again, then shoved up her glasses and rushed on.

"I was born the same year Ethel Holloway died. I know that because the villagers talked for a long time about how 1912 was a bad year in the village. My own brother died in a boating accident that year— so I never knew him. I wasn't even three months old. He was my half-brother, really, the son of my pa and his first wife, who died when Hob was a baby."

Molly bit her lip to keep from crying out. *Hob!*

"My pa married again when Hob was about twelve, and my ma tried to be the mother he never had. I was born quite a while later—my ma had a lot of trouble carrying a baby and there were three who died before I came along. Isn't that sad? My claim to fame is that I was born on April 14, 1912, the very day the *Titanic* sank. And poor Hob drowned in the cove just about two months later. Not a good year for people in boats, was it?" Miss Wilkins stood, her forehead creased in a frown. "Now, I know we have a good book about the *Titanic*. It's here someplace. Would you like to see it, dear?"

Molly took a deep breath. "Maybe another time." She tried gently to manuever Miss Wilkins back on track. "Can you tell me more about Hob? And the family in the Holloway House? What happened to them? Why don't they still live there?"

"Oh—yes," she said, sitting down again. "Well, the girls—there were four or five of them, I think— they all went to finishing school and then married into rich families in Bangor or down east. The boys were sent to boarding school in Boston. A few went on to college—Harvard, I think—and the others worked for their father's company until they got fed up with it and moved away from Hibben. All but Abner." She stopped and heaved a great sigh. "Oh, he was a challenge to his father, Abner was. Your basic pain in the you-know-what."

"Abner?" Molly winced. She remembered the piping young voice she had heard outside the study door.

"He was one of the younger children. Always running away from his governesses to come down here to the village. He liked the village children and loved the boats. When he was older and Wallace wanted to send him to boarding school like his brothers, Abner begged to stay home. He said he wanted nothing more in life than to stay in Hibben and be a fisherman!" Miss Wilkins laughed. "Of course, Wallace didn't like that idea at all. When Abner was sent off to school, he actually ran away and came home again. His father was livid, but the boy made such a fuss that in the end he was allowed to stay home with a private tutor." She smiled sourly. The light from the window caught her glasses and made them flash. "He escaped to the village every day as soon as his lessons were over, and soon he and I began keeping company." At Molly's blank expression, she elaborated. "Courting, really, I guess you could say. He said we'd marry when I turned sixteen."

"But wasn't he much older than you?" asked Molly. "If you weren't born until after his mother died—"

"Oh, he was about four and a half years older. But when I was fourteen and he was eighteen we pledged our lives to each other." Her lips tightened. "He gave me a ring that had been his mother's. He knew his father would never give him permission to marry into a village family—as if Wallace's own father hadn't been born right down here in the village!" She shook her head. "So we kept it our secret. By that time all the Holloway kids but Abner were off to school or married or working, and Wallace often went to Boston and Bangor to visit. Maybe he was lonely in that big house after his wife died. He started courting a wealthy Boston widow he had met through his eldest daughter's wealthy connections down there. When they married a year or so later, the woman wouldn't hear of moving away from the city to live in a place like Hibben, so Wallace closed up the house. Abner wanted to stay on alone, but Wallace insisted he move to Boston, too. Abner promised he would return for me when he was twenty-one. I would have been seventeen by then, and the perfect age for marrying." Her eyes behind the glasses looked moody. "Or at least I thought so then."

"Did Abner come back?"

Grace Wilkins shook her head. "He was a scoundrel. That's all I can say. I heard a year later that he had gone to sea as a merchant seaman. Left me, just plain left me with a broken heart." Her voice was wistful. "And I never found anyone else I cared to marry, although one or two asked me."

"I'm sorry," said Molly. "That must have been very hard for you."

"Oh, well, time heals all wounds, right?" Miss Wilkins shrugged. "That's what they always say. I wondered about him for years, picturing him off sailing the seven seas, having a high old time, while here I was cleaning the fish my dad brought home each day."

"Did you ever find out what happened to him? Did he ever come back?"

"Not to stay. And Wallace Holloway never came back at all. That big house just sat empty, falling into disrepair over the years. When he died, his eldest son, Arnold, inherited it but never lived here. About twenty years ago the grandchild of one of the girls inherited it and moved in with his family, but they didn't last long in that house. It's just too old and drafty. Too big for anything but a wealthy family with lots of kids—or else an innkeeper who can keep it full of tourists. I tell you, your dad has the right idea!"

"So you never saw Abner again?" asked Molly. "That's so sad!"

Grace Wilkins looked surprised. "Never saw him again? Did I say that? No, no, Molly. Don't go writing a tragic ending to my little story. Abner came back to Hibben after the war—the Second World War, that is. Stopped by to see me. We had a cup of coffee right here." She offered to refill Molly's cup, but Molly shook her head. "Brought his silly little wife, too. I tried to give back his mother's ring, but— to give him a little credit—he wouldn't take it. I hear he got divorced a few years later—no kids— and now he lives over in Benson. He was never a lad to make a commitment to anybody." She laughed wryly. "Lad! He's an old geezer now, same as me."

"What a story!" Molly thought it was a shame that the two old people couldn't have fallen in love again and made up for all the lost years. A hint of these thoughts must have shown in her face, for Grace Wilkins pursed her lips.

"Don't go getting all sentimental!" Miss Wilkins peered at Molly over the top of her glasses. "I saw him about a month back—funeral for a woman from his nursing home. I knew her because she had been the Benson librarian some years back. Anyway, Abner and I met up at the church. He's practically a cripple, the old seadog. A little bit senile now, I think, but in some ways still the same old Abner. Winked at me during the eulogy."

Miss Wilkins shook her head. "Don't know that I'd have wanted to spend my life with a man always setting out to sea, anyway. We had enough of that with my pa—and *he* came home at night. No, I have to say I've been content right here. I worked in the general store for years, then took over the library. And now here I am, working every day right in the little cottage that used to be my home. I was born right upstairs—in the children's book room. Fitting, don't you think? Of course it wasn't full of books then."

"This was your family's home?" asked Molly weakly. She remembered the woman she had seen in the garden—Mrs. Wilkins, Clementine had called her.

"Yes, indeed. We always lived here. After my parents died, I stayed on. I sold the house to the county about fifteen years ago when they wanted to relocate the library from the schoolhouse, and I moved into one of the modern condominiums right behind the church. They're much more comfortable than this old place ever was." Her smile was rueful. "Tourists love old places like this, but you'll see for yourself someday, my girl. Old bones need good central heating and nice hot showers. They don't care much about charm."

Miss Wilkins chattered on about this and that, somehow getting back to the sinking of the *Titanic* on her birthday in April 1912, but Molly scarcely listened.

She sat at the table, her limbs feeling as limp as wet seaweed. In her attempts at research, she hadn't opened a single library book this morning, and yet she had learned far more than she'd ever hoped to know. The Holloways *had* been a real family. Uncle Wallace and Aunt Ethel had truly existed, and so had their many children, all with names starting with A. Abner, the boy who pestered Clementine and found her secret cave and played pirates, was a real person. He had jilted Grace Wilkins and gone to sea, had married and divorced, and was still alive today. And then there was Grace Wilkins herself, flesh and blood, sitting at the same table with Molly. The facts added up to something impossible. School had never taught her how to solve equations like this.

Molly set her coffee cup on the table. She hesitated; she could still leave here and try to forget everything she had heard this morning. But instead she plunged bravely on. "Miss Wilkins, you've been a big help. But there's just one more thing I want to ask before I go."

Miss Wilkins broke off in midsentence—something about how, as a girl, she had begged her father to take her out in the boat, even though girls didn't go on boats. She blinked at Molly. "What is that?"

"You said they had a lot of kids—and that all the daughters married into rich Boston families, right? Well, I just wondered . . . well, whether all those girls were their own?"

"How funny you should ask." Miss Wilkins blinked. "Because you're quite right, though my family always tried to forget about her." She leaned across the table and lowered her voice to a whisper, although no one else but Molly was in the room. "There was a niece living with them once. She was older than almost all of the Holloway children. And she was the girl my brother, Hob, was sweet on. He knew her from school but didn't get much chance to be with her because she had to look after her little cousins. Abner told me once that she'd been more a mother to him than his own ever was. I think he was sweet on her himself, child that he was. He felt betrayed when she disappeared. Still feels betrayed, if you ask me."

Molly was trying hard to follow this story. "Disappeared?"

"The night Hob drowned. He went out in bad weather and was wrecked on the rocks in the cove. My pa could never understand such poor judgment. It wasn't like Hob, he used to say. He felt it was somehow because of that girl that our Hob died, though I'm not sure why. But years later when I told them about Abner, they said no good would come of a relationship with anyone from the headland house." Miss Wilkins shrugged. "Superstitious, I know. But my pa never fully recovered his good spirits after Hob died, and my ma wasn't able to give him any more children."

Molly swallowed. She had to ask. "The girl—" she whispered. "That niece. What was her name?"

"It was Clementine. Clementine Horn."

Without warning the humming began in Molly's head—that horrible Clementine tune. She stood abruptly. "Thanks for everything. I have to go."

"But you haven't found any books yet!"

"Oh, you've been so helpful, I don't think I need any books after all." Molly moved abruptly toward the door, gulping out a good-bye to Grace Wilkins.

"You're sure I can't help you find some books to take now? They found the *Titanic,* you know, only a few years back. Sent a submarine robot or something down to search. Now, I never! Amazing things go on these days, don't you think?"

That was exactly what Molly thought. But she didn't want to read about the *Titanic.* The humming was getting louder in her head, and her voice sounded hollow, as if it were coming from down a deep well. "I—I'll have to come back for books another day. I really have to get home now. Thank you . . ."

Then she started walking back down Cotton Lane. The humming receded, but her eyes, when she blinked, felt fuzzy. The sounds of the sea gulls wheeling overhead were muted. *I'm in a daze,* she thought. It was the sort of thing you always read people were in, without having any real idea what being in a daze meant. Now she knew.

Numbly she turned the corner onto Main Street and headed back up the hill. She passed the low stone walls built by the early settlers. There was the old building that had once been Clementine's beloved school. Now it was the antique shop. The next building was the church. Molly could see the modern condominiums where Miss Wilkins lived just beyond. As Molly trudged past, she glanced at the graveyard, and then she stopped. Here was her chance to cut through the fog and do some real research.

The headstones—most old, but a few new—seemed to beckon her inside the low stone wall. Hob Wilkins would be buried here. An inexplicable feeling of guilt penetrated Molly's daze at the thought of Grace Wilkins's half-brother—the feeling was just as mysterious as the hollowness that assailed her sometimes when she was with Jared Bernstein. Without planning her route, Molly left Main Street and walked slowly along the side of the wooden church. Could there be some answers here?

She stepped over the low stone wall and stood amid the graves. The grass was scrubby but green and neatly trimmed around the headstones. A few of the graves had small bunches of wildflowers at their bases, arranged in plastic containers. One gravestone, larger than the others, was a memorial to the boys from Hibben who had died overseas in World War II. An American flag fluttered nearby. Molly walked around the memorial stone and saw that the other side was dedicated to the boys from Hibben who had died in World War I. Hob Wilkins might have been one of those young men from Hibben, she realized, if he hadn't died so young. Long life was something she'd taken for granted until her near drowning, but now she knew there was no guarantee at all. Not for anyone. You lived until you died, and that was it.

Or was it? Paulette would say no, that the soul

had many more chances to live long lives. In other bodies. Maybe she should have asked Miss Wilkins for books on reincarnation.

Molly stepped around a few headstones, searching for Hob's grave. She found other Wilkins stones first, marking graves of babies who had died in 1906, 1907, and 1910. They had each lived only a few days. These might have been the babies Grace Wilkins's ma had lost before Grace was born on the day the *Titanic* sank in 1912.

And then there it was, a headstone larger than the ones marking the babies' graves, with a ship carved into the curve above the words:

HOBSON JOHN WILKINS

Our Beloved Son and Brother
Departed this life July 1, 1912
Aged 17 years

HE SAILS THE ETERNAL SEAS

Molly knelt at Hob's stone and traced the letters of the inscription with her finger. Her stomach tightened against the sudden hollow anguish. "I'm sorry, so *sorry*," she whispered.

Here in the graveyard anything seemed possible. Molly sat cross-legged on the grass in front of the stone and closed her eyes. The sun beat warm on her head, and she could hear the buzz of bees in the flowering bushes at the side of the low stone wall surrounding the graveyard. But then the buzz changed slowly to a hum, and it was the same old tune, humming through her head.

Her daze had lifted; now she could hear the scream of sea gulls as they flew overhead toward the wharf at the end of Main Street. She could hear the thud of hooves on the street in front of the church. She could hear the laughter of children in the schoolyard next door. She recognized the high-pitched voice that called out excitedly: *"There she is, Janie! Over here! Hello, Clemmy!"*

8 Clementine

On the last day of school, the graduating class tested the younger children in the traditional schoolwide spelling bee that marked the end of term. At noon the families started gathering in the schoolyard for the commencement ceremony. City high schools might put on fancy ceremonies in big auditoriums, but Hibben's village school kept the celebration to a simple afternoon of speeches and songs, with a picnic and dance afterward. The schoolchildren gathered in self-conscious groups, waiting for their families to arrive. The fathers of most of the children were absent, out with the fishing fleet as they were every day. But the fathers of the graduating seniors, on a rare day off, attended the ceremony dressed in their Sunday best.

Clementine wore a new white lawn dress, with her dark braids coiled tightly at the nape of her neck and interwoven with pink ribbon. She stood with the other five seniors just inside the school door, pink cheeks glowing even more vividly than usual as she peeked out into the yard to watch everyone assemble. Aunt Ethel and Uncle Wallace would not attend a village function, of course, but Janie had permission to bring the children—a rare outing, indeed. Little Abner especially loved the village. He'd told her the other day that he was going to be a fisherman when he grew up. Silly little boy—here he had a father wanting to send him to the best school in Boston, and all he wanted to do was fritter away his life in a boat. She knew Uncle Wallace would never allow it. In that, at least, she agreed with her uncle. If only he had the same plan for her as he had for his sons.

She heard Abner's excited voice now as he caught sight of her through the open doorway: "*There* she is, Janie! Over here!" He waved frantically and caught Alice's hand so she could run with him. "Hello, Clemmy!"

Clementine stepped outside. Janie smiled at her. "You look a right picture, Clementine. You really do."

"Thank you," she said, knowing it was true. "You all should go find places to sit. If you hurry, you may still get chairs together."

Anne and Amity, holding hands, stepped back in their lacy dresses and surveyed the yard. "Oh, Clementine, look how dirty these village children are!" said Anne. And Amity nodded.

"Our dresses are much prettier," observed Amity.

Clementine shushed them. "They don't have fancy

clothes like yours, but some of them are very smart. Smarter than you two!"

The girls flushed. Janie led everyone away to the wooden seats set in rows before the stage. Miss Kent and Miss Reddy, the two teachers, stood on the makeshift platform. Abby Chandler, the fifteen-year-old orphan girl who had come to Hibben a year ago and lived with Miss Reddy, sat at an upright piano. At a signal from Miss Reddy, she began playing the march that meant the seniors should walk onto the stage.

As head student, Clementine led the way. Jilly Peters followed, turning behind her to dimple at the boys. Then came Gilbert Hanks, Sam Sawyer, Earl Wallings, and Hob Wilkins, all looking unaccustomedly formal and grown up in their Sunday suits. The families of the graduates sat in the wooden seats, while the other villagers sat on the grass, on blankets, and on wooden folding chairs. Miss Kent had made a cake in honor of her six graduates and decorated it with a rolled diploma and tassled cap cleverly crafted of marzipan. The cake sat in the center of the plank table at the back of the yard. The village women had baked other cakes and pies and all manner of fluffy muffins (many of them blueberry, since the berries grew rampant on the headland in summer) and sweets of spun sugar. Frosty pitchers of lemonade waited to quench nearly a hundred thirsts.

When the seniors were in their places of honor on the stage, Miss Kent signaled everyone to stand for a prayer led by the Reverend Beasley. Then the minister began his speech about the responsibilities of adulthood, his booming voice carrying as it did in church over the fidgets and chattering of the assembled children and the *shush*ing of their parents.

The boys were men now, he said, and would soon be marrying. They would need to work hard out at sea to provide for their wives and children and to support the economy of the village. There was no more time for tomfoolery or boyish pranks. The girls were young women now, and ready for marriage. They would need to be steadfast keepers of the home, bearing children and guiding them through childhood, with God's grace. There would be no time now for flirting and games.

Clementine thought he made it all sound rather awful. She resolved that *she* would never marry and bear child after child like Aunt Ethel. There were other things to do in life. Other fish to fry. She smiled at her own wit, then listened with interest to Miss Kent's speech about how the graduates would take forth to use in life the wisdom and knowledge they had gained in the village school. And then Miss Reddy presented each graduate with a book. Clementine's was a leather-bound copy of *Hard Times* by Charles Dickens. Clementine stroked the soft cover and thanked Miss Reddy, sighing to herself at the aptness of the title. These *were* hard times. But they would be better soon.

The younger pupils came forth at the end amid the tumultuous applause of parents, bearing gifts for the new graduates: wildflower bouquets and home-made pen wipers and sweets from the general store. Abner pushed through the crowd to hug Clementine, and Alice and Anne gave her a small box wrapped in shiny pink paper.

"This is from all of us," Anne said. "Father gave us the money, and Janie took us to the general store. I wanted to order something really fine from Bangor, but this was the best we could do."

"It smells lovely anyway!" added Amity. Clementine pulled off the wrapping paper and opened the box to reveal three sachets of lavender and rose, tied with ribbon.

"You can put them in your wardrobe to scent your clothes, or even pin one inside your dress," Anne said.

"Mmmmm," sniffed Abner. "It smells as sweet as you, Clemmy!"

"My sentiments exactly," said a deeper voice appreciatively, and Clementine glanced over her shoulder to find Hob Wilkins grinning at her.

She tossed her head and looked away. She'd known Hob for years and liked him well enough. When they were younger, before she'd put her hair up, he'd pestered her the way all the boys pestered the girls—dipping the ends of her braids into inkwells, chasing her at lunchtime, hiding spiders and frogs in her desk. She ignored him the way she ignored her small cousins when they bothered her. Clementine had come in for more teasing than the other girls. Jilly Peters said that was because she was from the big house on the hill and the boys wanted to make sure she didn't act too fancy.

Although Clementine didn't look down on the villagers because of their lack of wealth and social position, she nonetheless felt set apart. They didn't share the same goals; they didn't know what was important in life. She felt alternately amused and depressed by their collective lack of ambition. The girls all wanted to get married. The boys all wanted to be fishermen. Hob Wilkins's goal in life was to be exactly like his father, to spend his days out in the cove trailing lobster traps through the water. How could she take his attempts to court her seriously?

At Christmas he presented her with a tiny wooden boat he'd whittled himself. In February a silly homemade Valentine, unsigned and still oozing glue around the paper lace doily stuck onto red paper, lay on her desk when she arrived at school. The card, its message cut from newspaper words and pasted onto the doily, vowed eternal love. Hob had given himself away just before lessons began by asking permission to go out to the pump to wash his sticky fingers. And this past spring, on her seventeenth birthday, he had presented her with a bouquet of wildflowers picked from the hillside as she started home from school.

She thought later she should never have accepted the first gift (she'd given it to Abner one day as a bribe to make him stop pestering her) because Hob seemed to think something had been decided between them. He acted now as if he had the *right* to her attention. He offered time and again to walk home with her after school and carry her books—"So many books!" he laughed. "What a silly, studious girl!"—but she always turned him down.

She knew Aunt Ethel and Uncle Wallace would frown on her association with a boy from the village, but that wasn't the reason she ignored Hob Wilkins. She just wasn't interested in flirting with empty-headed boys. Hob looked confused when she told him her plan of going on to college. He'd asked how she could even *think* of ever leaving Hibben for somewhere else.

She'd wanted to ask how he could even *think* of staying but had held her tongue. Now, spying Miss Kent across the yard, she hugged her little cousins and thanked them again for their gift, then headed over to talk to the teacher. Miss Kent was the most educated woman in the village, and she was Clementine's one oasis in an intellectual desert.

The teacher stood at the plank table, cutting the big cake into pieces for everyone. "May I talk to you a moment?" Clementine inquired in a low voice. "In private?"

Miss Kent wiped the knife on a napkin and set it down carefully out of reach of the little children. "Why, yes, dear. I think we can find a minute now." They walked over to the low wall that separated the schoolyard from the graveyard behind the church.

Clementine explained about her longing to attend college and how her uncle and aunt forbade it. She explained how they insisted she work as their unpaid governess-cum-household drudge. "They should pay me, at the very least," she declared. "Or let me leave here and earn money for college by being someone *else's* governess. But my uncle and aunt won't hear of it. They say I shall stay home with them until I marry. But I don't want to work for them—and I'm never going to marry!"

Miss Kent wrinkled her forehead and put her hand on Clementine's arm. "But, Clementine, dear, of course you shall marry! Even girls who go on to college marry eventually—unless they want to become dried-up old maids like me."

"You aren't dried up at all," said Clementine, shocked. "You're educated and independent. I intend to be the same."

Miss Kent shook her head slowly. "My dear, I know how you have loved your studies. I don't think I've ever had a more eager or more brilliant student in all my time teaching. But family duty must come first—before all else. I cannot help you go against your family's wishes. Didn't you listen to the Reverend Beasley's speech? It's important for a girl to help out at home, where she belongs."

Clementine felt tears welling in her eyes. How could Miss Kent say these things? How could she—a teacher!—believe that staying home with a passel of little cousins could be as important as getting an education? Clementine simply stared at Miss Kent until the teacher patted her hand and walked over to chat with some parents. Then Clementine stood there, cheeks blazing, and stared blankly at the grass. The tears in her eyes made her unable to focus. When she blinked them away, she found she was looking at Hob Wilkins and Sam Sawyer wrestling companionably without a care in the world. When he saw her watching, Hob grinned.

"Care to join us, Clementine?" he called. "Let's see how strong you are!"

Behind her she heard Jilly Peters's sassy voice: "You know he's sweet on you, Clementine. He just wants to get his arms around you. I bet you two are married within the year!"

Clementine stalked away, bitter, but not before she'd heard Hob's laugh. "I hope you win that bet, Jilly. There's nothing I'd like better than to wed Clementine Horn. And the sooner the better."

Clementine sat on the low wall and ate a piece of Miss Kent's cake. She barely tasted it. She watched the schoolchildren cavorting in the yard and noticed most of her own cousins hung back, too shy and unfamiliar with other children to join in. Only Abner and little Alice seemed comfortable. Alice examined a village child's rag doll, while Abner kicked a ball around with some of the little boys.

Abby Chandler's crashing chords on the piano signaled that the dance was to begin. The village doctor, Dr. Scopes, jumped up onto the platform with his fiddle. The villagers cheered. The running children were rounded up and the schoolyard cleared for dancing. Abby and Dr. Scopes played popular tunes that set everyone's toes to tapping. The Reverend Beasley asked Miss Kent for the first dance, and everyone clapped when they moved into the circle. Then Sam Sawyer asked Jilly Peters to dance, and Earl Wallings asked his sister. Clementine watched from the wall. She was too sunk in misery to want to join in. These people were so . . . so provincial! This sort of entertainment was all they cared about. An orphan girl plunking out tunes and a second-rate fiddler trying to keep time! She looked on dispassionately.

Miss Reddy relieved Abby Chandler at the piano, and the music changed from popular tunes to waltzes. Gilbert Hanks and Hob Wilkins both crossed the yard, and Clementine could see the desire in Hob's eyes as he neared her. Jumping off the wall, she walked straight over to little Abner. "Let's dance," she said, and turned pointedly away from Hob. As she spun off with the child in her arms, she saw Hob, his face crimson, ask Abby Chandler to dance instead.

Soon the schoolyard was full of couples moving across the grass. Even the Holloway children joined in enthusiastically. Little Abner danced with his sister, Alice. Amity danced with Aaron, then with Anne. Andrew bowed and asked Janie to dance. Laughing, she accepted.

Clementine danced with Gilbert Hanks, then Sam Sawyer, then Earl Wallings, taking no joy in it. She danced with Andrew and Aaron and little Abner again, who clung to her white dress. "You look so pretty today, Clemmy. Will you marry me?" He gazed up at her with his usual expression of adoration. She hugged him automatically, her thoughts elsewhere.

"Sure I will. You're my own sweet little man."

Clementine smoothed her skirt as the Reverend Beasley approached. But just as he was about to speak, Hob Wilkins cut in. "Pardon me, Reverend, but Clementine has promised this one to me!" And he grabbed her arms and pulled her against his chest.

"Hob Wilkins! Let go of me!" She struggled against him.

"This is our graduation, Clementine," he said, releasing her enough that she could stand back to look up at him. "You can't mean to end your school career without a single dance with the man who loves you best!" His tone was teasing, but she saw in his blue eyes how seriously he meant the words. *Oh well,* she thought. *One dance.* And she stopped struggling and let him lead her around the schoolyard. As they circled, his arm tightened around her waist. She heard him sigh.

"Oh, Clementine, you know I'd do anything for you, don't you? I'm not kidding. You're so special to me." His voice murmured in her ear. She could see his own ears were bright pink. As the glimmer of an idea began to form, she felt a thrill of power. She deliberately relaxed her body against his. He lowered his head to press his cheek against her soft dark hair. When the song ended, he kept his arms tightly around her and continued dancing, singing the song he had often hummed in the past to tease her: *"Oh my darlin', Oh my darlin', Oh my darlin', Clementine . . ."*

Over his shoulder she could see Janie and Alice beckoning her to come. They were ready to leave. Smiling at Hob, she excused herself. She was ready to leave, too. She needed time to think about her budding idea. "Thanks for the dance, Hob."

"Oh my darlin'—may I have this next dance, too?"

"No, I have to leave. But I'll see you soon."

He brightened. "You promise?"

Clementine nodded, then hurried over to her cousins and Janie. On their way out of the schoolyard she stopped to say polite good-byes to the Reverend Beasley, Miss Reddy, and Miss Kent. When Clementine held out her hand to Miss Kent, the teacher hugged her instead, quite hard. "Be sure to come back down and visit the school," she murmured into Clementine's ear. "I am going to miss you."

Hope leapt up in Clementine's heart again. "Oh, Miss Kent," she whispered. "Do you suppose I could come and help you with the children? I could teach math to the little ones and geography—it would be no trouble at all. I could save the money you pay me toward college!"

Miss Kent pulled abruptly away. "Oh, Clementine," she said sadly, "please don't go on this way. Your job is to tend to your uncle's children. You must do as he says. That is your duty."

Clementine turned and walked after Janie without a backward glance. There would be no help at all from Miss Kent. How she had overestimated the teacher! Hob Wilkins waved, watching her leave with longing in his eyes. On any other day she would have turned her back on him. But now she waved and smiled.

That evening she sat numbly through a celebratory dinner in her honor, with Uncle Wallace presiding in fine humor. The older children were permitted to eat in the dining room for the occasion, and Clementine was allowed a half glass of wine. Aunt Ethel even made the trip down the long flight of stairs and sat for the first time in months with her family, although she merely pushed the food around on her plate.

"You need to eat more, my dear," reproved Uncle Wallace from the other end of the table. "Remember that you're eating for two. You need to keep your strength up."

"Yes, Wallace," said Aunt Ethel softly. "I do try, you know."

The new baby was due around Christmas, Janie had whispered to all the children. But they must wait patiently and not tire their mother with questions about it. Little Augustus was not yet a year old, and he needed their attention, since their mother was too weak to take any interest in the poor lad.

Janie came in from the kitchen to clear their plates. They sat silently until she reentered bearing a tray laden with two wild blueberry pies, a bowl of whipped cream, and a stack of serving bowls. She set the tray near Aunt Ethel and began slicing the pie into thick wedges.

"None for me," Aunt Ethel told her, then caught her husband's eye. "All right, then. Just a small portion."

"A small portion for me, too, please," said Clementine, when Janie had moved around the table to her place.

"Clemmy's trying to keep her figure," announced Anne. "I saw how one of the boys from the village was looking at her! He even said right out loud that he'd like to marry her!" Anne's thoughts had recently turned to romance, and she often speculated to Clementine about their future husbands and what being kissed would be like.

Uncle Wallace set down his fork and cleared his throat. "And who might this village boy be, Clementine?"

She shrugged lightly. "Oh, Uncle Wallace, it's nothing to worry about. It's just Hob Wilkins—he graduated today, too, you know. He always has a crush on one girl or another."

"I certainly hope you don't return his affections, Clementine."

"Not at all, Uncle Wallace," she replied honestly.

"That's good." Uncle Wallace shook his head and picked up his fork again. He looked around the table at all the children. "You all know how your mother and I feel about the village children. They're not our sort."

"Of course, Father!" Anne's voice was merry. "I'd

never want to marry a villager. Why, they smell of fish and lobster all the time. And we'd have to live in a little cottage and—well, I think it would be awful! Wouldn't it, Clemmy?"

But it wasn't the smell of fish or the small houses that Clementine objected to. It was the pattern of small-town life. It was the lack of opportunity.

"Father will find all you girls suitable husbands in Boston or New York," said Aunt Ethel softly. "You too, of course, Clementine, dear."

Her aunt and uncle were no better than the villagers.

"I hope it wasn't a mistake to allow Clementine to attend the village school all these years," worried Uncle Wallace. He frowned at Clementine. "Make sure you avoid the Wilkins boy in the future, niece. I'm sure he's a very worthy young man and will work hard on his father's fishing boat, but he's not of our class." He peered around the table at all the children. "I will cut off any one of you who lowers herself— or himself—to marry down in the village. Your mother and I would be so ashamed . . . you would have to leave our home. We would want nothing to do with you. Do I make myself clear?"

"Yes, Papa," they chorused. And Anne added: "Marrying a villager—what a disgusting thought, Papa!"

But Clementine's heart began racing. Cut off? If she married a villager? A blossom of hope unfurled. She smiled around her mouthful of pie and pondered her new plan of escape.

Clementine awoke very early the next morning with her sheet and blanket tangled around her legs. She listened in the darkness. No child stirred. She sat up and kicked off the covers. An escape route! At dinner Uncle Wallace had unknowingly set her on a path of escape. But she must hurry.

She dressed swiftly in her simple gray cotton school dress and coiled her braids around her head. When they were securely pinned, she shook the mending out of her sewing basket and rolled another dress and a change of undergarments up tightly to fit in the basket. It wouldn't hold much more, but she pressed *Hard Times* on top and forced the wicker cover down till she could latch it. She picked her woolen shawl up off the chair. Early mornings in Hibben were chilly even in the middle of summer. The winters were unbearable. But soon she'd be living somewhere warmer. Anywhere but here.

Then she knelt and pulled her hatbox out from under the bed. She couldn't leave these mementos of her happy family behind, no matter where in the world she traveled. She peeked inside at the doll, the red-bound atlas, and her mother's locket. The locket would be especially useful if ever she needed money. She would hate to sell it, of course, but if her plan worked, she wouldn't have to.

She crept down the hallway, pausing for a minute outside the doors of the children's rooms. She would have liked to say good-bye but knew she could not trust her young cousins to keep her secret. They would beg her to stay; they would call for their parents to stop her. She liked sweet Abner best, but he, even more than the others, threatened to weigh her down with his puppy-dog devotion and tie her to this place. She would not stay and be their unpaid governess. She would not marry and follow in Aunt Ethel's pattern of having a baby every year. She would be on her own, pursuing her education and seeing the world. The children would forget her as easily as she would forget them.

She padded downstairs to the kitchen to pack a few slices of bread, cheese, and meat to keep her going until she had work. Then she froze in the back hallway as she heard a soft footfall. Someone was awake!

She turned to flee—never mind the food—but had to stop at the sound of Janie's soft voice.

"Why, Clementine! Up so early—and there's no school for you today, nor any day now, is there?"

"Oh . . . good morning, Janie. I didn't realize you arrived so early."

"Why, whoever else do you think it is that gets your breakfast ready in the morning?" The young woman pressed a thin hand to her mouth and laughed. "Maybe the little doll in that hatbox you treasure so much?"

"I want to have breakfast out on the headland," Clementine improvised quickly. "A picnic to celebrate the ending of school. To finish school was something my parents always wanted for me. I feel close to them again when I look at all I have left of them." That was true enough and would explain why she was carrying the hatbox. Clementine hurried on: "Do you have something I can pack?" She held up her sewing basket.

"Land sakes! At this hour? My girl, it's barely light enough to see out there. You don't want to get the pages of your papa's nice book of maps wet in the dew. Or soil your pretty little doll. And I suppose you'll go to that little cave Abner was telling me about. I don't like the sound of it. Too dangerous. You ought to be sure to keep those children away from the cliff."

"I will," said Clementine.

Janie turned back to the kitchen and Clementine followed. She watched while Janie sliced roast salted beef and thick slices of homemade brown bread. The young woman wrapped these in grease paper and set them on the table. She fished two pickled eggs from the jar in the pantry and added a peach from the bowl on the counter. "Will that do you?"

"That'll be fine, thanks."

Janie took a cotton napkin from the hutch and wrapped the food, tying the ends of the cloth into a neat knot. "Here, let's put it in your basket."

But of course her basket was full. "I will," said Clementine, picking up the corners of the cloth bundle and hurrying toward the door before the hired girl could reach for the basket and see all the clothes packed inside. "I'll be back when the children awake," she lied, and rushed out the back door. Just out of sight around the side of the house, she stopped to dump the bundle of food into the hatbox. She replaced the lid and, picking up both the box and her sewing basket, hurried on.

The morning wind was cool and fresh. It blew over the headland, rippling the grass. Gulls swooped overhead as Clementine moved toward the cliff. She looked back and realized Janie was watching her. Clementine waved in what she hoped was a cheerful gesture. Janie waved back, then stepped inside again and closed the door.

As soon as she felt sure she was not being watched, Clementine changed direction, veering sharply away from the cliff path and back around the side of the house. She tried to keep out of sight of the windows, just in case any member of the family inside happened to look out. She hurried behind the shed, behind the chicken coop, and then down the road to the village.

The road into town was rutted. It always turned to mud in the rain but was hard packed now and dry. The usually frequent summer rains had held off for three weeks, and people were saying that when the storm finally did come, it would be a humdinger. First she passed the church, then the school. The small houses lining the street had neat picket fences in front and well-swept stone steps. Housewives in the village prided themselves on the sheen of their entranceway. Most had planted flowers along the short walkways to their doors. The sight of morning glories just opening for the day made Clementine feel cheerful as she hurried past. Soon the soft, flowery air was overpowered by the sharper smells of salt and fish and lobster.

The townspeople were just opening their doors to bring in the milk and coal that had been delivered at daybreak. Clementine drew her shawl up over her head, tying it securely beneath her chin. She hoped it hid her face.

She knew exactly where to find Hob Wilkins. She turned off Main Street and headed down to the wharf. The fishing schooners were tied up at the rock wall. Their lowered sails billowed and flapped in the morning breeze. Men crawled and jumped and climbed over every inch of the vessels, checking knots, scrubbing decks, loading the hundreds of lobster pots on board. The pots looked like chicken crates made of oak and were stuffed with bait to attract the lobsters, which entered easily but couldn't get out again through the nets. This would be Hob's life, Clementine thought, her mouth twisting. Catching lobsters, throwing the females back so they could lay more eggs, bringing the males triumphantly home to sell or eat. It was no life at all.

The fishermen were packing the barrels with salt for their catch and ordering everything for the day at sea. Their voices rang out across the harbor, laughing or quarrelsome or simply brisk. Soon they would be on their way, and Hob would be taking his place as a new fisherman among them. Clementine had to find him first.

She stood at the railing along the wall and peered at each ship, searching for Hob's blond head. She saw some of the men who worked on her uncle's fleet mending nets, and she drew her shawl forward. It wouldn't do to be seen by them and have one mention to her uncle that she had been here. She saw the bright red hair of Sam Sawyer in a cluster of young men near some smaller boats out on the pier and jumped away from the railing. She ran down the steps to his side and placed her hand on his arm.

The young men stopped talking and looked at her. "Hey, it's Hob's darlin' Clementine!" said Sam. "What are you doing here, darlin'?"

"I want to find Hob. Where is he?"

Someone hooted. The others shuffled their feet at the interruption.

She pressed Sam's arm impatiently. "Is he with his father? Where can I find him?"

Sam pointed, grinning. "See that beauty at the end, there? That's the *Undine*. But you won't find Hob going out today, not in his condition."

She pushed back the shawl so she could see him clearly. "Why? What's happened?"

"Me and him were up on the cliffs with the other boys last night having, you know, a celebration. It's a pretty big thing, being all graduated now. I guess you're the only one sorry to leave that old prison. Anyway, we were horsing around and Hob fell."

She asked tightly: "Is he hurt?" Would her careful planning come to nothing? Perhaps it was only a little sprain.

"Old Hob slipped on a loose stone. He's home in bed with his leg wrapped."

She breathed an inward sigh of relief. "So he'll mend."

"Oh, yeah. He'll be out on the boat as soon as he can convince his ma to let him walk. She's really only his stepma, you know, but she does carry on as if he were her very own." Sam glanced back at his small group of friends. "So, you going to accept? I want to be best man at the wedding, that's all I ask."

"Which is his house, Sam? It's on Cotton Lane, right?"

"Ha!" Sam leered at her. "You aren't really going to take him up on his proposal now, are you, Clementine? What a pair you'd make, the two of you! 'The Brawn' and 'The Brain'! I just can't see it working out, myself. But Hob's always had a thing for you, that's for sure." He was laughing.

She stood there, silent, looking at him, thinking that his chipped front tooth and wild red hair made him look like a pirate. He'd probably turn out to be a fine seaman.

"It's the stone cottage with the blue door. You can't miss it." Sam turned back to his friends.

Clementine ran back up the stone steps to the street. She drew her sewing basket higher on her arm and held the hatbox tightly against her chest. She hurried up Main Street to Cotton Lane, juggling her burdens to reach one hand up to tug the ends of the shawl tightly under her chin.

She nearly collided with a stooped man dressed in sober black just at the corner of Cotton Lane. She jumped aside. "Oh, pardon me!"

"Well, if it isn't the high school graduate herself!"

Dr. Scopes beamed at her. "Saw you dancing at the school yesterday. I hadn't seen you for a long while, my dear. You're usually out with the children when I'm up at the house."

"Oh—Dr. Scopes!" Her heart pounded. "Your fiddling was wonderful," she said politely.

"So what brings you to the village so early? I would have thought with school out, you'd be home with your family."

"Oh . . . I'm doing some errands for my aunt."

"I'm headed up to the big house now to check on that poor lady. You're looking overburdened, my girl. Here, let me help you carry some of your things." He shifted his black bag and held out a hand. "The basket? Or the box? We can walk along together, I should think."

"Oh, thank you, Dr. Scopes. But I'm not done with my errands yet." Her mind raced to come up with a plausible explanation for such an early morning visit to the village. "Our hired girl needs a few things at the general store. I'm trying to help out now that I have more time at home."

"Well, give me the box, anyway. I'll carry it home for you."

"No, really," she protested. "I'm fine." She wished he would get on with his rounds and leave her. She hoped desperately that he would not mention this encounter to her uncle or aunt but knew it was most likely he would. Well, she would just have to make sure she was well on her way by then.

The doctor nodded. "I'll let you get on your way,

then," he said. "It's only right that you should help out after all your uncle and aunt have done for you. I'm sure you are a great comfort to them."

Clementine gripped her hatbox tightly. She had to get to Hob! She smiled politely at Dr. Scopes. "It has been pleasant to see you again."

"Good morning, then," he said, and she turned away. As she hurried along up the street in the opposite direction from the general store, she could feel his eyes on her back.

There was the cottage with the door painted robin's egg blue. The low garden gate was also blue—a departure from the stone walls or traditional white fences of the other cottages in Hibben. A plump, fair-haired woman was sweeping the stoop as Clementine approached the blue gate. Clementine recognized her from the school picnic the day before. This was Hob's mother—or stepmother, as Sam Sawyer had said.

"Mrs. Wilkins?" Clementine untied her shawl and settled it loosely over her shoulders. She put up a hand to check that her braids were still neatly pinned.

"Yes, dear?" The woman leaned on her broom. "Oh, you're one of the Holloway girls! How are you this morning?"

"Clementine Horn," she corrected. "And I'm fine, thank you. I was in the village doing errands for my aunt—she isn't at all well, I'm afraid, with this new confinement—and I heard the frightful news about poor Hob's fall. I'm so sorry he has suffered such a terrible accident."

Mrs. Wilkins laughed, her eyes twinkling. "The villagers tend to exaggerate, I'm afraid. But it is true that Hobbie's still in bed this morning. He fell yesterday along the cliff path and bruised his leg. His pa and I thought he ought to wait till the swelling goes from his knee before letting him spend a whole day out in the boat."

"Oh, what a relief. I'm glad it's nothing very serious." Clementine lingered by the rosebushes. She was counting on traditional village hospitality, and Mrs. Wilkins did not disappoint.

The fair-haired woman reached out and placed a plump hand on Clementine's sleeve. "Since you are already here so early, perhaps you'd like to come in for a cup of coffee? The baby will be waking up soon and I'll need to feed her. You can visit with Hob while I tend her, if he is awake."

Clementine smiled with satisfaction and answered quite calmly: "Why, how very pleasant."

She followed the woman into the small house. So far, so good.

The houses in the village were much alike—frame cottages of two stories—two rooms up and two down, nestled against the rocky hillside. From the harbor it looked as if they might tumble down right into the sea. "Little mouse holes," Aunt Ethel labeled them disparagingly. Mrs. Wilkins led Clementine into the back room, which was the kitchen. It was crowded, though cheerful, with a stone fireplace set in one wall and blue-curtained windows along the back. The house was built up almost against the hill, and the kitchen windows looked out at the rise of rock dotted with wildflowers. In the center of the room was a round table covered in blue checked oilcloth. Simple crockery, pitchers, and bowls were stacked upon a shelf that ran the length of one wall. Clementine heard a whimper and noticed for the first time a wooden cradle near the large black stove that dominated one corner of the room.

"There, there, little one, just wait another second and Mama will feed you." Mrs. Wilkins clucked at the infant and reached for the blackened kettle that sat on the stove top. She poured Clementine a mug of steaming coffee and handed it to her. "I can sympathize with your aunt, my dear, having had a difficult confinement myself. We women do have a lot to bear." Then she bent over the baby and her eyes were warm with love. "Still, don't think I'm complaining! Little Grace is only two months old, but she's the light of my life." She tickled the baby under her fat chin. "Aren't you a little angel?" The baby chortled, and Mrs. Wilkins glanced up at Clementine. "Isn't she a dear?" She turned back to the baby and smoothed the blanket. "And look at those blue eyes. Aren't you Mama's sweet blueberry?"

Clementine had never seen a mother fuss over a tiny scrap of baby. Aunt Ethel always handed her new babies over to a servant girl immediately after their births. Clementine watched in fascination as Mrs. Wilkins settled herself comfortably in the rocking chair by the hearth and offered baby Grace her breast. Then she smiled at Clementine. "There's cream in the pitcher on the shelf, dear. Help yourself. Can you reach it? Pour Hob a cup, too, why don't you, with plenty of cream, and go on up. I'll join you soon as I'm finished here."

Clementine poured a cup of coffee for Hob, added cream to her own cup and his, and listened to Mrs. Wilkins croon and chatter to baby Grace. She felt a pang in her heart and for the space of a second missed her own mother fiercely. She left her basket and hatbox by the door to the garden and hurried up the narrow stairs, sloshing coffee over the rims of the cups she carried.

At the top of the stairs were two rooms. The one at the back of the house was small, with a sloped ceiling dropping low to meet the outside wall. Hob lay in this room in an iron frame bed, his head turned to the window. Like the kitchen windows, the windows in this room looked out to the rocky hill.

"Hello, Hob," she said in a low voice.

"What—oh, *Clementine!* My word, it's *you!*" He struggled to sit up. "I've been lying here daydreaming about you—and here you come right though the door! I must be a magician."

She handed him a cup of coffee, wondering how to begin. "I heard you were hurt. I was so worried, I came as fast as I could."

"I thought I heard voices downstairs," he said, gazing at her wonderingly, "but I never thought— It boggles the mind, my darlin'. Fairly boggles the mind." He was grinning at her now, blue eyes twinkling.

How thick should she lay it on? What would he believe? She gave him her sunniest smile. "I felt just awful at the thought of you lying injured in bed," she said. "And I realized—well, I realized that I'd been a fool."

"A fool? How?"

"A fool for trying to push you away from me. A fool because I—I really *do* care for you."

He stared at her. "You do?"

She nodded, eyes cast down shyly, and glanced at him from under her lashes. He was lapping up every word!

"Clementine Horn, really? You do?" When she nodded again, he laughed. "Pull over that chair there, girl, and come talk to me!"

She carried a ladder-back chair over from the wall and set it near his bedside. She sat down and took a deep breath, raising her eyes and gazing directly into his. "Yes," she said. "I *need* to talk to you. I've been thinking we really ought to spend more time together, now that we're out of school."

Hob brushed back his fair hair. "You must be heaven sent, my darlin' Clementine."

She didn't need Jilly Peters to tell her Hob Wilkins was sweet on her. And Uncle Wallace had unknowingly set her plan to escape in action when he said last night that he'd cast out anyone who married a villager. Cast out! She would marry Hob Wilkins if that's what it took to be rid of her uncle forever. But she hoped it wouldn't actually come to marriage. Clementine thought briefly of the atlas down in her hatbox at the foot of the stairs. She had vowed to herself long ago that she would one day travel to the very places shown on those maps. Her father would have wanted that for her. And if Miss Kent wouldn't let her stay here to earn money as an assistant teacher, there were other teachers at other schools who might. Benson, for instance, was only a few miles across the cove and a far more bustling town than Hibben.

But Benson was too close. Hob would find her in Benson. As her husband, he could take her back to Hibben with him. No, she would have to go farther away. Out of Maine entirely. The new big buses that ran from Boston to Bangor now drove up the coast, passing right by Hibben, to the new depot in Benson. So Benson was the escape route, the point of departure for a better life, and all Clementine had to do was get there.

She smiled archly. "So come on! Get up!"

He reached for her hand. "You know this is music to my ears, darlin', don't you?" His voice was husky. "How about this for a first date? How about you and me going berrying?"

Berrying was not what she had in mind.

She would make Hob take her across the cove today. The road along the headland led to Benson, but the journey by land was much longer than by water. There was more chance that Uncle Wallace could find her if she walked. No, she must get Hob to take her in a boat. And then Clementine would go by bus down to Bangor, then on to Boston and

New York. Somewhere, someplace out in the wide world there would be work—work that paid—and money to be saved for college. In her determination she had come to this plan: she must get to Benson today and move on to a new life.

"It's a gorgeous day," he continued, "and I'm sure I can hobble around now. The blueberries are just busting off the bushes. Ma will make us a pie."

"Oh, I don't know," she demurred. "You mustn't strain your leg. I was thinking, well, I was hoping you'd take me out in a boat. For a picnic. I've got one packed, just downstairs."

"Clementine, you take my breath away." He set his coffee on the chest of drawers, then lay back on his pillows and grinned at her.

This was going to be a snap. "So you'll do it? Take me out in a boat—and sail right over to Benson?"

"All that way? We can have a picnic closer to home, my darlin'." He reached for her hand and held it. "Picking berries isn't going to hurt my leg any more than hiking all the way down the hill to the wharf will."

Her hand felt small in his, and she turned it so their fingers could twine together. "But you're such a"—she glanced at his muscled arms—"an able-bodied seaman. It would be so *romantic* out on the water together. Oh, *Hob*. Think of it. *Alone*."

"Clementine Horn, you're a girl full of surprises." His eyes looked puzzled, but she sensed his eagerness.

She leaned toward the bed. "Come on, Hobbie. You don't want to waste a beautiful day indoors. I'll go down and see if your stepmother objects. I'll tell her I'll take splendid care of you."

Hob flung back the sheet and swung his legs over the side of the bed. He wore loose red-and-white-striped pajamas, with the left trouser leg folded up and pinned above the knee. Thick linen bandages were tied around the ankle and knee on his left leg. "Don't even bother to ask her. I'm going! If you're that ready to be out in a boat with me—well, Clementine, there's no man or woman alive who can stop me! We'll have to take the rowboat. It's flat-bottomed and will do for a picnic. I don't think we'll get across to Benson in it, but we'll eat in the boat, though, and have a nice long chat."

"But I want to go to Benson! Right now!" She smiled to take the sharpness out of her tone. But desperation crept in anyway. *"Please!"*

"What's in Benson anyway?"

She had to go *today*. What would make him ready to sail? She thought fast, a fixed smile still on her lips. She widened the smile and leaned toward him. She placed one hand on his arm, then boldly reached the other up to brush the fair hair off his forehead. She was surprised his hair was so soft, as silky as little Abner's. Beneath her hand, she felt his arm tremble. And then she knew what to say next.

"We have to go today," she whispered. "It's our best chance. My uncle will be looking for me soon, if we don't start off now."

"What are you saying?" he asked in that husky voice. "Clementine, *why* do we need to go over to Benson?"

She drew in a long breath, then let it out slowly, never taking her eyes from his. If this didn't work, she would leave here now and start walking. It would take her all day to hike the road to Benson. She made her voice light and stroked his long fingers. "Hobbie, we can't marry here, you know—the Reverend Beasley wouldn't perform the ceremony without my uncle's permission. But over in Benson, no one knows us. We could find another minister, or a justice of the peace, or somebody—"

"Clementine Horn, are you saying you want to *marry* me today?" Hob's voice broke with a squeak of surprise. "Are you having me on, or what?" He glanced around the room as if he thought he might find Jilly Peters hiding to share Clementine's joke. "Have I died and gone to heaven? What is this?"

"This is just my clumsy way of trying to tell you how much I care for you! It's taken me ages to get up the courage to tell you. I've felt this way a long time, but I've just never been able to show it before. Not until this morning, when I heard you were injured. That was when I, well, I realized my true feelings." She said this all in a rush, hoping it sounded plausible. Had she gone too far? But maybe she could ditch Hob at the Benson wharf—send him off to look for a minister—while she raced off to the bus depot. If she couldn't shake him off, she'd go ahead and marry him—at least that would get Uncle Wallace off her back. Then she'd run off from Hob, her new husband, the first chance she got.

"Right now? Today?" When she nodded, smiling, he said in a voice choked with emotion: "Clementine, I don't understand you at all. But I'm not going to pass up the chance to marry you. Just hang on a second while I dress, and we'll be on our way. *Whoopee!*"

Clementine glanced in consternation at the closed bedroom door. Mrs. Wilkins would be up any moment. What would she say if Hob told her the plan?

"We'll get there somehow," he was saying now as he started unbuttoning his pajama shirt. "Even if I have to steal a sailboat! And tomorrow we'll come back home, man and wife. Your uncle won't be able to do a thing about it, and my pa will be so pleased. We'll live here, of course, to start. You can help my ma with baby Grace—and soon we'll be starting our own little family!"

He threw his shirt down on the bed and grabbed her hands again and pulled her up from the chair. She stared at his bare chest, her cheeks growing redder than ever. His big hands reached up to cup her chin and tilt her face to his. His hands were warm and gentle, and she closed her eyes as he drew her to him and held her snugly against his chest. He seemed so simple and good—she really didn't mean to hurt him. But it was the only way. And soon she'd be gone from here—and he would find some other girl in the village to marry and have babies with. Maybe that orphan, Abby Chandler. She had seen Abby looking enviously at her whenever Hob teased her in school.

Now Hob was murmuring his favorite song into her hair: *"Oh my darlin', Oh my darlin', Oh my darlin', Clementine—"*

She was already lost to him, though he couldn't know that, and she would soon be gone forever—once they got over to Benson. "We'll both be 'dreadful sorry,' " she teased, quoting from the song and pulling away from his embrace with a deliberately lighthearted giggle, "if we don't get going *now!*"

But he drew her closer, hard against his body, heedless of his bruised knee. He wrapped his arms around her more tightly and breathed a sigh of deep contentment. "To be with you, Clementine, all our lives long—I couldn't ask for more," he murmured. He took her chin in his hand again and tipped her head. She saw the expression in his eyes then, and with the teasing gone it was pure longing that shone out. His lips pressed hers warmly in a soft kiss, her first kiss.

Then there was a clattering of footsteps on the narrow wooden stairs, and the bedroom door opened. She struggled out of Hob's embrace and turned to face Mrs. Wilkins.

But it was Uncle Wallace who stood there in the doorway. He held her sewing basket and hatbox, and his face was dark with anger.

"Clementine Horn!" he barked, and Clementine stood there, trembling.

Mrs. Wilkins, behind him in the doorway, pressed

her hands to her round cheeks. "You see, Mr. Holloway, here she is—safe and sound! Just visiting my boy, who has hurt his leg."

"Hello, Uncle," Clementine began in a soft voice. "It's just as Mrs. Wilkins says. Poor Hob has twisted his knee in a fall. I heard about the accident and thought I should see if I could help in any way—"

"Yes, I see you have your way of cheering him up!" His sarcasm filled the room. "You told Janie you were off for a sunrise picnic on the headland, but Dr. Scopes told me he saw you down here in the village!"

"I was running errands for Aunt Ethel. She—"

"So you told Mrs. Wilkins. And the doctor, too, I understand!" He opened her wicker sewing basket, and her dress, undergarments, and *Hard Times* flew out and dropped to the floor. He opened the hatbox and dumped the contents onto Hob's bed. Mollydolly's green velvet party dress fluttered to the floor.

"Errands, you say, girl? With a change of clothes and your little box of treasures?" His hard voice made her wince as if he had struck her. She felt her face flushing deeply as she bent to gather up her scattered belongings.

"You owe me an explanation, Clementine. I'm taking you home at once." He ignored Hob entirely, nodded curtly to Mrs. Wilkins, and stepped out into the tiny hallway. Clementine picked up her hatbox and turned desperately to Hob, who had reached for his pajama shirt and was pulling it on again, his face stricken.

He cleared his throat and manfully stepped toward Uncle Wallace, his injured knee nearly buckling. "Sir, I can explain," he began. "Clementine and I plan to marry. We love each other, and—"

"Silence!" roared Uncle Wallace. "Get back in bed, boy. You're not marrying anybody."

Before Hob could speak again, Clementine turned to him. "Meet me at the wharf tonight," she mouthed, her words mere wisps of breath aimed in his direction. "Eleven o'clock."

She thought she saw him nod just as Uncle Wallace's fingers dug into her shoulder and turned her back toward the door. He kept his heavy hand on her shoulder as they descended the steep stairs, then he pushed Clementine outside the door ahead of him into Mrs. Wilkins's carefully tended garden. He moved his hand to Clementine's arm and propelled her through the blue gate, out onto the lane. She stumbled, her head lowered in embarrassment and fury, but said nothing. She could feel Mrs. Wilkins's eyes on her and knew the woman was watching worriedly from the doorway.

Her uncle reached for the sewing basket. "Running off to be married, Clementine? After all we've done for you these past seven years? After we've told you how we need your help with the children? Not to mention what you told me at the dinner table last night!" He shook her arm as he led her along. "Lying to me through your teeth, weren't you? I told you only last night to keep clear of the village boys, and this morning I find you right smack in the lap of that

half-naked village lout. I thought we could trust you!"
She stumbled along beside him, hugging the hatbox,
determined not to say anything.

"This will not go unpunished, my girl," he said
coldly, and he kept his fingers tight around her upper arm all the way up the steep road to the headland.

9

"Will you please stop this and tell me what the hell is going on?"

Molly blinked at the voice, rubbing the place above her arm where she felt the imprint of Uncle Wallace's fingers. She turned slowly away from Hob's gravestone, trying to restore her sense of the present. And then her hands flew to her mouth as she saw Hob himself standing at the low stone wall.

"I saw you come in here," Jared explained in a flat voice. "I called to you, but you didn't answer. I've been . . . listening." The strained tone disappeared as his voice rose. "My God, Molly! You're freaking me out!"

And she lowered her hands. It wasn't Hob Wilkins—of course not! How could she ever have thought it? They looked nothing alike. This was Jared Bernstein. Just Jared—or was it? She widened her eyes; his tousled dark hair and swimmer's muscled body dressed in cutoff jeans and a green T-shirt was superimposed for an instant over the image of Hob as she'd last seen him—straight blond hair, wiry body dressed in baggy pajama bottoms.

Whoever he was, he leapt over the wall and walked toward her. The image of Hob seemed to flicker, then melt away. He stood right in front of her, clearly Jared now, not Hob at all. Angry Jared, frightened Jared, Jared whom she felt sure she had somehow wronged quite terribly.

But wait—what did that mean? Molly pressed her hands to her stomach. She felt hollow. She sank down onto Hob's gravestone as her knees gave out.

"Hey, are you okay?" Jared knelt in front of her. "Stupid question—obviously you're not okay. But what's going on? I was walking up to your house when I saw you standing here in the graveyard." He paused and searched her face. "You look like you've seen a ghost. Is that what you're going to tell me? Were you muttering to ghosts?"

She drew a shaky breath. "Would you believe me if I said I just don't know?"

She had seen *something*, been talking to *something*, all right. Felt *something*. Molly shivered, remembering the warmth of Hob's embrace. But that hadn't been *Molly* he'd held—it was *Clementine*. Still, Molly could sense Hob nearby. She could feel Clementine, too. Call it spirit, or call it soul—or call it just some tiny piece of consciousness that existed apart from bodies—something was reaching out to Molly with a message. She felt it as a tiny nudge inside her head.

A push toward Jared, who knelt in the grass to read the inscription on the gravestone where Molly perched. Head down, his face was shadowed. Molly blinked in the bright sunlight and reached out her hand. She could not pretend to herself any longer that he was not somehow connected to her, to this— to all that was happening. She touched his dark curls and felt them spring soft under her fingers. As he reached up his own hand to touch hers, she knew with a quick certainty that his hand on hers was no different from Hob's hand on Clementine's, and that their bond ran deeper than any of them remembered.

"Hobson Wilkins," Jared read in a hushed voice. "Is that—I mean, the name you called me, *Hob*—is that him?"

Molly nodded and knelt next to him, tracing the inscription with her finger. "It's Hob, all right." A weak smile flickered across her face. "I guess it really is time that we talk," she said softly. "You ask about ghosts? I'm being haunted by hundreds of them. A whole village, actually. And what's more, I don't just *watch* them—nothing so ordinary. *I'm one of them.*"

"Better tell me about it. I mean *really*, Molly. Tell me everything you know. This seems to concern both of us, but don't ask me how."

She left Hob's stone without a backward glance. "Not in here. Let's go somewhere else."

"How about walking down to the wharf? I just got hired on at this little fish shop called Day's Catch. It's across from a little café. We can have lunch."

Jared smiled slightly. "My treat—in exchange for a real conversation with you. At long last."

She shook her head. She'd been on her way home from the library—it seemed so long ago. "I've got to get back up to the house. My dad and Paulette will be back from Benson soon, if they're not back already." She explained about Paulette's appointment at the hospital.

"Then I'll walk you home," he said. "We can talk on the way." She nodded and they stepped back over the wall and out onto Main Street side by side. "Do you promise you won't run away screaming again?" he asked as they paused by the church and antique store.

"At this point I have no idea what I'm going to do," Molly replied. She glanced in the window, half expecting to see Miss Kent conducting a geography lesson in the village school. But the school was full of antique furniture and tourists. They moved on.

"*Yoo-hoo, Molly Teague!*"

Molly and Jared wheeled around, and Molly recognized Grace Wilkins striding up the road. She moved very fast for someone so old.

"Thought that was you! With your boyfriend, how nice!" Miss Wilkins caught up to them, panting. "I found the book about the *Titanic* you wanted and signed it out in your name."

"Um—thanks," said Molly.

"The *Titanic?* Where does that come in?" asked Jared under his breath.

Molly introduced Jared. "Miss Wilkins, this is

Jared Bernstein. He's from Ohio, too. Miss Wilkins is the librarian. She was born on the same night the *Titanic* sank."

"My single claim to fame," added the old woman.

"Nice to meet you," Jared said politely, holding out his hand to shake Miss Wilkins's. "I haven't been to the library yet. I've been looking for a job and just found one this morning—down at Day's Catch. I'd like to come in and get a library card, though, when I have time." His voice was politely neutral, but as he held Miss Wilkins's hand, a change came over his face. Molly watched his cheeks flush and his eyes grow bright.

Miss Wilkins seemed similarly affected. She left her hand in his, looking puzzled as she studied his face. Her own wrinkled face was pink with—could it be excitement? "I think we've already met, young man. But not at the fish shop."

"You look so familiar to me," Jared agreed. "I know we must have talked before."

Miss Wilkins gently withdrew her hand from his and reached up as if to touch his cheek. "Strange," she murmured. Then she smiled and withdrew her hand. "I was a fisherman's daughter and ate fish pretty nearly every day of my life while my parents lived—but now I can't stand the stuff. It's pork chops or roast beef for me these days, sometimes sausages. Oh, I know what the doctors say about red meat and fat and all that. But I figure when you're my age, you can eat anything you like. Do you like sausages?"

Molly was relieved when Jared flashed his swim-star grin, even white teeth bright against his tanned face, and allowed the odd moment to pass. "Love them," Jared said. "Sausages and eggs for breakfast." But his eyes remained puzzled and his cheeks were pink as they chatted.

"Come visit me at the library. I like a boy who reads. Too many kids today just stick themselves in front of the box. Terrible thing." Miss Wilkins pointed back down the hill. "Library's just up Cotton Lane."

"I could use something new to read in the evenings," Jared told her. "I'm living over in a tent at the campground now, and I read by my campfire every night before bed."

"My gracious, a campground! I've got an extra bedroom, my boy. Maybe you should move right in with me." She stopped suddenly and looked surprised at herself. Molly could imagine she was wondering whatever possessed her to invite a young man she had only just met to come to her house.

"Um—well, thanks. I think I'm just fine in my tent . . ."

"Look, we need to go now," Molly said hastily. "Maybe you two can talk at the library later and arrange things."

"What?" But Jared couldn't drag his eyes from Miss Wilkins's.

"If you come to my house, look for number sixteen," she told him. "Look for the red door." She reached out and pressed his arm, then walked along to the condominiums behind the church. Molly hurried up Main Street with Jared behind her. He kept glancing back.

"I don't know what it is about that old lady," he said, shaking his head as they walked up to the drive across the headland. "Maybe it's just because I miss my grandma or something. She died last year." But then he shook his head. "No—I don't know. I just feel I've already met her. It's weird." He frowned over at Molly. "Just another weird thing to add to the collection of things that have happened since I met you."

"You want to hear about weird? You don't know the half of it." She slanted a smile at him. As they walked slowly up the hill, Molly searched for words.

The story was not an easy one to tell. In fact, she had never before thought of it as a story at all. Stories have a start and a middle and an end—but this one didn't. She tried to begin the story with the day—that fateful day—when she'd met him on the steps. Or when he'd tossed her into the pool. But that wasn't the real beginning, either. She had to backtrack, tell him how she'd always had a fear of water. She told him about her dreams of the long hallway and of the girl in the house—the girl she now knew was Clementine. She'd thought that her dreams were just the products of an active imagination—at least that's what Jen had told her—or were due to the stress of the swimming lessons and near-drowning. Yet here in Maine the dreams blurred with reality. She'd been brought up to believe there were no such things as ghosts, and she knew very little about reincarnation—the two explanations Bill and Paulette had offered. But how else to explain what was happening? She *knew* she wasn't having any sort of breakdown.

No beginning to the story, and no ending. There was only the middle, and that's where they were now. The middle of the middle, sort of like being in a maze, lost, looking for the exit.

Finally, Molly stopped talking altogether. They were at the steps of the porch, and the van was nowhere in sight. She stared at the stone steps, not daring to look at Jared for fear of what she'd see in his face. Ridicule? A sneer? Even simple disbelief would be hard to take now that she had allowed herself to put words to all that consumed her.

He remained silent so long that she had to look up. He was staring across the headland to the cliff. "Well?" she asked.

He turned to her, frowning. It was the same frown she remembered from the moment before he threw her into the pool. She got a good grip on his arm, just in case he had any ideas about hurling her down into the cove. But he just kept standing there, frowning fiercely. Then he closed his eyes and sank down onto the steps.

"The middle of the middle," he murmured. "Molly, either we're both totally crazy—or else you're really on to something."

It felt as if a great, oppressive weight rolled suddenly right off Molly's chest. Slowly, he touched her cheek with one finger. Molly remembered the feel of Hob's hands when he held Clementine's face, how he kissed her lips. She spoke quickly. "My mother would disown me if she could hear us." Her laugh was shaky.

"I really *did* feel I already knew Miss Wilkins," he marveled. "And now you're telling me Grace Wilkins is Hob's baby sister. But her brother died when she was only a baby. She wouldn't be able to remember him, anyway."

"Who knows what people remember?" Molly found her voice. "Maybe there's some essence of Hob—some *Hobness*—about you that she recognized."

" 'Hobness.' That's a good one."

"Maybe—somehow—it's what I recognized in you, too. When we first met on the school steps, I mean."

Jared was leaning back against the stone steps, staring up at the sky. "I've never thought about reincarnation before. Never had to. But there's got to be some solution to all these mysteries, and maybe that theory fits better than any other." He hesitated, thinking it over. Molly could hear the surf pounding against the cliff walls in the distance. "It's all got to fit together somehow, you know, because there are just too many coincidences. Too many connections between you and me and this place for it all to be just *chance*. I read somewhere that when you get past a certain number, coincidence can't be called coincidence anymore. There starts to be a pattern. It has to be part of a plan. Facts add up."

"What plan? What facts?" she asked, her heart thumping.

He looked at her and held up one finger. "Fact: you're terrified of water. And now we know that Hob drowned."

"But you're the one connected with Hob. And you're not afraid of water."

He nodded. "True, but the water must figure in somehow." He held up another finger. "Fact: You have bad dreams about a big house. Then you come here to visit your dad and stepmother, and you recognize this house. There's another connection."

Molly held up a finger, too. "The girl I see in dreams—the girl I become in my visions—has dark hair in braids and really red cheeks, and her name is Clementine. And today I learned that a girl named Clementine Horn really did live in the house. That's a fact." The reed grass rustled in the breeze. "I forgot to ask Miss Wilkins what Clementine looked like."

"And the name itself is unusual. Clementine— just like the song," mused Jared. "I don't know why I keep singing it, but whenever I see you, it pops into my head."

"It's the tune that keeps humming in my head, too. It was in my head even before I met you." Her voice came out a whisper. She held up another finger; it trembled slightly. "It's the same song Hob used to sing to tease Clementine."

Molly stood and moved into the driveway, staring up at the big house. It loomed above them, all angles and windows and chimneys. Jared stood next to her, and they faced the house together as they talked. Molly felt they were working on a puzzle. One of those giant puzzles with five thousand pieces and lots of blue sky and blue water. Almost impossible to fit together—but then a piece would slip in perfectly and you'd be encouraged to keep on.

They walked along the headland. Molly led Jared through the reed grass to the cliff's edge. She told him about how Clementine used to escape from the children by coming out here. She stopped a safe distance from the cliff's edge, and together they leaned carefully forward to peer out at the spray.

Molly shivered. "Clementine used to play out here with her doll—the doll named Mollydolly, isn't that creepy? She had a game that she was a giant. And sometimes she would actually climb over the edge of the cliff down to a ledge where there was a cave. Can you believe it? She had a lot more guts than I do. Nothing in the world would get me over the side."

"A cave?" asked Jared. He looked intrigued. "Where?"

Molly pointed. "Just down there, I think. It had a shelf you could stand on—about five or six feet wide. I guess it was safe enough, if you could get down there without falling into the cove."

She didn't go any closer to the edge, but Jared did. He lay on his stomach and scooted along so that

211

his head was hanging over the side of the rock. Molly moved back a few feet. The height of the rock and the proximity of the cove made her nervous. She turned to look back at the big house.

"Hey, Molly, I see it," said Jared, still at the cliff's edge.

"Will you come away from there? You're making me nervous."

He stood up and stepped back from the edge. "Looks like eighty-odd years of erosion from the spray has pretty much worn the shelf away. I bet it's only about three feet wide now. Too bad. I wanted to see the cave."

"*Ugh,*" said Molly. "Come on, let's go back. There's the van."

The blue van crunched up the driveway. As Bill parked in front of the steps, Molly jumped up to open the door and help him out.

"So how did everything go?"

"Everything seems to be all right." Paulette grimaced. "But I'm feeling pretty rotten."

"Just seasick, probably," said Bill. "The cove was rough."

They greeted Jared politely, though Paulette raised one eyebrow at Molly behind his back.

"Maybe you'd better go up to bed," Bill said to Paulette, opening the front door.

"Maybe," she said. "I sure don't feel like eating lunch." She climbed the steps to the porch.

"Would you like to stay?" Molly asked Jared. She didn't miss the look her father and Paulette exchanged.

"Can't," Jared said, glancing at his watch. "I've got to be down at the wharf to work in about twenty minutes. It's my new job," he explained to Bill and Paulette, "at the fish shop near the wharf."

Bill and Paulette said good-bye and turned to go inside. Paulette looked wan, and Bill was limping badly. Molly hurried to hold the door for them, then turned back to Jared. He was standing behind her, and she nearly bumped into him. He caught her by the shoulders.

"I seem to keep doing this, crashing into you on steps." She started to laugh, flustered by his sudden nearness and by her reaction to it. They stood together, each searching the other's face.

The sea breeze picked up and the reed grass swayed. "There's that wind," Jared said. "I've noticed that whenever I'm thinking about you, I feel wind."

"The wind is blowing, that's why you feel it," Molly reasoned.

"Yeah, but ever since the thing with the pool, I've felt the wind start blowing whenever I think about you." He tightened his hands on her shoulders. "Whenever I touch you."

He wants to kiss me. I know he does.

The day had been sunny and warm, but it seemed to her as they stood there that the breeze picked up, grew cooler. "I felt the wind as soon as we met," she told him. "Even before the—the *thing* with the pool, as you so eloquently put it."

He looked away. "It's just . . . hard for me to say, okay? I can hardly bear to say it—that I threw

213

you in the pool. Knowing you couldn't swim. Knowing you were afraid! It—it was a horrible thing to do, Molly, and I don't know why I did it, and it scares me. You're not the only one with nightmares, you know."

He looked so miserable, so perplexed by his behavior, that she understood something she hadn't before: *Weird things are happening to him, too, and he doesn't know why, and it's just as awful for him as it is for me.* "Jared, it's all right now." She said the words firmly. "I forgive you, okay? But when will you forgive me?"

"Forgive you for what?" His dark eyes glinted.

She hesitated; it seemed the answer was on the tip of her tongue, but then it was gone. "I don't know." She sighed. "Yet."

He bent his head and kissed her hard on the mouth, wrapping his arms tightly around her. She felt dizzy with the sense of having done this before, with Jared but *not* with Jared. He released her and stepped back. "I've been dying to do that since the moment I met you," he said. "But now—I've got to go to work."

"Call me tomorrow?"

"Absolutely. Nine o'clock in the morning—sharp!"

Tingling from his kiss, Molly went to the kitchen. Bill was assembling sandwiches for himself and Molly. "Paulette's in the study," he said. "Lying down. She says she's feeling queasy. But she hasn't had anything to eat for hours."

"How about if I make her a cup of mint tea?" Molly suggested. "And maybe a bowl of chicken soup or something? You go on into the study and sit with her," said Molly. "I'll bring the stuff in when it's ready."

He nodded, looking relieved, and hobbled from the room while she searched the pantry for a can opener. She waited for the soup to heat and looked out the window at the sunny headland. No wind now at all.

Outside, while she and Jared were tossing out facts and bizarre coincidences, it had seemed to her that a pattern really *was* forming into a completed puzzle with all the pieces of sky and water firmly interlocked. But here inside, with her father and Paulette waiting in the other room, with the cheerful, everyday whistle of the teakettle filling the kitchen, all the fragments seemed ephemeral again. It was as if Jared's departure had sent the puzzle pieces all floating off into the air.

After they ate lunch, Bill settled Paulette on the study couch, where she lay for most of the afternoon, sipping iced herbal tea and watching soap operas. Molly set to work stripping paper in the dining room. Two walls were ready to be repapered now, and she still had two more to strip. She dragged the ladder over to the windows and began ripping the old pattern off. She closed her eyes against the flurry of yellow dust from the ancient glue.

Her father joined her, holding the ladder for her while she worked.

"So Jared Bernstein isn't on your hit list anymore?" he asked, smiling up at her.

She pulled a long strip of floral paper away and tossed it down onto the drop cloth covering the floorboards. "I guess not." She remembered the feeling of Jared's lips on hers. "Not at all, anymore. You know, Dad, the strangest things keep happening to him, too. We don't know what it's all about, but it's a relief to know it's happening to both of us."

"Kind of rules out needing to see a psychologist—is that what you're thinking?"

"Well, doesn't it?"

"Your mother would be delighted if it were true."

"I don't know about that." She threw down several more strips. "I mean, there are things that make her even more uncomfortable than the idea of talking to shrinks."

"Ghosts, you mean?" he asked.

"That sort of thing." She sent down more strips and a shower of yellow powder.

Bill handed up a knife, and Molly scraped more flakes of glue off the wall. They worked companionably for another hour or so until the remaining walls had been stripped. Then Molly carried in the rolls of new paper from the hall. She unwrapped one and looked at the pattern of green vines. "Oh, this will be pretty."

"But we won't start till tomorrow," Bill said.

"You're a regular workhorse. Come on, let's stop now. Go on in and see what's become of Paulette. Too much of those soap operas and she'll turn into a vegetable. I'll get us a snack."

Molly walked through the library into the study. Paulette lay on the couch with her hands covering her gently swelling abdomen. Her face was pale and her eyes were red-rimmed. Her carrot-colored hair stood in spikes, as if she had been running her fingers through it. The television was on, but she was not watching it.

"Hi," said Molly.

"Come and get cozy," Paulette invited. "I haven't seen you all day. And I haven't even had a chance to tell you who we met today at the hospital." She punched a button on the remote control panel and the television screen went dark. "In an elevator. You're going to die when you hear."

"Who?" She sat down on the couch next to Paulette.

Paulette grinned. "His name is Mr. Holloway."

Molly's eyes widened. "*Holloway!* Is he related to *my* Holloways?"

Paulette nodded. "We were on our way up to see my doctor and stopped at another floor. This ancient man hobbled in with a nurse, and she was saying, 'Mr. Holloway, you come along now,' and *of course* my ears pricked right up. So I just barged in and told him—even though most people usually never say anything to other people in elevators, have you noticed that, Molly?—I told him we'd bought a house over in Hibben called the Holloway House. I asked him if it was any connection to his family—and guess what?"

"He said yes?" A little thrill of excitement tickled the back of her neck.

Paulette shifted carefully on the couch. "He said he actually was born in the house and grew up here. He said he hadn't been here for years and years and would love to see the place sometime, and how about *today?* His nurse jumped in and said of course not, and that he wasn't being polite—honestly, she talked to him as if he were six years old! He lives in a private nursing home near the hospital and was just going for a checkup today, but aside from being kind of trembly, he didn't look so sick to me."

"He *couldn't* be that man I saw in the visions, you know—that awful Uncle Wallace? Or could he? No, Uncle Wallace has to be dead by now. Miss Wilkins said—" She tried to remember what Miss Wilkins had said earlier that day.

"Miss Wilkins?"

"She's the librarian. That little cottage where the library is now was her house when she was a girl, and today she told me all about the Holloway family—" Molly broke off at the sudden flash of pain in her stepmother's face.

"Paulette!" She jumped off the couch.

"Wait . . . it's just . . . a cramp." Paulette closed her eyes for a long moment. "Gone now."

"Should I get Dad?" Molly asked worriedly.

"No, that's okay."

"Should we call the doctor?" She adjusted the pillow at Paulette's side. "Do you want anything?"

"No, I'll be fine."

Bill came into the room carrying a pitcher of iced herbal tea and a plate of crackers topped with sliced cheese. "Are you hovering, Molly? Give poor Paulette some room to breathe."

Molly sat back down next to Paulette on the couch. Bill poured them all glasses of tea and then settled himself into his recliner, propping his ankle up with a sigh.

Paulette balanced a cracker on her thin knees and sipped some tea from her glass. Molly watched her drink, noticing how delicate the bones of her face were and how fragile her hands looked holding the heavy glass.

Paulette noticed her scrutiny. "Hey, I told you something fascinating—now it's your turn to tell me something."

"She wants to know why you were out with Killer Bernstein," growled Bill.

"Well, I have to admit I was surprised when we drove up and there you both were. What happened today? How did you link up with Jared, if you hate him so much?"

"Link up," echoed Molly. "Like links on a chain." Bill and Paulette both raised their eyebrows. And then, of course, she had to go on to explain all that had happened to her that day.

Bill lay stretched out in the armchair in perfect repose, listening. Paulette, on the other hand, seemed to come to life as Molly spoke. Her weariness dropped away, and she shifted this way and that on the couch, interrupting several times to ask questions or to press for details of what Grace Wilkins had said, or what Molly had seen at Clementine's graduation ceremony, or what Uncle Wallace had looked like. Her hair stood up around her head like a halo as she scrubbed her hands through the strands.

"Oh, Molly, Molly!" Paulette said when Molly concluded her account with the talk she and Jared had had out on the headland. "This is wild. *Really* wild."

"There are even more weird connections." Molly held up one finger. "Fact: I just heard the story of the Holloway family today." She held up another finger. "Fact: You met Mr. Holloway at the hospital! That's just too weird to be another coincidence."

Paulette nodded with excitement. "It's *astonishing!* That means it's not just you and Jared having these connections. It's like you said—links on a whole *chain* of coincidences, and we're all part of it." Her eyes sparkled. "I mean, just think of it! All your life, you're afraid of water . . . then just when you're having major trauma with your mom and that coach about swim lessons, Jared shows up in town and tosses you in a pool. And you're there in Battleboro Heights having bad dreams about a house . . . and you come to Maine and find *this* house. *Ooh!* It gives me the creeps, but isn't it wild?" She looked delighted.

Wild, thought Molly drily. A wild chain of coincidences. All leading her—here? But where did the water come in? She crossed her arms across her body protectively, quite sure she wouldn't like to find out.

"You want to know what I think? I think my theory is right. Reincarnation," asserted Paulette. "It's the only thing that makes sense, right, Bill?"

"It's an interesting idea," he said, sounding unconvinced. But at least he was polite. Her mother, Molly reflected, would be laughing so hard she'd be rolling on the floor.

Molly frowned at Paulette. "How is reincarnation supposed to work? I mean, I know the theory goes that when a person dies, his soul is born again into a new baby. Right? And so the soul lives on—a whole different life. Right?"

"That's it exactly!"

"But why? I mean, what's the point?"

Paulette grinned. "Horatio, do I detect a glimmer of new philosophy?"

Molly slumped back into the couch cushions.

"Your mother will have ten fits," said Paulette, smiling at the thought. "When you go home you'll be talking about oversouls and karma and astral travel like this psychic I know in San Francisco. She's the one who taught me what little I know about this stuff. There's a theory, she told me, that says the reason we're born again and again is to work out situations and relationships with people. And if something—or someone—cuts our life short before we have worked out what needs working out, we'll be encountering those people and those situations—

in one guise or another—again and again in other lives until we've learned how to work out what we need to learn."

Bill leaned forward in his chair. "So what do we have to work out together, sweetheart?"

"Oh, I'm sure *we've* got everything figured out this time around, Billy." She laughed. "We're absolutely the most perfect couple I know. Don't you think so, Molly?"

"Sure," said Molly absently. She was busy following another train of thought. "Listen, Paulette? What was that old Mr. Holloway's first name? Did he say?"

"Didn't I tell you?" asked Paulette. "His name is Abner."

Without warning the humming began in Molly's head, and a child's voice piped the words. She stood up in a daze, putting her hands to her temples and pressing. *Lost and gone forever, Dreadful sorry, Clementine!* The tune in her head held memories of salt and seaweed, a subtle smell of fish, the thrum of waves dashing on rocks below the headland. Then the song disappeared as abruptly as it began.

Bill pushed himself out of the recliner and came to stand near Molly. He kissed the top of her head. "You know, honey? I think you're at the end of your rope with all this weird stuff going on all the time. Maybe you and Jared ought to go to Benson tomorrow and visit this Abner Holloway guy in his nursing home. It can't hurt—and maybe he'll have some answers. All I know is, I don't think you can take much more of this."

"I think you're right, Dad. Whenever I try to figure things out, I just feel like going to sleep for a thousand years." Molly walked toward the door. "I'm going to take a nap. Wake me up before the next millennium." She passed through the library into the big hallway. Bill and Paulette came out of the library after her, heading toward the bathroom. Bill's arm was wrapped protectively around Paulette's shoulders. She walked with her hands pressed against her abdomen.

"Just a few little cramps," she was saying.

In the hallway there was the acrid smell of a pipe. The humming began again in Molly's head, at first faint, then growing ever louder. Molly shook her head vehemently. "Please, no," she murmured. But as she started up the stairs to her room, she felt the swish of long skirts around her ankles. As she opened her door and crossed to the bed, she heard children's voices calling to her: *"Oh, Clemmy, were you really running away?"*

10 Clementine

Oh, Clemmy, were you really running away?" Abner looked frightened.

All the children crowded behind them in the front hallway, their expressions mixed. Anne tossed her head and looked disdainfully at her wayward cousin. The others seemed excited by their cousin's disobedience.

Uncle Wallace ordered Clementine into his study. She took a deep breath and walked through the library. All the young cousins, as well as the hired girl Janie, followed, but Uncle Wallace closed the door to the study firmly in their faces. Clementine could imagine them all pressed to the door, eager to hear what happened. She could hear the rustling and whispering as they waited. Abner's voice was loudest: "What's he going to do to Clemmy?"

Uncle Wallace stood with his back to the fireplace, with Clementine in front of him. He did not speak for a long time but busied himself filling his pipe with fresh tobacco, tamping it carefully down into the smooth wooden bowl. She kept her eyes lowered, hoping a show of meekness would appease him.

Finally he struck a match, cupped his hands around the pipe to light it, then sucked hard to get it burning. When thin blue smoke curled up to his satisfaction, he withdrew the stem from his mouth and frowned at her. "Niece, you are a disgrace to the family. What do you have to say for yourself?"

She remained silent.

Her silence angered him further, and he began to pace back and forth in front of the fireplace, puffing on his pipe.

Uncle Wallace spoke at length about how ill Aunt Ethel was, and how the children depended on her, Clementine, and how her selfish insistence on going her own way was hurting everyone who counted on her. If Clementine would not stay home willingly and help with the children, Uncle Wallace pronounced, she would remain locked in her room until her duty became clear to her.

She stood with her head bowed, trying to make his words bounce right off her. She imagined she could see them, all the words, falling into the corners and ricocheting off the ceiling. She vowed she would not be held prisoner by her uncle, no matter what.

"Are you hearing a word I've said, girl?" her uncle asked roughly and snapped his fingers under her nose.

Her head jerked up and her eyes blazed with hostility. "I demand obedience from you. We'll see how many days up in your room it'll take to make you see reason!"

He reached for her arm, but she pulled away defiantly. Rage boiled in her belly at the thought of how he hoped to break her will and keep her from living her own life. He would lock her in her room, he would lock her in this house with all the children to look after, and her life would wither away! No books, no school, no job teaching, no college education!

"Don't touch me!" she yelled at him. "I *won't* stay with you! I don't care about any of you! I just want to be away from here, learning something useful about the world!" She heard a gasp from the children behind the closed study door.

She used her haughtiest voice, one that sounded like Miss Kent's voice when she spoke to recalcitrant children. "I tell you, I'm leaving here, Uncle Wallace. And there is nothing you can do about it. You have no right to try to stop me."

For a moment she feared he would strike her. His eyes blazed and he choked on a mouthful of smoke. Then he set his pipe carefully down in its stand and grabbed both her arms. He yanked them behind her back. "You and your fancy education." His voice was low and dangerous. "To your room, niece."

She didn't say another word as he pushed her in front of him toward the door, holding her arms behind her back as if she were shackled.

Janie gathered the silent children around her in the library and they all watched Uncle Wallace march Clementine back out into the hall and up the stairs. But Abner pulled free and raced up behind her. When he saw his father step out of Clementine's room and lock the door, he waited in the shadow of the hallway until his father disappeared down the hall into the master bedroom. Then Abner crept forward and whispered through the keyhole: "Clementine! I'll help you get out if you promise you won't leave me. You said you would stay for always. I need you, Clemmy!"

Pesky little Abner. But she knew she could count on his loyalty and devotion. He might be able to help her. She made her tone light. "Of course, I promise, Abner. You're my own sweet boy, aren't you? How could I ever leave you?"

"You won't?"

"Never. Now come closer and listen to me. I have a special job for you to do."

They held a whispered conference. There was no way to remove Uncle Wallace's keys from his vest pocket without his knowledge. But Janie always left after supper and hung her ring of keys on the nail behind the pantry door. Abner would stand on a kitchen chair and steal the keys and bring them upstairs. He would open the door and free his beloved cousin.

Clementine spent the rest of the day preparing her escape. Uncle Wallace usually ate with Aunt Ethel in her room on the days she could not make the journey downstairs—Clementine hoped today would be one of those days that Aunt Ethel felt especially indisposed. Abner would open the door around seven o'clock, and she would leave immediately. But she had a whole day to get through first, locked up here in her room. She'd be surprised if they could manage without her help even half the day. No one was as good as she at calming fussy Augustus when he cried. She hated Uncle Wallace, hated him and weak Aunt Ethel. She wished they were dead. She flopped across her bed, listening for sounds of life in the big house.

She heard Aunt Ethel moaning down the hall. She heard the children's voices through the open window, laughing and shrieking outside on the headland. She heard Janie's voice nagging at them. She wished she had something to read. Her favorite book, the *Atlas of the World*, was down in Uncle Wallace's study. He had confiscated her sewing basket and the hatbox. She lay across the bed, thinking about the atlas, planning where she would travel once she finished college. Europe appealed—a nice long tour of the Continent. And then a journey through South America.

Clementine must have slept for a while because when she woke up the clock in the hall was striking seven. Evening already—and her stomach was rumbling. She had not eaten all day. She remembered the picnic Janie had packed her that morning—was it only this morning she had run off to talk Hob into taking her to Benson?—and looked around the room for the wrapped bundle of food, but it wasn't there.

Then she remembered it was stowed inside the hat-box. She must retrieve her things, of course, before making her escape. She could eat then.

Seven o'clock meant supper was over and Janie would be leaving. Anne would be the one to get the children ready for bed, since Clementine couldn't. Abner would be coming any minute with the key.

But Abner didn't come for another hour, and when he did, he whispered through the door that Janie was still at the house and Anne was putting them to bed.

"Mama's very sick," he hissed, sounding scared, and then ran off again when he heard his father and Janie coming. Clementine sighed. Silly little boy—she thought she'd be able to count on him. And Aunt Ethel—*damn* that woman for her weakness!

She crossed the room impatiently to the windows and stood looking out across the headland. If only she dared climb out this way. She didn't care about anyone in this house as much as she cared about getting herself out into the world. There was a tree just a few feet too far from the house—she'd checked earlier whether she could fix a rope out of bed sheets and swing down to freedom. But no, the only way out was through the door.

She flopped back across her bed to wait for Janie to leave. She hoped Abner wouldn't forget and fall asleep or something. He was so little. He couldn't really be trusted, devoted to her though he was.

She closed her eyes and imagined the boat ride with Hob to Benson. They would sail right across the cove, then she'd break it to him that she was having second thoughts about marrying so young. And off he'd go. Maybe he'd be angry. Certainly he'd be disappointed—he was so head-over-heels about her. But in the end it didn't matter how *he* felt—just as long as *she* was safely away from Hibben. She knew she was selfish in this but didn't care. Her desperation to move on with her life was too great. And Hob was the means to the end.

If somehow she couldn't get away, they might have to get married after all and spend the night in a hotel. Well, that would be too bad, but in the morning she'd sell her locket and head straight to the depot to get the big bus to Boston or New York—wherever the bus went. It didn't matter. There was bound to be work in the city, and soon she would have a paying position at another school, or maybe as a governess to a wealthy family that would pay her for her services. No one from Hibben would ever find her. And when she had enough saved, she would apply to colleges. Her life would finally begin!

She heard a rustling noise and ran to the door. "Abner? Is it you? Did you get the key?" Clementine held her ear to the door.

His childish voice seemed loud in the nighttime hush of the big house. "I couldn't get it, Clemmy! Janie's still here and she hasn't hung her keys back up on the nail."

"Janie shouldn't be here now." She rattled the door handle. "Why hasn't she gone home?"

"I don't know. She's in the bedroom with Mama.

Janie said we're all to stay up in the playroom. She said Anne is in charge."

"Oh, Abner!"

There was the sound of shuffling. "I'm *trying,* Clemmy. I want to help you! Maybe I can get one of the others." His little voice sounded sad. He loved her so. He wanted to be her hero.

"Don't tell Anne." Anne was becoming more and more troublesome lately, always bossing and telling on the younger children, and Clementine didn't trust her anymore. Anne was too prim. Clementine had been looking forward to the time Anne would go off to boarding school in the fall. But now it was turning out that she would be gone before Anne. "Maybe Andrew or Amity will be able to get the key. Go look for them," she ordered Abner. "Don't let me down. You're my little sweetheart, aren't you? I don't want to leave my sweet boy, but if you don't let me out of here, I might have to get out some other way, and then, well . . . you might never see me again." That ought to make him try harder. "Now, I'm depending on you, Abner. Go get the key—and hurry!"

"Oh please, Clemmy," he sobbed. "Promise you won't—oh—!" He broke off suddenly and she heard the small thuds of his footsteps as he darted down the hall. Then came the murmur of voices—her uncle's deep rumble and Janie's high-pitched one.

Clementine rattled the doorknob again, then stood leaning against the door with her forehead pressed upon its smooth, paneled surface. Time passed. She moved to the window and stood there, looking out at the shapes of trees, planning her future. She heard the clock in the hall strike eight-thirty, then nine. The evening outside her window grew dark. She paced the room, stopping every few minutes to rattle the door handle. She felt faint with hunger. Did her uncle mean to starve her, then? Had everyone just forgotten her? Finally she pounded on the door with clenched fists. "Janie! Uncle Wallace! Please open the door! Let me out!"

But no one came.

The children would all be in bed by now. Abner had failed her. So much for loyalty and true love!

She resumed pacing. Soon Hob Wilkins would be waiting for her at the wharf, and she wouldn't be there! Clementine began to cry helpless tears of rage. She then heard the slam of a door and the heavy, measured tread of her uncle's footsteps in the hall-way. They stopped outside her door. She heard the beautiful sound of the key scraping in the lock.

Then Uncle Wallace stood there. His hair was wild, as if he had been out in a boat in the middle of the stormy cove. His face was haggard. "Clementine, girl," he said in a choked voice, "you must be hungry. Come with me."

She followed him down the stairs. From her aunt's room she heard a cry. Uncle Wallace winced.

"It seems your aunt may lose this baby," he said softly. "We have been attending to her all day. Janie stayed as long as she could, but she has just left to go home to care for her own old mother. I have telephoned down to the village for the doctor, and he is on his way."

Clementine didn't answer. All she could think of was how hungry she was. Even a slice of bread would be heavenly—and a tall glass of milk.

"We need your help here tonight, Clementine. That is why I am releasing you from your room early." He directed her to the kitchen and nodded at the table, where a bowl of soup and a hunk of bread sat waiting. "I had thought two days in solitary confinement would be punishment enough for your adventure this morning, but if you can promise me you will be a dutiful and proper member of the family, then I will not lock you in again. Am I making myself clear?"

She nodded quickly, not looking at him, eyes fastened on the soup. She could already taste its fragrant broth.

"Clementine!" His rough voice made her look up. "On your knees!"

She just stared at him. "Excuse me?" she asked weakly.

"*On your knees,* Clementine! I want you to promise to do your duty to your family. Come along now." He held out his hand.

She wouldn't take it, she wouldn't! But there seemed no other way to get at that soup, and then to get out of the house. She sank slowly to her knees at his feet. He placed his hand on her head.

"All right, niece. Promise."

"I promise," she said, shrugging.

His fingers tightened in her hair. "What is it you promise, girl?"

"I promise to obey you and my aunt in all things and to fulfill my duty to your family."

"Look at me when you say it!" But now his hand was gentle on her head. "And remember, my dear, this is *your* family, too."

She looked up at him and tried to keep her voice steady. "I promise to obey you in all things and to fulfill my duty to *my* dear family."

He stared down at her, blue eyes probing. She lowered her eyes meekly so that he wouldn't see any challenge in them. Satisfied at last, he took her hand and helped her to her feet. She stepped quickly to the table and sat down.

"Eat quickly, then," he said. "I need you to attend to the children. Several of them are still awake and worried about their mother."

"Yes sir," she said through a mouthful of soup.

She finished her small meal and followed her uncle up to the children's rooms. Amity and Alice were awake, clinging to their dolls. Anne was holding a howling Augustus, trying to calm him. Clementine crossed the bedroom and took the baby from Anne. "He needs another bottle," she said. "And he's wet! No wonder he's crying."

Anne looked at her resentfully. "Well, I tried my best! But how am I to know how to tend an infant? That's Janie's job—or yours!"

"We did sing to him, Papa," offered Alice. "But

he wouldn't go back to sleep. He's not used to sleeping in a basket. He wants his bed in Clementine's room."

"I'm sure you tried your best," Uncle Wallace said. "But Clementine will take over now. I need to wait for the doctor. Your mama is having a hard time tonight."

"Go down and fill his bottle, Anne," directed Clementine, patting Augustus's small back. "I'll change his clothes. And Amity and Alice, hop back into bed. I'll tell you a story in a minute."

Uncle Wallace left them and hurried back to his wife's side.

Soon Anne returned with the baby's bottle. Clementine settled herself in the low chair between the little girls' beds and fed him. While he sucked, she began a story. She had sat in this chair many times, sometimes tending the girls when they were sick or had been sent to bed early for some naughtiness or needed comforting after a bad dream. Tonight, if God were on her side, was the last time she would ever sit here. She listened to the clock chime the half hour and closed her eyes in despair. Already past nine-thirty, and here she was, no closer to the wharf and Hob's boat than before.

Anne settled on the window seat to listen. Clementine took a deep breath and forced her voice to be soothing and slow. "Once upon a time," she began, "there was a girl named Mollydolly. She was young, but she wasn't little. Do you know why?"

"Because she was a *giant* little girl, right,

Clemmy?" All the children knew Clementine's stories about the giant girl.

"That's right. And she lived high up on a cliff above a dangerous, rocky cove."

"Like us, up here on the headland, right, Clemmy?"

"Right. Now you girls close your eyes and listen." They did, and Clementine continued the familiar tale. "One day she was hungry and wanted to make a good supper. She thought that soup would taste good. So what did she put in her caldron?"

"Trees!" squealed Alice.

"*Shhh,*" said Clementine. "That's right. She just pulled up some big trees and tossed them down over the cliff into her boiling caldron. Just like Janie puts celery into the pot when she's making soup. And then Mollydolly sprinkled in a few boulders for seasoning and threw in part of an old fence—"

Her voice droned on, telling the story of the giant girl. Soon Amity and Alice were asleep, baby Augustus was asleep in Clementine's arms, and Anne was dozing on the window seat. If Clementine went right now, she might still be able to meet Hob after all. She stood up to carry the baby to his crib in the room they shared.

But then there was a commotion in the hall and the bedroom door flew open. Uncle Wallace ran in, his face above his beard flushed. "Clementine," he hissed. "Go straight to your aunt! Hurry, girl!"

Clementine clutched the baby. "But, Uncle Wallace—I—"

"Remember your vow, girl! I need your help!"

Anne stirred on the window seat, then opened her eyes and hurried over to her father. "Is it Mama? Is she all right?"

"She is having a hard time," he said in a choked voice. "Clementine must help. You stay up here, Anne. It's not something I want you to see."

Wordlessly, Clementine handed the sleeping baby to Anne and followed her uncle from the room.

"The doctor isn't here yet, and no one answers his telephone. Perhaps he's on his way—I can only hope so. But you, you've attended the births, Clementine. You must know what can be done to help Ethel. You've helped her so many times before."

He pushed her along the hall ahead of him down to Aunt Ethel's room and opened the door. Clementine had assisted at half a dozen births, it was true. But this was not a birth. Nothing could have prepared Clementine for the sight of her aunt writhing on the bed, her white nightgown hiked up around her waist. Blood had seeped onto the white gown and onto the bed sheets. Clementine started to back out of the room, but Uncle Wallace pushed her forward. "You must help her!" he insisted. "She's in terrible pain."

Clementine could see that for herself. But she stood motionless as he left the room and closed the door. She knew tricks to help turn a baby that was stuck or to get a blue-faced baby started breathing. But this wasn't a baby yet, and it didn't look now as if it ever would be. She approached the bed slowly and reached out to pull the quilt over Aunt Ethel's bare legs. When her aunt moaned and kicked the quilt off again, Clementine backed away. She spied a pitcher of water on the bedside table and poured some into the glass. "Would you like a drink of water?" She held the glass out. Her aunt groaned and opened her eyes.

"Clementine?" The voice was a whisper.

"Yes—"

"You must promise to—you must—stay with the children." A spasm crossed her face, wrinkling it with lines of pain. Aunt Ethel reached out one thin hand to her niece. "Promise me, promise to take care of my babies." The pale eyes were pleading.

Clementine backed away. Aunt Ethel was trying to trap her! And in the meantime, Hob Wilkins was waiting for her down at the wharf. He would think she wasn't coming. But she was—oh, she was! She made her voice gentle. "Of course, I promise," she told her aunt. "But you'll be fine in no time, Aunt Ethel."

"Clementine, there's so much blood. Clementine, do something to stop it—!"

Clementine sidled out of her aunt's room, ignoring her mewling cries, closing the door softly behind her. She started down the back stairs but saw a light in the kitchen and heard her uncle shouting into the telephone. So she went back along the hallway to the main staircase and hurried down. She needed only her hatbox and then she'd leave, free as the wind off the ocean.

She crept through the library and into her uncle's study. The room smelled of smoke—not the pungent odor of her uncle's familiar cigar but of woodsmoke. Odd, on a summer's evening. But she had no time to think about that. The hatbox sat open on a glass-fronted bookcase. Her doll and her mother's necklace lay inside, but the atlas was nowhere to be seen. She hesitated, looking over at the desk. She pulled open all the drawers, searching for her atlas. What would Uncle Wallace have done with it? The atlas wasn't in any of the drawers, but in the top drawer she found several bills and a handful of coins in the tray with the pencils. She stashed the money in the deep pocket of her skirt, then turned to leave. As she passed the fireplace, something caught her eye. It was the remains of a fire, which explained the smell of smoke. And although she was in a terrible hurry to be away, something made her bend down to look more closely into the grate. What she saw made her flush with hatred: there were burnt pages of text among the ashes and twisted shreds of red leather.

So this was how Uncle Wallace thought he would stop her from pursuing an education, was it? By burning her beloved *Atlas of the World*—her only legacy from her father? She stuffed a shred of the leather into her hatbox along with her doll and the locket and ran from the room, rage sending her climbing the stairs to tell her uncle just what she thought of him before she left forever.

She threw the door open, heedless of disturbing the Eternal Invalid, words forming on her lips to berate her uncle for his selfishness and petty vindictiveness. But the words turned to a cry of horror when she saw all the blood.

There was blood, blood everywhere—on the bed sheets, on the floor, on her aunt who lay so still atop the coverlet, and on her uncle, who bent over the bed.

At the sound of her cry, he whirled around. His face was white, teeth bared. "I told you to stay with her!" he spat out. He jumped up and shook her by the shoulders, then grabbed for her hands when she frantically tried to pull away. "I told you to help! But you didn't! You *wouldn't!* And now we've lost them both. *Damn* you!"

The blood from the sheets, from her aunt, seemed to swirl up and fly at her. "No!" she gasped. She ripped her hands out of his, horrified to see that they, too, now had blood on them.

And then she ran. She ran on shaky legs down the stairs, clutching her hatbox. She threw open the front door and nearly collided with the doctor, who had tied his horse to the hitching post.

"*Whoa,* girl!" began Dr. Scopes, reaching out for her. The startled horse whinnied softly.

She darted around them, barely seeing them, and hurtled across the headland. Horrible Uncle Wallace, trying to lay blame! And stupid, ignorant Aunt Ethel, who didn't know when enough children were enough, who didn't have anything else to do with her life but lie in bed and grow thick around the middle. Month after month. She spent her whole life propped on pillows, sipping tisanes, gazing vacantly out the window—never holding a book, never wondering about the world. It was lamentable, but it was nothing to do with Clementine Horn! She would have no part of it, of them—they were nothing to do with her. "I don't care," she whispered.

Blood seemed to swirl all around her as she ran— she saw it running down the road like a river ahead of her. *No!* She felt it dripping down the back of her dress. She smelled it in the night air. It tasted sour in the back of her throat. *It wasn't her fault! It wasn't her fault! It had nothing whatever to do with her!*

"I don't care! I don't care!" she screamed and nearly fell along the rutted lane. She leaned against a tree to catch her breath, reaching one hand up to push back her hair. And though the night was dark, in the fragile moonlight she thought she could see the bright smear of blood staining her palm.

"No!" She screamed her denial to the dark night sky and kept running.

11

$\mathcal{J}$f Aunt Ethel had died, how could she still be moaning? Molly lifted her head groggily and listened, peering around her bedroom. The room was in near darkness, illuminated faintly by the moonlight through the open window. The curtains stirred in the night breeze. Her head was throbbing and her legs ached from running—but no, it had been *Clementine* who had been running. *Hadn't it?*

There it was again—the moan that had awakened her. Heart hammering, Molly sat up and slid off the high bed. She opened her bedroom door and stepped out into the long hallway. She stood tensely, listening to the silence. The terrible scenes she had witnessed in Clementine's time were still with her. Molly longed to bolt down the stairs and out the door the way Clementine had done. Molly pressed her hands to her temples. If she went to the room at the end of the hall and opened the door, what would she find?

She heard a cough from the bathroom next to her bedroom and the sound of water running into the sink. Then, while she stood in the hall, eyes still wide with alarm, the door opened and Paulette stepped out.

"Thank God it's you," Molly said in relief.

"Oh, Molly!" said Paulette. "You startled me. You must have been sleeping like the dead. We called you earlier for dinner and you didn't answer. We figured you'd come down if you were hungry. Anyway, I'm sorry I woke you." Her face was pale, her orange hair limp.

"What's wrong?"

"I was having a few really bad cramps. But I think they've stopped now."

Molly closed her eyes. The image of Aunt Ethel on the bed flickered behind her lids. "You should call your doctor."

"Billy already called. Diagnosis: pregnancy woes. The prescription: sleep until morning and call again only if the cramps get worse." She shrugged. "The doctor didn't seem worried, so I suppose I shouldn't be."

"I guess not." Molly hugged herself, chilled in the long hallway. She reached up to draw her shawl more tightly around her shoulders, then realized there was no shawl. She was still wearing her rumpled shorts and T-shirt. She felt confused, trapped between two times. It took great effort to make her voice sound normal. "Sleep until morning? Sounds like a good prescription for anybody, really. I ought to follow it myself."

"You do look exhausted," Paulette said. She peered more critically at Molly's face. "Are you all right? Has anything else—you know, happened?"

Molly didn't think she could bear recounting the horror of Aunt Ethel's death just then. She shook her head. "Nothing."

Looking unconvinced but too ill to press for an answer, Paulette said good night and started down the hall.

After breakfast Molly went straight to the phone in the pantry and called the Benson operator. "I'm trying to get in touch with Mr. Abner Holloway, who lives in a nursing home in Benson," she said. "Can you help me? Are there a lot of nursing homes?" She'd call them all if she had to.

"Checking," said the operator.

After a moment she gave Molly the name of two places: a nursing home and a convalescent center connected to the hospital. "Thank you," said Molly, then hung up. She decided to call the place connected to the hospital. That made sense, since Paulette and Bill had met Abner in the hospital.

But the receptionist in the Benson Hospital Convalescent Wing and Nursing Home did not have a listing for Mr. Abner Holloway. So Molly dialed the other number. She fingered the end of her long braid as she listened to the ringing.

The receptionist at The Breakers Senior Home put her on hold for a full five minutes. Molly sucked impatiently on the end of her braid, then pulled out a few long blond hairs and nervously twined them around her thumb. Her father shambled into the kitchen in cutoff jeans and a rumpled shirt and dropped a pile of mail onto the table. Then he went to the stove and put the teakettle on to boil.

"How's Paulette?" she asked, covering the receiver.

He gave her two thumbs up. "Looking perky as ever. I'm treating her to breakfast in bed. Looks like the scare last night was"—he reached for the china teapot—"a tempest in a teacup."

Molly watched him slice peaches into a large bowl. The receptionist spoke into her ear. "Sorry to keep you waiting. Now, how may I help you?"

"I'm looking for a patient—a resident? named Abner Holloway." Molly spoke all in a rush as if afraid the woman would put her back on hold.

"Who may I tell him is calling?"

"Oh, wait, don't tell him anything yet! I mean— well, my name is Molly Teague, but he doesn't know me. I'd like to come see him."

"Shall I connect you to his room?" asked the receptionist patiently.

"No! I mean, not yet." God, she sounded like an idiot. She took a calming breath. "What I'd like is to visit him today. Would that be possible?"

"We have visiting hours between ten and noon and again this afternoon from three till five. Unless you're a family member. Then you can come whenever you like—*if* Mr. Holloway wants to see you. You'll need to ask him."

"Would—would it be possible for you to ask him for me? Just tell him my name is Molly, and I live in his old house in Hibben, and I want to talk to him about . . . about Clementine. Clementine Horn. Could you tell him that, please? Tell him I'd like to come this morning. I'll wait."

"This is highly irregular," said the receptionist. She put Molly on hold. Molly watched Bill make a cup of coffee for himself and fill the small pot with herbal tea for Paulette, then set them both on a tray. He came to the pantry, and Molly stepped aside so he could get the milk from the refrigerator.

"Want to join us for breakfast upstairs?" he asked.

"No thanks." She shook her head. "But I'd like to take the van and go to Benson this morning. Would that be all right?"

He nodded. "Sure. We're not going anywhere." He set the tray on the table and sorted through the morning's mail, laid a few pieces on the tray to take up to Paulette, and waved one envelope at Molly. "Hey, this one's for you." He balanced the tray carefully and carried it up the back steps.

After another few minutes the receptionist returned to the phone. "Mr. Holloway says he will look for you at ten o'clock," she said. "But when I gave him your message, he became most agitated. We cannot let our residents be upset by visitors. You must be careful not to agitate him when you come. He is not very strong."

"I'll be careful," promised Molly, and after asking the receptionist for directions to the nursing home and scrawling them onto a piece of scratch paper, she hung up with relief. She checked her watch. Almost nine. Jared would be calling any minute.

She ate a peach while she opened the letter from Kathi:

Dear Molly,
I was going to call you at your dad's, but I'm getting a rejection complex, you know? So I thought I'd just write. That way if you tear up the letter unopened or something, I won't have to know about it. I wanted to write to say I miss you, and I'm sorry, REALLY SORRY, that I just stood by while Jared tossed you into the pool at Michael's. I wish I could convince you that I never really thought you'd sink like that. I guess I thought you'd even like it. Anyway—I was wrong. I hope we can still be friends. By now you know that Jared has come up to Maine to look for you. He was so desperate, my parents said he should go. He was tearing his hair out, panicking about stuff. I tried to keep him from going—I knew you'd be really mad, and probably at me, too, for letting him come. I know you hate his guts, but he didn't mean to hurt you. I don't really understand any of what's going on, and I hope someday you'll explain.

Anyway, I hope you'll write. It's Dullsboro Heights around here without you. I went to a movie with Michael last night. He swears you and he really aren't, you know, dating or anything hot

*and heavy. I hope that's true, because I think he's
kinda cute.*

Love from your faithful old buddy and pal,
Kathi

Molly reread the letter, then folded it neatly and replaced it in the envelope. So much had happened since she arrived in Maine only a few days ago, she hadn't given Kathi a thought. She'd never even thanked her friend for saving her life. Poor Kathi had been beating herself over the head, feeling bad because she couldn't stop Jared from going to Hibben. And yet here Molly was waiting urgently for his call so the two of them could go over to Benson together. She would have to write later in the afternoon and try to tell Kathi what was going on.

If only I knew *what was going on.*

The phone rang at last and she grabbed it. "You have to come with me," she began as a greeting. "It's all set."

"*Whoa!* Let's slow down and start over," Jared teased. "I call and you answer and say hello. I say, 'Hi, this is Jared. Remember I said I'd call at nine? Well, here I am. Shall we get together today?' And you say, 'Yes, Jared, that would be totally fantastic.' Okay? Now let's try it. You start. Say 'Hello, Jared.'"

Molly cut him off in exasperation. "Listen, Jared, you won't want to play games when you hear what's going on. I had another vision last night—well, I'll tell you about that later. But yesterday my dad and

Paulette met Abner Holloway in Benson. Can you believe it?"

His response was excited jabbering on the other end of the line. When he had calmed down, she told him the story of how Paulette and Bill met Abner in the hospital elevator, and how Bill had said Abner would be a good one to ask about Clementine, and how she, Molly, had just made arrangements to go visit the old man. "Now, if you'll tell me how to get to your campground," she finished, "I'll pick you up in the van in about fifteen minutes."

"Why don't we just take the ferry? It's a lot faster to Benson across the water than along that coast road."

"Uh—I'd rather not."

"Oh, yeah. I forgot. Too much water out there, is that it? But, hey—what if I promise I'll hold your hand the whole way?"

She winced. "*Right,* Jared." She wanted to trust him now, but the memory of the near-drowning was too vivid.

He was silent a moment. Then he spoke in a soft voice. "Okay, we'll drive. I'll be waiting at my tent. Just take the road toward Benson along the cliff, and turn left on the first dirt road you see. There's a sign that says Blueberry State Park. The tent sites are just past the ranger's office."

She dressed carefully in a striped sundress and white sandals. In the upstairs bathroom she re-braided her hair neatly, glancing at her face in the mirror. Maybe a little lipstick? She wanted to look nice for Abner. Or was it for Jared?

As she leaned closer to the glass and smoothed the gloss over her lips, the reflection shimmered and Clementine's face looked back at her. Molly backed away, her heart pounding. But the other girl was smiling. And in an instant the reflection was gone. Why was Clementine smiling? Was it that she approved of the lipstick—or the reason for it? Was Clementine happy that Molly was going to see Abner?

Molly said good-bye to her father and Paulette, then hurried out to the van. She drove carefully down the drive, thinking that when she'd last taken this road, she'd been running in the dark, imagining blood on her hands, blood everywhere. But no—that had been *Clementine* running away from Aunt Ethel. And this was *Molly* going to visit Abner. How had that little boy felt when he lost both his mother and his beloved Clemmy in one night? Had Clementine ever come back to Hibben and seen him after she got her precious education? Molly hoped she would soon know.

The road around the cliff was treacherous, and Molly had to slow to a crawl at several places. Then she turned off onto the dirt road into Blueberry State Park, and there was the ranger's office, just as Jared had said. She drove into a grove of pines dotted with colorful tents. Vacationing families were eating breakfast at the picnic tables. A few small children played in the pine needles. Jared jumped up from his seat at a picnic table when he saw the van.

"Want to see my humble home?" he asked through the window when she'd parked near the picnic table.

His face so near her own made her tingle. "Well, for a second. Visiting hours start at ten." She opened the van door and climbed down.

He led the way to a small orange tent with a steeply pitched roof. He knelt to unzip the flap and stepped back so she could look inside. "Go on in, if you want," he invited her. "It's small, but it's cozy."

She stooped, then peered in at the rumpled sleeping bag, blanket, and pillow and shook her head. "That's okay. It looks—nice, though. Like a little nest." She backed away and stood up, bumping right into Jared. "Oh, sorry!"

He wrapped his arms around her. "Is this another sign you're falling for me?" he asked, and her face grew warm, but she didn't pull away. They stood like that for a moment, her hands on his shoulders and his arms tight around her, and she had a dizzy memory of Clementine standing like this with Hob in his bedroom just before Uncle Wallace burst in.

She extricated herself and walked to the van. "Where do you cook?" she asked, determinedly casual. "Do you make a campfire?"

"Well, there's this little grill. I keep planning to cook fish on it. And hot dogs." He climbed up into the passenger seat. "But so far I've been eating stuff you don't have to cook. Bread and cheese. And picking blueberries. There's a little café down by the wharf in Hibben. In fact, I called after work to see if you wanted to come into town and have dinner with

me, but your dad said you'd gone to bed really early."
He looked at her. "Maybe we can have our first date
there."

"Haven't we already had our first date?" She
turned the van carefully in the small dirt clearing and
headed back out to the cliff road.

"Those weren't dates. Those were—confronta-
tions, or something."

"Or something," she murmured.

As they drove to Benson, Molly told Jared about
the most recent vision—how Uncle Wallace had
locked Clementine in her room, how he'd burned
her atlas, how Abner had tried to help by getting the
key but failed, and how Aunt Ethel had died after
her miscarriage. Her voice trembled at the last.

Jared reached over and tugged her braid. "Poor
Clementine," he said slowly. "What a guilt trip! But
you know it wasn't her fault Aunt Ethel died. Not
really."

"But maybe if Clementine had stayed, the way
Uncle Wallace told her to, she could have done something. She just ran away. It was terrible!" She edged
the van around another curve.

"She was scared. She ran away because she didn't
know what to do."

Molly was silent a moment as a car in front of
them pulled into a lookout point, then she shook her
head. "She didn't run away because she was scared.
I was in her head and I know. I'm beginning to think
that deep down she wasn't a very nice person at all.
She ran away because she didn't want to bother with

her aunt. She just wanted to get away from that family and the responsibilities they were heaping on her, and so she left. She didn't *care*."

"But maybe *later* she felt guilty."

Molly shrugged, though his words struck a chord with her. Later? How much later? Was it possible that Clementine felt guilty about neglecting Aunt Ethel and wanted Molly somehow to help make things better? But that didn't make any sense. Aunt Ethel was long dead. She was beyond help.

From her perch in the driver's seat, Molly could see over the sheer drop to where the sea pounded the cliffs, waves exploding into plumes of foam. It seemed to her the sea was especially rough today.

The road wound on for miles and miles until at last it descended steeply into Benson. Benson was larger than Hibben and had made more headway with the tourist trade. The wharf at Benson was crowded with camera-toting visitors. Tables topped with gaily colored umbrellas dotted Hill Street, Benson's main road, where merchants sold local blueberry jam and pies, fresh fish, handcrafted jewelry, whittled ships inside bottles, and wooden toys. A man with a bassoon voice stood near a boiling vat of water, bellowing that fresh lobsters could be had at a bargain price. Molly piloted the van carefully down Hill Street, consulted her hastily scrawled directions, then turned up a steep lane to arrive at a white clapboard building with a wide front porch. Two old women wrapped in shawls sat in identical rocking chairs, knitting and listening to the radio.

The receptionist took their names. "Oh, yes," she said to Molly. "Mr. Holloway will be down in a minute. You can wait in the lounge."

They followed her down a hallway to a large, pleasant room. The floor was covered with a luxurious Oriental carpet. The walls were lined with books, and the long windows were fitted with cushioned window seats beneath. At one of the two long tables against the wall, a woman in a wheelchair sat reading the day's newspaper with a magnifying glass. Another woman sat crocheting in the far corner.

The women looked up when Molly and Jared entered. The one reading the paper waved her magnifying glass. "Make yourselves right to home," she called. "Nice to see some fresh faces around here. Not that I can see much, anyway."

"*Um*—thank you," answered Molly uncertainly. The woman turned back to her newspaper.

Four overstuffed armchairs, several straight-backed chairs, and a long couch were grouped at the far end of the room near the fireplace. Molly and Jared perched in two of the chairs and waited, looking at each other steadily. Outside the windows Molly could see attendants pushing men and women in wheelchairs across the lawn toward the building. Dark clouds blew across the sky and obscured the sun. Wind whipped the tree branches. The woman with the magnifying glass coughed a few times and rustled her newspaper. "Looks like rain," she announced. "Even I can see that."

Molly and Jared didn't have long to wait before a tall, white-haired man entered the room. He gripped a cane and walked slowly, his head hanging low to watch the floor as he crossed shakily to greet them. Molly and Jared looked at him expectantly. *This is little Abner?* thought Molly. *I can't believe it!*

He wore a pair of faded black pants and a long-sleeved white shirt buttoned up to the neck, and his long bare feet were encased in black corduroy bedroom slippers. He shuffled to their armchairs, stooping over his cane. When he reached their chairs at last, he raised his head. And with a start, Molly recognized him: *the old man on the plane!* She saw that he remembered her, too.

He smiled broadly and reached out to shake her hand. "You're the young lady from the airplane! Now what in the world brings you here?"

She brought forth her most gracious smile. "I'm Molly Teague. It's nice to see you again, Mr. Holloway, and it's an astonishing coincidence that we've already met." *But I don't believe in coincidence anymore.*

He gripped her hand with his thin, cool one. "Now, doesn't that beat all?"

Molly introduced Jared, who shook hands politely, then murmured to Molly with unconcealed amazement in his voice: "You already *know* him?"

"He sat in front of me on the plane to Bangor."

"I was in Boston for some special heart tests they don't do way up here," Abner explained. "Spent four days in the hospital walking on treadmills and getting strapped into all sorts of outlandish contraptions."

"Did it help?" asked Jared politely.

"Well, I'm still able to get around, and that's what counts, isn't it?" Abner eased himself down onto one of the straight-backed chairs. "Can't sit anywhere else," he muttered. "Otherwise I'm there all night— maybe stuck for good! Have to call one of the nurses to fetch me out again." And then he looked straight over at Molly. "Nice-looking girl—thought so on the plane, too."

There was a long pause. She could hear the rustle of the newspaper as the woman in the wheelchair turned a page. She could hear the whistle of the rising wind outside. Both Abner and Jared were waiting for her to speak. She realized this was her show, but she had not rehearsed how to go about asking what she needed to know.

She cleared her throat and leaned toward Abner. "Mr. Holloway, I'm staying with my father and stepmother over in Hibben," she began. "In your old house, you know? And yesterday, I met Miss Wilkins. You know, Grace Wilkins, at the Hibben Library? She mentioned she knew you and said that you'd grown up in the house my father bought."

She'd thought he was trembling before, but now, quite suddenly, he was shaking with new violence. "Ah, Gracie," he said, and gripped the wooden arms of his chair tightly. The shaking subsided. "But the receptionist said you wanted to talk to me about Clementine Horn. It must be Gracie, then, who told you about her. Who else would even know the name anymore?" He rubbed his hand across his eyes, then leaned forward. "You mustn't believe a word any-

256

body says about Clementine," he said, his eyes burning fiercely. "It's all lies."

Molly and Jared exchanged a glance.

"Are you on about that old cousin of yours again, Abner?" called the woman from the wheelchair. "Like a stuck record, you are."

"You keep out of this, Thelma!"

Molly wiped her palms nervously on the skirt of her sundress. "Miss Wilkins said that her brother, Hob, and Clementine Horn were—"

"They were not! Don't you believe it for a minute! Clementine was a virtuous young girl."

"All Miss Wilkins said was that her brother Hob was in love with Clementine. But her brother died out in the cove, and no one knows what happened to Clementine."

Abner released his hold on the chair and his arms began trembling again. "She was kidnapped." He shook his bent finger in their faces. "I know, I know, people said she ran away, but she promised she would stay and take care of me, and I believed her. She would never lie to me."

"Kidnapped, my foot," called the woman who was crocheting. "That girl ran off just like everybody said she did."

"No she didn't. She never would have done that to me."

The woman reading the newspaper looked over at Abner with a wry smile. "That's it, Abner. You hold fast to your dreams."

"You two keep out of it!" His voice rose to a

childish whine. He rubbed his hands together, and Molly winced at the dry, sandpapery sound. "Don't pay any attention to Sarah and Thelma. They don't know a thing about it."

"Did Grace Wilkins tell you how old Abner ran off on her?" the woman named Thelma asked Molly. "Ditched her just the way his cousin Clementine ditched him."

The old man struggled to rise from his chair. His face was alarmingly red.

"But that isn't what we came to talk about," Jared said quickly. "We just want to know what Clementine's connection is to *us*. Especially to Molly."

"What do you mean?" barked Abner. "Why should my cousin be connected to you kids in any way at all? You never even knew her."

"Come on, Molly. Tell him about the visions."

"Eh?" shouted Abner Holloway. "Tell me about *what?"*

"Visions, Abner! The young man said *'visions'!* Why don't you get yourself a hearing aid and stop being so confounded vain!" called Thelma, rattling her newspaper. She was making no pretense at reading anymore and sat listening avidly. The other woman, Sarah, continued crocheting, but Molly could tell from the way she kept darting glances in their direction that she was eavesdropping, too.

"It's this," Molly began hurriedly. "I've seen things up at the house. And other places, too. I know it sounds crazy, but we think—that is, Jared and I think—well, that I'm being haunted by Clementine

Horn. I've seen her and her aunt and uncle—your parents, Mr. Holloway—and all the children. The visions frighten me, and I want to know . . . I want to ask you to tell me about Clementine. I'm trying to find out whether she's trying to contact me—or whether, well, whether we're just imagining things." She stared down at her hands.

"Molly's not imagining things," Jared added. "You see, I've had visions and dreams, too."

Abner sat back, looking confused. "Taken by the kidnappers, maybe killed."

"What kidnappers do you mean?" asked Molly faintly.

"She was kidnapped, the night my mother died. Had to have been. She would have come to me if she could," said the old man staunchly. He crossed his shaking arms tightly across his chest. "Since she never came back, it means she *couldn't* come back."

"He can't bear to think she just ran off and met somebody and didn't think twice about a little kid back in Hibben, Maine," said Thelma.

But now Abner was nodding. "Little kid, yes, that was me. She was seventeen and I was just turning five. She was half mother to me, half sweetheart. I used to ask her to promise she would wait for me till I grew up. I wanted to marry her as I've never wanted anyone else. She promised me, you hear me? I know I was only a child, but my feelings were stronger and truer then than any time after." His voice grew ragged. Molly glanced over at him with concern.

"Nobody ever loved me as Clementine did," Abner whispered. "Nobody ever could. That's why I always waited for her. I waited for Clementine to escape from her kidnappers and come back to me."

The woman crocheting snorted indelicately.

Abner sat staring at his feet, shaking his head back and forth. His wrinkled hands gripped his knees tightly. "Someday the kidnappers may let her go," he whispered. "Or she'll escape. Just wait. Clemmy is very clever."

Jared looked over at Molly and raised his brows. She cleared her throat. "Mr. Holloway, about the girl in my dreams? She's short and thin and about seventeen, with very pink cheeks and long dark hair in two braids coiled on top of her head. Is that anything like your cousin?"

"She said she wanted to look taller," Abner said suddenly, his hands gripping his bony knees. "She always wore her braids up high. I worshiped the ground she walked on—" He broke off.

"All you kids seemed to love her," Molly told him. "Well, Anne wasn't so affectionate, but all you others were jumping on her all the time, asking her to play with you—"

"I always begged to go down to the harbor to see the boats," he said, his eyes staring across the room. Molly knew he wasn't seeing her and Jared at all but was looking back in memory to happy times with Clementine. "Sometimes we went to my favorite place—the secret cave." He fell silent.

Molly's heart raced. Everything he said corroborated things she had seen or dreamed. Here was proof that the girl was letting Molly see scenes from her life. What Molly still couldn't figure out was *why*. And not knowing made her afraid.

Then Molly's words seemed to register with Abner and he jerked his head up to stare at her. "Hold on just a second. What are you talking about, girl? Are you saying you saw me and my brothers and sisters in your dreams?"

"Well, in my visions," said Molly. "Yes. I don't understand it, either."

Both women were staring at her, frankly fascinated. Abner was clenching and unclenching his hands on his knees. Molly looked over at Jared and felt reassured by his nod.

"I saw this girl in my dreams," Molly tried to explain. "But in the visions, it was as if *I* were Clementine. Looking out of her eyes."

"*You* were Clementine? Nonsense!" Abner's voice sounded strangled.

Molly hurried on, determined to tell him what she'd seen, determined that he would at least hear about it all. "It was as if I were looking out of Clementine's eyes, as if I knew the things she knew and felt what she felt."

Abner's face had grown very pale. Molly spoke gently, glancing toward the doorway to see whether the nurse were nearby. "In some of the visions you were wearing a little felt cap—you were very sweet. Clementine played pirates with you up in the playroom. You had a wooden sword." She felt a sense of unreality as she remembered the boy Abner—at the same time speaking to the man Abner, grown so old. "Clementine was just finishing school, and she was totally miserable because she wanted to go to college. She had big fights with your parents about it. But they said she had to work in the kitchen with Janie and look after all you kids as well. She hated all the work. I think she did more work than Janie and Miss Finch put together."

"Janie! Miss Finch!" cried the old man, hands clenching and unclenching now on the arms of his chair. "I haven't heard those names in nearly a century. How could Gracie Wilkins tell you about them? She never even knew their names. They were long gone before I started courting Gracie."

Molly sighed. "I'm trying to tell you, Mr. Holloway. Miss Wilkins didn't tell me these things. I *saw* them. Ghosts or visions—or something. I've seen Clementine at the house, and I've *been* Clementine at the house and also out on the headland and in town. I know now I've been dreaming about her for as long as I can remember, back in Ohio—where I live when I'm not visiting my dad. I've seen her in mirrors, too."

"Then you must be a crazy girl," Abner said, now smiling horribly. His teeth were stained and yellowed. He struggled to stand. Jared rushed to help him, but Abner shooed him away. "Any little girl comes in here and says she's turned into my cousin Clementine—why, I'll tell you what that means. She's off her rocker. Maybe it's drugs!"

"I am not on drugs." Molly sighed. She signaled Jared: They'd better leave now. This was going nowhere. Molly could see out the window that it had started to rain. She did not relish the prospect of driving back along that narrow road in a thunderstorm.

"You're on drugs or else stark-raving loony!" Abner shouted. "Clementine was kidnapped years and years before you were born. If she's dead, it's because the kidnappers killed her. She never had a chance to escape because if she could have gotten away, she would have come back to me. She promised. She promised!"

"I'll get the nurse," said Sarah from her corner. "He starts carrying on like this, you know it's time for his pills." She reached over to the table and pressed the intercom buzzer.

"Thank you for talking to us," said Molly politely to Abner as the nurse hurried in with a brown prescription bottle, announcing that Mr. Holloway needed his medication now and would be taking a nap afterward. Jared and the nurse eased Abner into his chair again, and the nurse popped a pill in his mouth. Abner gulped the water she offered him, then subsided with his eyes closed.

Molly and Jared said good-bye and started walking out of the lounge. They had reached the receptionist's desk when they heard a voice behind them.

"Children, wait a moment."

They turned and saw Thelma in her wheelchair rolling after them. They waited for her.

"He's not always like this," Thelma began. "Most of the time he's as rational as anyone else. I don't know what it is you're seeing or dreaming, honey, but I do know that Clementine Horn has a powerful hold over Abner and always has had. Whatever it was happened so long ago, I can't see how it matters to anyone—but it sure does seem to matter to Abner. He was so betrayed, you see. I think he's been waiting for that cousin of his all his long life. Couldn't hook up with that Grace woman he was engaged to because he kept thinking Clementine would come back someday. Months can go by and he's fine, but comes along any little mention of Clementine, he starts talking about kidnappers again. We had a folk-song sing-along one night last winter—some of the folks here have a really good little band—and one of the fiddlers started playing that 'Oh my darlin' ' song—you know, about the girl called Clementine? Well, if that didn't set Abner right off. He stood up and hollered she wasn't 'lost and gone forever' at all because the kidnappers stole her away, but she'd be coming back as soon as she could. Of course, even if there had been kidnappers, which I don't believe for a second, the girl was twelve years older than Abner anyway and would be dead by now in any case. But Abner, no, he can't bear to hear it." She paused and looked up at them. "I just wanted you to know because—well, he's a good old fellow, Abner is, as long as you don't bring up the past."

Sarah, the woman who had been crocheting, walked out of the lounge in time to hear Thelma's last comment. "You've got a thing for old Abner, haven't you, Thelma? You can't hide it from me!" She smiled at Molly and Jared. "I'm sorry you had to see him like that. The receptionist should have warned you not to talk about Clementine Horn. He always falls apart."

"That's what I was just telling them," said Thelma.

"Well, he's gone up for his lunch and a nap," said Sarah. "You'll see, he'll be right as rain this afternoon."

A crack of thunder made them all jump. "Did you say rain, Sarah?" Thelma grinned.

Everyone laughed. Then Molly and Jared thanked the women and said again they were sorry to have upset Abner. They stepped out into rain falling in sheets and raced for the van. Inside, they sat silently for a few minutes, listening to the pounding water on the roof, each lost in thought.

Jared broke the silence: "Well, that was useless."

When Molly spoke, it was hard to hear her over the rain, and Jared leaned close. Molly's lips curved in a smile. "It wasn't totally useless. You saw how rattled Abner got when he heard what I'd seen. It was all true, everything I saw. We don't know what happened to Clementine, and we don't know what she wants from me—but at least we know I'm not imagining all this."

"Maybe that's been your big worry, but it wasn't mine. I just want to know how we can figure out what all the weirdness means—and get it to stop.

And we still don't understand a thing." He looked out the window and frowned. "My big worry now is getting back to Hibben. I don't think the cliff road will be very safe in this weather."

"Then let's stay here till it stops," said Molly. "We can go eat lunch somewhere and wait it out."

"I have to get back. I work at one o'clock." He shifted in his seat. "Let's hit the road—but take it slow."

Molly started the van and headed out along Benson's narrow streets. The windshield wipers, on high speed, cut a blurry swatch through the downpour of rain. Molly leaned forward to see better, but the going was very slow. With the windows up, the glass grew cloudy. She turned on the defroster and cracked her window. Water drizzled in through the crack and blew in her face. "This is terrible, Jared!"

"You can say that again," he said and pointed.

She squinted out the window to see what he meant. The road to the right, the only road leading back up the hill to the cliff, was blocked by two police cars. Police officers were lighting flares and laying them in the road to keep vehicles away.

"Oh, no." Molly clenched her hands around the steering wheel.

Jared wound down his window and leaned out, ignoring the rain that pelted his head. He shouted over to the police: "What's going on?"

"Road's closed! There's a rockslide about a quarter mile along the way toward Hibben," one officer called back. "This rain just washes the hills into the sea.

It's dangerous. Better take the ferry, if it's still running."

Jared pulled his wet head inside again and shut the window. He turned to Molly with droplets glistening silver on his lashes. "What can I say? Police orders."

Molly pressed her forehead to the steering wheel. She felt like screaming.

"Come on, Molly. It's perfectly safe. I told you, I'll hold your hand the whole way." Jared's fingers massaged the back of her neck. "With pleasure."

She gritted her teeth as rain pelted the van. She followed the line of cars back into town, down to the wharf. She wasn't afraid of boats, she told herself; she was afraid of the substance they floated in. "Probably the ferry isn't running anyway. Not in a storm."

"This isn't a storm," he said. "It's just rain. Anyway, let's go see. Drive down to the wharf. If the ferry isn't running, I'll have a perfect excuse for my boss. But if it is—then we're getting on it. All right?"

Slowly, windshield wipers on high, Molly drove the car down Hill Street to the wharf. There were several cars ahead, all waiting to drive up the ramp onto the ferry docked at the pier with its doors like a giant mouth open to swallow the vehicles. She unrolled her side window and paid for their tickets. Then she drove smoothly up the ramp and parked on the bottom level of the boat. Out of the rain now, a silence fell. The people from the other cars were all getting out and climbing the steps up to the passenger deck. Jared reached for Molly's hand and squeezed. Without speaking, she followed him.

Upstairs, she had to admit the ferry seemed solid. It rocked gently across the waves once they'd pulled away from the Benson pier. Jared sat next to her on the padded wooden bench inside the windowed cabin. She had chosen a seat that did not look out over the water. There were only a few other passengers— mostly tourists with small children, who stood at the windows or outside on the covered deck, enjoying the ride despite the rain. Molly could hear the great engines churning beneath her.

After they had traveled halfway across the choppy water of the cove, Jared stood. "Let's go outside," he suggested. "We won't get wet if we stay under the overhang."

"You go right ahead. I'm sitting here until we land."

"*Dock,* you mean. This isn't a plane."

"Believe me—I know it." She crossed her hands in her lap and closed her eyes. *So far, so good,* she thought. She allowed herself a little thrill of pride. She was here on a boat in the middle of the cove, and she was all right. Holding in the panic, but all right. Still, there was no sense pushing her luck. If she set foot outside, the sight of the sea might ruin her careful control.

Jared shrugged. "I'll only go out for a minute, then." He stepped out onto the deck.

As they churned across the cove, Molly was increasingly aware of the dark, deep water all around. The fluttering in her stomach grew stronger. She looked out at Jared through the glass door. The rain was still coming down but drizzling now rather than pouring. Jared was leaning over the railing, staring out at the water and at the cliffs along the shore. As she studied his back, the hollow feeling expanded. She stood and walked to the glass door. As she pushed through the door and stepped out onto the deck, the buzzing hum started up in her head.

Somehow he looked so familiar, standing there that way, hands on the railing, head lifted into the wind. She remembered seeing him just like that once before—only not in broad daylight with the sun high overhead breaking through the clouds. She had seen him in moonlight, leaning over a railing. She remembered how the moonlight illuminated his face as he heard her coming and turned, remembered how her heart leapt in excitement and gratitude that she hadn't missed him after all, that he had waited for her.

12 Clementine

Somehow Clementine's sheer determination to be away from that house of horrors propelled her shaky legs down the rutted lane to town and through the late night streets. She headed straight to the wharf, pausing only a moment at the corner of Cotton Lane to wonder whether Hob were back home already, tucked up in bed while she braved the night wind. She was already more than twenty minutes late. She might have lost him.

She breathed deeply as she walked, smoothing her skirt with her palms and reaching up to repin her braids securely. If he were there, she wanted to look neat and presentable, someone he would want as a bride. Someone he would take across the cove without delay.

She passed the office where Uncle Wallace worked and saw a light burning. Through the uncurtained window she could make out the shape of Mr. Wallings, her uncle's bookkeeper, working late at his desk to record in his ledger the amount of fish each schooner in the Holloway Company had brought in that day. He wouldn't have news, yet, of what had happened up at the house.

Her legs throbbed and her eyes ached. She must not think about the house.

It was hard to see. The sky was covered with scudding black clouds, moving swiftly in the path of the wind. She hurried past the Holloway Company and down to the seawall. She hugged her hatbox and stared out into the blackness of the cove. The wind picked up, whipping her skirts against her legs and tugging at her coiled braids. The moon shone down, revealing the dark shapes of the fishing schooners bobbing up and down on choppy water. No one was there.

Tears came to her eyes and were blown immediately onto her cheeks by the brisk wind. Hob did not love her enough—he had not waited. But then she saw a figure, its back to her, leaning against the railing of the seawall, staring out at the windswept sea. Holding up her skirts with one hand, the other keeping a good grip on the hatbox, she walked steadily forward.

She recognized the long, thin back. He was wearing loose dark clothes and his feet were bare. The moonlight illuminated his fair hair and wind ruffled it into a yellow thatch.

"Hob!" she cried, running up to him, and he turned and caught her up in his arms, a great grin splitting his face.

"Clementine—you came after all! I was about to give up on you."

"Of course I've come, my love. I just had a hard time getting away. They locked me in, can you believe it? But now I'm here and all ready for our journey." She could feel the muscles in his arms like ropes around her. She gave him her best smile. "I can't wait to begin our new life together, Hob . . ."

He stepped back to look at her. He glanced at the sky, then shook his head. "Clementine, I can't wait, either. But I'm worried about this weather. It isn't a good night to be taking a boat out all alone. It looks to me like there's a storm brewing."

"Oh, Hob—you promised! And a promise is a promise!" She pulled away and gazed up at him, seething inside with anger that after all she'd been through, her plan might come to nothing. She made her eyes sad and round. "Don't you love me?"

"Of course I do! But, Clementine, must we go tonight? What about your aunt? I saw the doctor riding up the hill. If she's so sick, maybe you should be home with her—?"

She shook her head. "No, Hob, she'll be fine. This is my only chance to escape them. You don't know how they watch me! I spent the whole day locked in my room, all because my uncle doesn't want me to be with you. But once we're married, they won't be able to keep us apart. We need to go right now, tonight, before they come looking for me. I thought I could count on you!"

"You *can* count on me. You're my future, Clementine. But it's farther than you think across the cove." He reached to pull her back into his arms, but she stepped away and hugged her hatbox.

"If you want to marry me, Hob, we have to go to Benson this very night."

He frowned at her. "But I can't sail the *Undine* alone, and the waves are too rough for a smaller boat."

"You could handle her. You're big enough. And *so* strong. Stronger than other men."

He shook his head, but she could see he was flattered. "You're daft if you think that I can do the work of four men," he said.

"Then don't take the schooner. I can help you with a smaller boat. We'll be fine. You just tell me what to do." She walked along the pier, inspecting the small crafts tethered near the larger vessels. "Look, what about this one?"

"That's Sam Sawyer's dinghy! It's nothing more than a rowboat with a sail. It would never take those waves."

"Of course it will." She bent and lifted the heavy line tied to the iron mooring. "We just take this and—"

"Clementine!" He had to raise his voice as the wind whipped the words out to sea. "You stop that!"

She narrowed her eyes and peered down at the waves. "Hob Wilkins, you listen to me. If you want to marry me, you are taking me to Benson this very night. Or else I just might change my mind."

"You really *are* daft!"

"What's the difference between daft and desperate?" she asked him, tears spilling onto her cheeks. "I want to be with you for the rest of my life. But if I don't get away tonight, my uncle will find me and lock me away, and I'll never see you again!" Her tears—tears of rage and frustration—mingled with the salt spray.

Hob cleared his throat, clearly anxious at the sight of her tears.

She dropped the heavy rope and shifted her hatbox. Then she slipped one arm around his waist and leaned against him. "I trust you, Hob. There's no one like you. I . . . I love you."

He looked away, down the pier to where the *Undine* was tied to the mooring. Clementine felt his arms tighten around her again as he pulled her against his chest. She could feel his heart pounding—or was it her own? Then he put his hand on the back of her neck and lowered his face to hers. His kiss nearly suffocated her; she couldn't breathe. She felt their hearts pounding together louder and louder until she thought hers must surely burst.

"All right. I'll try." He indicated a boat twice the size of Sam's little rowboat, fitted with a mast and also with oars for rowing. "Your uncle owns the *Undine,* but this little lady belongs to my pa, every beautiful inch of her. We can take her, I think, if we hurry across before the rain starts." When the moonlight gleamed down through a hole in the thick cloud cover, Clementine could read the name painted on the bow: *Grace.*

"She's perfect." Clementine climbed aboard the

Grace before he could change his mind. "Oh, thank you, Hob!"

The *Grace* was about twelve feet long, with a single mast. Its deck was crowded with dozens of wooden lobster pots and carefully folded nets. Hob lit the oil lamp that hung on a hook at the bow. Then he untied the heavy rope from the iron mooring and cast off from the pier. He hoisted the sail up first, then pulled the ropes tight as the sail filled with the brisk night wind. "Hold the tiller steady while I get this up," he ordered. Clementine stood at the stern and gripped the wooden tiller. As the heavy sail flapped hard, the vessel turned in the water. "This is crazy," he said. But his eyes glowed at the sight of her. "Pa always says it's bad luck to bring a woman on board a ship." He was grinning now. "Bad for the day's catch."

"Well, good thing we're not planning to catch anything," she replied, smiling at him.

"Oh, we'll catch it all right, when people find out what we've done!"

They laughed together as he raised the mainsail. "They'll be happy enough to welcome such a nice couple back to Hibben after our wedding tomorrow morning," Clementine told him, raising her voice to be heard over the flapping of the heavy cloth. "We'll have to be as respectable as they come to make up for this adventure."

"What a great story this'll make for our children," added Hob, tending to the myriad of lines and pulleys. "Not to mention our grandchildren!"

She held the tiller steady, caught up in the story—

275

for a moment almost believing that they would marry in the morning and return to Hibben. "We'll go back to Benson every year for our anniversary celebration," she said. "And take all the children and grandchildren along!"

The mainsail and jib filled with wind, and the *Grace* moved silently out over the water toward Benson. Clementine sat next to Hob as he took the tiller. The wind that filled the sails also blew the clouds away for a few minutes, and the moon was bright. Far across the water she could see lights twinkling on the cliffs. When the water grew even more choppy, Hob competently luffed over the waves. He scanned the sky.

"We'll make good time if the wind keeps on this way," he said. "Maybe you're not so daft after all, Clementine Horn!"

Then he frowned as the cloud cover rolled back across the sky.

"Is it going to rain?" she asked. She didn't really care, just as long as the boat kept on its course away from Hibben. Freedom! She would never see Uncle Wallace again—not if she could help it. And the children . . . well, they would get along fine without her. She resolutely pushed all thoughts of Aunt Ethel from her head.

"I hope it'll hold off until we dock," he said. He shifted course slightly to ride the waves more smoothly. "As long as a fog doesn't come up, we should be fine." She sensed that despite his worry, he was enjoying this challenge. She touched his arm gently.

"I like a man who can master the elements," she said. "That's the kind of husband for me." In the light from the lantern, she saw his ears turn red.

He was a nice boy, and she hoped it wouldn't take him long to get over her once she escaped him in Benson. He'd go home again and apologize to his pa for taking the *Grace* without permission, then start work again with the fishermen. He'd marry a nice girl in another year or so. He'd spend his whole life in Hibben, with fishing filling his days and family filling his nights. She supposed he would look back on this night as an exciting high point in an otherwise humdrum life.

She, on the other hand, would be working somewhere, earning money for college. She would get a degree. She would travel the world and think only sometimes of Hibben and her old life there. From time to time she might drop Hob Wilkins a line from far-off lands. That would cause a little excitement!

Hob was singing as he changed direction by shifting the sail so the wind struck the other side. They must keep clear of the rocks. The boat tacked a zigzag course across the cove, and Hob sang louder, shouting out the words to be heard above the wind: *"Oh my darlin', Oh my darlin', Oh my darlin', Clementine. You are lost and gone forever—"*

She laughed, and the wind whipped her laughter up into the sails. It seemed for a moment that her laughter, derisive and careless, filled the sails and sent the boat skimming along even faster. She joined in his song, shouting her excitement. *Gone forever! Hooray!*

Keeping a hand steady on the tiller, he reached his other around to hug her. "But you won't be gone at all, sweetest girl. We'll be together forever!"

"Forever!" She laughed harder, drunk now on the wind and spray, on the danger, on the night. What an adventure this was! She grew more and more giddy with the sense of her own power over this boy. And her power made her careless. "I'll be sending you postcards from Africa, Hob!" Her words were swept out over the choppy water. They were halfway across the cove. She could see the lights of Benson each time the wind blew a hole in the fog, and she threw caution, as it were, to the wind. "I'll write whenever I have time. I'll never forget my darlin' Hob."

"What was that about postcards, Clementine?" shouted Hob over the roar of the wind. "What do you mean?"

"Oh, I'm just a silly girl," she giggled, nuzzling his cheek. Then she pulled her shawl tightly around her shoulders and mentally kicked her own shin. *Shut up!* she told herself. *Do you want to give it all away so soon? He'll learn quickly enough once we dock in Benson that the marriage is off.*

After a while she grew cold in the wind and huddled low on the polished deck. She was surprised that the deck had been scrubbed so clean. She would not have thought that the burly fishermen cared how the floor looked. But then she remembered how Uncle Wallace once told her that the simple fishing folk believed each vessel had a soul and must be

278

treated with respect by the men who sailed her. Clementine wedged her hatbox under a net beside her so it would not slide with the motion of the boat, then drew up her knees beneath her long skirt and wrapped her arms around them. She sat there thinking about the reactions of Hob's wife and children when they received picture postcards from exotic places.

The boat dipped sharply, its starboard side lifting high before slamming down into the water again, and Clementine peered up at the dark shape of Hob, struggling to hold the lines as the wind buffeted the craft. She would help him if she could—but no use both of them getting cold. She closed her eyes and tried to blot out everything but the thought of her future. She planned to ditch Hob as fast as possible once they docked, then head for the depot. In Boston or New York or wherever the first bus took her, she could sell her mother's necklace and live on the money until she found work with a family who could pay her well. There would be books and books and books, and a new atlas to replace the one Uncle Wallace had burned. She tasted the bitter anger again as she thought of all the times she'd lain across her bed, poring over the maps in her father's atlas, and she hated Uncle Wallace with fresh vigor. How dare he!

She closed her eyes, lulled by the rising and falling of the boat as it made its way across the waves toward Benson. But then the boat rose sharply again, smacking hard on its port side, and she heard Hob shout. Her eyes flew open as the spray showered her, dousing the lamp. Now she could barely see him at all.

She struggled to her feet and was thrown against the mast by the choppy dance of the *Grace*. "Hob!" she called, kicking aside the nets and hanging on tightly to the boom.

"Sit down!" he yelled back. "It's blowing too hard." The roaring wind tossed his words to the sky. "We're turning back. We'll never keep clear of the rocks in this weather."

"Oh no! You mustn't turn back, Hob! I thought you would take care of me!"

"Believe me, I'll be taking care of us both if I can just turn her around!" She saw now he was standing on deck, pulling frantically on the lines to lower the sails. "Help me! We have to get these down!"

"But why?" she cried, fighting against the wind to reach him. The first hard drops of rain began to fall. His hair was already wet from the sea spray, his shirt plastered to his chest. "We must keep on!" Across the cove lay Benson, though she could no longer see the lights of shore through the fog and darkness.

"Hold the tiller while I reef the mainsail!" he shouted, hauling on the line to shorten the amount of sail exposed to the wind.

"You promised!" she wailed, wanting to strike him, seeing all her dreams disappearing into the clouds that now covered the water. She would be her uncle's prisoner forever, slave to him and his motherless brood. She grabbed the tiller. "You promised!"

The wind roared fiercely, blowing fog away. She

could see the lights of Benson again, far across the inlet. They had not covered as much of the distance as she'd thought. Damn Hob for letting her down!

The boom swung sharply around and the *Grace* spun windward.

"I hate you!" Clementine screamed at Hob, but the wind dashed her words into the waves. "You mean nothing to me! Nothing!" The rocks loomed up now on their left, and Hob battled to turn the boat from the sharp peaks. An awful scraping sound rose above the wind.

She huddled in the stern, head down, both arms aching as she tried to hold on to the tiller, which threatened to wrench itself from her hands with every lurching movement of the boat. Waves splashed onto the deck. She let go of the tiller and covered her head with her arms.

"For Christ's sake!" Hob shoved her away roughly. "Do you want to capsize the boat?" He dropped the lines to grab the tiller, hoping to jerk the boat around. But it dove sharply and Clementine slid forward across the deck, crashing into the mast. She screamed. The boom broke free of the lines and swung to the starboard side, smashing her down on the deck.

"Oh, God, no! Hob, save me!" She was dreadfully afraid now. All her plans of escape, all her dreams of her glorious future dissolved in the churning water. What remained was a longing to live, to live and be safe, never to touch water again.

The *Grace* spun like a gypsy, whirling wildly in a crazy dance. A splintered board from a broken lobster pot flew into Clementine's face, gashing her forehead. She cried out as she felt blood streak down her face from the wound.

"Hang on, Clementine," yelled Hob, still desperately fighting wind and rain to right the boat. "Hang on for dear life!"

Down in the darkness of the cove the *Grace* floated on her side, moving back with the rush of waves, then surging forward again, crashing wood against rock. There was no sign of Hob. Not anywhere. Clementine hung onto a piece of splintered wood and called for him until she was hoarse, but her voice, thin and weak, was swallowed in the roar of waves. Her head ached fiercely from the blow to her temple when she was swept overboard. She tried to kick her legs but they seemed as heavy as lead weights. She put up her hand and thought she could feel blood, sticky and warm on her fingers. She lay her cheek in the water and closed her eyes against the pain. Behind her eyelids she saw blood—the blood-red cover of the atlas in the fireplace, the blood on the bed in Aunt Ethel's room, the blood on her conscience as Hob Wilkins's young, strong body was sucked down deep with the seaweed into the churning black water when the boat capsized. She opened her eyes once more before she joined him. The clouds parted and the moon shone down, and what she saw was her hatbox floating out of the cove on a crest of white foam—floating out to sea.

13

Molly coughed and gagged, straining to expel the water that was choking her—but no water came out. She felt strong arms tighten around her, and the thought exploded gratefully in her head: "He's alive after all. We're *both* alive."

Then she heard his voice. It was half gasp, half whimper. "Clementine?"

She opened her eyes, coughed again, and felt the hard metal railing of the ferry deck press into her stomach. The arms clutching so desperately and the head—with dark hair, not fair—pressing against her chest belonged to Jared. *Jared,* not Hob.

He moaned as the ferry bobbed gently against the Hibben pier.

Then Molly glanced up and saw the ferry pilot walking toward them. "Okay, kids, enough schmooching. Time to get off, unless you want to pay for the return trip. We leave in ten minutes."

He stopped when he saw Molly's face. "Is something wrong? Is the boy sick?"

Her voice seemed to come from far away. "We—we're all right." *We're all right!*

Molly tried to step away from the railing, but Jared's weight pinned her in place. He moaned again, eyes tightly closed, still lost in a nightmare as bad as Molly's. She looked back at the man. "We'll leave in just a minute. He's okay."

She only hoped that were true.

As the ferry boatman walked off, glancing back over his shoulder, she mustered her strength and towed Jared to the glass door. Jared gripped her hand tightly, and when he spoke, his voice was groggy. "Clementine—"

"*Shhh,* it's me. It's Molly." She staggered along with Jared hanging on her. They stumbled together back through the door and down the steps to the parking deck. "Come on, Jared," she said worriedly when he moaned Clementine's name again. "It's over. We're back in Hibben now."

She led him to the van and helped him into the passenger seat, where he slumped with his head in his hands. Then she drove down the ramp, off the ferry, and parked near the seawall. The rain was only a mist now and already the sun was trying to come out. Rolling down her window, Molly sucked salty air into her lungs. It felt so good to fill her body with precious air, to exhale heavily, to breathe in again. She studied Jared, who was doubled over with his head between his knees. She reached over and rubbed his back in small circles, staring out at the same deep gray water where the *Grace* had gone down.

Jared raised his head suddenly and coughed. His body shook in spasms. "You wouldn't let me turn back!" he gasped, turning to her. "Why didn't you hold the tiller—? Oh, I tried, I tried . . . but we shouldn't have gone out, I *told* you it wasn't safe."

"Jared, stop! I'm Molly, not Clementine. We shared a vision, I think—but it's over now. You're here and you're safe. We're *alive!*"

He lifted his head slowly and stared at her. "How can you stand it?" he asked raggedly.

Stand being alive? Stand knowing now that Clementine had been responsible for Hob's death as well as her own? Clementine had recklessly, uncaringly led Hob Wilkins out to sea that night. And they had both paid for her selfish determination. Molly bowed her head over the steering wheel as tears filled her eyes. What a waste of two young lives. "I'm not sure I *can* stand it," she murmured.

"How can you stand having visions like these?" he persisted, sitting up and looking out the window. She knew he was back with her now.

"When I'm having them, it's not weird at all. I'm looking out of Clementine's eyes. I am her. I feel only what she felt. Desperate to get on with my life, resentful of people who are trapping me. I don't even think about the people I use to get what I want, really. I just use them."

"What do you mean? Whom did you use to get what you want?"

Molly looked away from him. Out in the now

calm water of the cove she could see bobbing markers for the lobster pots.

"I—*I* didn't use anybody. But Clementine did. Don't you know? Or were you stuck completely in Hob's head, just as I was in hers?"

He rubbed his eyes. "I don't know exactly what happened. I mean, I remember standing out there on the deck, leaning over the railing. Then I heard your voice, only you called out: 'Hob!' And when I turned to see what was going on, there you were, Molly, standing in the doorway. And suddenly, it was like another girl was superimposed over you. And the whole day turned to night. It was dark, but there was a moon—and I wasn't on the ferry anymore at all but standing with you on the pier back at Hibben. You wanted to go out in a boat, but I thought it wasn't safe."

Molly was nodding. "It's the same vision. But how can that happen?"

Jared's eyes were wide and frightened, and Molly wished she could do something to erase the expression in them. She felt she was an old hand at having these visions now, but it was new and scary territory for Jared.

"I was Hob—I wasn't me at all!" he continued. "And Hob had been waiting, worried, longing for you. For Clementine, I mean. When I heard your voice, I grabbed you and I was so excited that you'd come—I'd been hardly daring to hope you'd really come. You'd said eleven o'clock, but it was much later by the time you finally ran up. Oh, I was so in love with you. I've never felt that way before—"

He was speaking fast, then broke off, staring at her in wonderment.

"You weren't in love with *me,* Jared," Molly said, dropping her gaze. She couldn't bear knowing how she had betrayed him. Or rather how *Clementine* had betrayed *Hob,* she corrected herself swiftly.

The rain started falling again, enclosing the van in a curtain of gray mist. Molly reached for Jared's hand and squeezed it. He put his arm around her shoulders, and they sat that way for a long time without speaking.

Finally Jared raised his hand and stroked Molly's braid. "Clementine let go of the tiller, true; but Hob shouldn't have been out with her in that boat in the first place." Jared was speaking slowly, carefully distancing the girl and boy in the past from their own present. "He knew the weather was rough. But she made him feel like a man. Big and powerful. Hob was so head-over-heels in love with that girl, he thought he could do anything."

If only that were what had happened. If only it were a simple tale of passion ending in unexpected tragedy, with the two young lovers going down together to their watery graves. But Molly knew better, and she shook her head bitterly. She pulled her braid away. "It wasn't like that, Jared."

"I was there, too, Molly. I know exactly how Hob felt."

She faced him. "You know how Hob felt, but you don't know how Clementine felt. You don't know the whole story at all."

Jared smiled. "I know she was like you, Molly.

Smart and pretty. She loved books, and she loved me. I mean Hob. But Hob was like me—he loved the water. I know everything Hob knew; I have all his memories, his history. I know he lived with his dad and stepmother. He had a baby sister named Gracie. He wanted nothing but to be a fisherman like his pa and to marry Clementine. He adored her, and I know just how he felt, Molly. In fact, I think that's what I've been feeling for you all along, ever since we met. Hob's love for Clementine." His smile widened. "Do you think maybe *that's* what this is all about? We died too young last time. This is our new chance to be together?"

Was it? She wished she could believe it. It would be so nice to be able to fall into his arms now and say yes, this was meant, this is our second chance. But it wasn't true. She knew what had been in Clementine's hard heart that night; she knew the plans Clementine was making even as Hob risked his life for her.

Maybe it would be better, Molly reflected, gazing into the dark pools of Jared's eyes, to let the truth lie buried at sea. If she told him now, wouldn't it just spoil everything? Wouldn't he hate her—or want revenge?

The word seemed to hang in her head. Molly looked out at the mist surrounding the van without seeing it. She smelled the sharp salty air and heard the screeches of sea gulls overhead. *Revenge?*

Jared didn't know why he had thrown Molly into the pool. Something had come over him, he'd said.

Could the something that had come over Jared have been Hob's anger at Clementine for lying to him?

It seemed the fates had conspired to bring everything together: Molly being forced to confront swim lessons; Molly meeting Jared; Molly coming to the big house on the headland and finding Jared there as well; Molly and Jared having visions of two other lives.

Too many coincidences, Jared had said, and you have a pattern. Molly felt a bubble of excitement float up into her throat. She felt she almost had it, almost understood the *reason* for all of this. What if this were Clementine's attempt to make up for what had happened? She was showing Molly and Jared how it had been because she knew now that it shouldn't have been that way at all. But wasn't it too late? You couldn't, after all, change the past.

Molly tried to see out across the water to the line of land that was Benson. The sea looked cold and gray. "Jared," she said softly, reaching for his hand, "I'm beginning to understand."

"Tell me. I'm nowhere near understanding any of this."

"What if—what if Clementine hurt so many people that she's sorry? Maybe she's showing me scenes from her life so I can do something about what happened. Fix it, somehow." Her voice grew even softer. Maybe what she said sounded crazy, but it felt right. "What she did to Hob. What she did to little Abner. Even what she did to Aunt Ethel."

"But then why is she showing me the scenes,

too? And why do I feel I was in Hob Wilkins's head?" He squeezed her hand. "I think we were those kids in a past life. And they messed up, but now we have another chance to love each other."

Molly took a deep breath, shaking her head. "You don't understand. Clementine didn't love Hob. She wasn't going to marry him at all. She was planning to run off as soon as they docked and head for the bus depot. She planned the whole thing. She used him, plain and simple. I was—I was *there,* Jared. In her head. I know this is true."

He was silent a long moment, staring straight ahead through the windshield. Then he said, "Well, if that's true, Hob never knew it. He loved her so much, even at the end." He paused, then added softly, "Maybe he was born again, loving her still."

"Then he's been loving a lie," she said. "All this time." Unable to look at him now, she, too, stared out over the water.

Molly wanted Jared to come back to the house with her. Now that she'd found comfort in talking, she wanted to hash everything out, try to figure out what their double dream meant. But Jared had to work. Before he walked up Main Street to Day's Catch, he put his hands on her shoulders and drew her toward him. Gently, he kissed her lips. And then again, and then her lips responded and she was clinging to him.

"That wasn't Hob kissing Clementine," he said huskily into her ear. "This is *us*. Here and now. Don't forget it."

When she arrived back up at the house Paulette and Bill were eating egg salad sandwiches in the kitchen with the plumber and carpenter who had come to work on the new bathrooms. Molly changed into dry clothes and joined them, glad they were busy talking about tile and pipes and drainage so she didn't have to answer questions about her visit with Abner. She felt fragile, as if caught between times again. After lunch she wandered out and sat on the front steps.

Raindrops sparkled on the headland grasses and dripped from the trees like tinsel. Molly looked pensively out at the reed grass. She had the strangest feeling that she was supposed to do something. But what? *You can't change the past,* she thought. *What's done is done.* It was the sort of thing Jen would have said. She sat outside, lost in her musings, but came up with no answers at all. When rain began pelting the headland again, she stood up and went inside.

That night she went up to bed early, feeling as bruised and battered as if she really had capsized in the cove that day. She slept restlessly, kicking off her sheet, dragging it back again, twisting it around her legs. When she awoke suddenly, she thought it was because she was wrapped so tightly she felt like a mummy. But then she heard the moaning down the hall and knew the sound must have reached her even in sleep. She extricated her legs and slid out of bed. Another moan filtered through the door, and she hesitated, confused, her hand on the doorknob. Was this real—or another vision?

But then, as she opened the door and saw her

father coming out of the bathroom carrying a towel, she knew it was real and happening now, and that Paulette was in trouble.

"Molly!" His eyes were wide. "She's bleeding! Please run down and call an ambulance!" He limped toward the master bedroom as fast as his injured ankle would allow.

She darted down the back stairs, grabbed the phone in the pantry, and realized she did not know the number for the hospital. Instead, she dialed 911, the emergency numbers burned into her brain since childhood but never used until this moment. She sputtered out that her stepmother was having a miscarriage, that they must send help in a hurry. When she gave the address, the person on the other end of the line said decisively that the coast road was blocked by rock slides and the ferry wasn't running. They would send a helicopter. She should stay on the line until help arrived.

But Molly hung up and stood there, trembling. She listened hard but heard no sound from upstairs. Memories of Aunt Ethel's death invaded her and she was loath to climb the stairs, scared to see what was happening to Paulette. There was nothing she could do, nothing they should expect from her. She opened the back door and stood in the doorway, every nerve in her body charged, urging her to flee out over the headland into the dark, wet night.

The rain had stopped for the moment, and the clouds were blowing hard, thinning out enough to let the moon shine through. She looked out over the moonlit headland at the dark shapes of trees and heard the drip of water off the roof. The wind rustling the grass seemed to whisper a message to her: *Don't run*. Resolutely, she shut the door. But she still couldn't bring herself to climb those stairs.

Molly lifted the teakettle off the stove. It was empty, so she added water at the sink before setting it back on the burner. She turned the flame up high. She would make tea. Paulette liked tea. And if Paulette couldn't drink it, maybe her father could. Maybe she'd drink some herself.

She pulled some mint leaves from the plant on the windowsill and washed them, then dropped them into the china teapot. While she waited for the water to boil, she made toast, buttering it thickly. Each of her movements was slow, deliberate. She sprinkled sugar and cinnamon liberally onto each slice, cut the toast into triangles, and arranged them on one of Paulette's rose china plates, listening for sounds from upstairs. What next? Napkins. And teacups. Maybe a few slices of lemon for the tea? Maybe milk? Did Paulette like milk in her tea?

She found a wooden tray painted with daisies in the pantry and assembled the cups and plates attractively. She poured boiling water into the teapot to steep the mint leaves. Finally she carried the heavy tray back up the stairs to the master bedroom. She concentrated hard on each step so she wouldn't trip, and so she wouldn't think of anything else but the moment at hand. She didn't know how she'd have the courage to step back into that bedroom at the end of the hall.

When she saw the pale figure on the bed, the

twisted sheets stained with blood, she backed away, dizzy. The present and past swirled around her like the lace at the curtained windows—intricate patterns woven in tight thread. Where did one thread end and another begin? She couldn't seem to keep hold of the present. Hadn't she been here before?

The urge to turn again and run was very strong. She could be out of the house in seconds, running free.

But she steeled herself. "No," she said aloud, her voice firm. Was she speaking to herself? Or was Clementine speaking? At that moment it seemed the same thing. "No running away." Paulette lay curled tightly into a ball, knees drawn up to her chest.

"Paulette?" Molly murmured and stretched out one hand to touch Paulette's hair.

"I need the doctor," whispered Paulette, tears streaming down her face. "I'm so afraid!"

Without the mousse to make it spiky, Paulette's hair felt baby fine. Molly smoothed it back. "I called for the ambulance. They're sending a rescue helicopter because the coast road is closed in places. And the ferry doesn't run this late. Just hang on. You'll be all right."

"You don't know that! Molly, I don't want to lose my baby . . . !"

"There's not very much blood," Molly said in as comforting a voice as she could manage. She didn't really know how much blood there was, since she carefully kept her eyes averted from the spotted sheets.

"I don't want to die!" wailed Paulette, reaching out a thin hand, clutching Molly's arm.

"Don't even think such a thing!" cried Bill. His face was ashen. He checked his watch. "Damn! Why don't they *hurry?*"

"Maybe you should have some tea, Dad."

He shook his head, distracted. "I'll get some things ready for the hospital," he said, and went to rummage in the closet.

Then Paulette moaned, and both Molly and Bill rushed over. She opened her eyes and tried to sit up. "Oh, no."

Bright red blood trickled onto the white sheets.

"Oh, Paulette." Bill's face was gray. "Molly, we have to do something."

But Molly, too, stood as motionless as a sailboat in a windless cove. What could *she* do? She didn't know the first thing about medical emergencies, she had no training, she couldn't stand the thought of blood . . .

She turned away from the bed and caught sight of herself in the big mirror above the dresser. The mirror flickered, and for a second Clementine's face looked back at her, then it was gone. But as Molly glanced back at Paulette, a vision of Aunt Ethel's haggard face blew through her mind, and with it came memory. Suddenly confident, Molly approached the bed. She pulled back the stained sheet, picked up a clean towel and pressed it between Paulette's legs. Then she shifted Paulette's body to position a pillow beneath her hips. She heard herself whispering gentle words of comfort to both her father and stepmother as she smoothed Paulette's hair. Paulette lay motionless, eyes closed. Bill strode to the windows.

Then Molly heard the helicopter whirring across the headland. "Thank God!" she cried, her strange competence shattered. "I'll go down, Dad."

She tore down the front stairs. She pulled open the heavy door and raced outside. The propeller blades chopped the air as the helicopter hovered in the side yard. Then it landed. Large and white, with the welcome words BENSON EMERGENCY RESCUE on the side in big blue letters, it crouched on the wet lawn like a giant insect.

"Here!" called Molly, running barefoot toward the chopper, waving both hands. "Hurry!" The wide arc of the helicopter's searchlight illuminated the reed grass, waving in the night wind, and the engine seemed to make the headland shudder.

Two paramedics, a man and a woman, jumped down, carrying a folding stretcher. "Stay back!" one yelled to Molly. "Watch out for the blades. We don't have room for another casualty in here."

She led them into the house and up the stairs, looking back over her shoulder as she ran up the steps two at a time. "It's my stepmother, she's having a miscarriage or something. There's blood, and she's fainted! Will she be all right?"

Without answering, the paramedics entered the bedroom. The woman went straight to Paulette, pulling away the towel to check the bleeding, then taking her pulse. The two paramedics eased Paulette onto the stretcher. Paulette opened her eyes as they tightened the straps around her thin body and smiled at Molly. Bill still seemed dazed as he lurched over and grabbed Paulette's handbag from the dresser, then limped down the hall after the stretcher. When he asked whether he could go along in the helicopter to Benson, it was clear in his voice that he fully intended to stay with Paulette whatever anyone said. The paramedics nodded. But there would be no room in the chopper for anyone else.

Outside on the lawn, Bill turned back to Molly, who stood uncertainly behind him in the rain-soaked grass. "I'm sorry, baby. I'll have to leave you alone for a while. But I'll call you as soon as I know anything."

She nodded. He ducked under the propeller blades and pulled himself up into the chopper. The door slammed, and the helicopter rose, its strong blades whirring. For a moment, before it swung away over the headland and out across the water, the air thrummed with noise, and Molly was illuminated in the bright searchlight. She was suddenly aware of her short nightdress and wet feet, and felt small and insignificant beneath the huge machine.

She hurried back inside, locking the heavy front door behind her. The big house seemed to welcome her back, its many empty rooms echoing voices from the past all around her as she climbed back upstairs. She ignored the whispers and went straight down the hall to the master bedroom. She didn't hesitate even a minute but moved to the bed and stripped off the sheets.

She left them soaking in the bathtub. She opened the tall doors of the hall linen closet and selected a clean set of brightly patterned sheets and pillowcases. She made up the bed in the master bedroom, smoothed the bedspread, then turned to leave the room.

But the tray of tea and toast caught her eye. Untouched, it sat where she had set it on the bedside table. She walked over and touched the pot. It was lukewarm. She poured a cup and cradled it in her hands. She was bone tired but less panicky, more peaceful now than she had been since her near-drowning. Her calm was something to do with Paulette, and something to do with Clementine, but her mind refused to analyze her feelings. She sat in the blue armchair by the window and sipped her tea. Then she ate a triangle of cinnamon toast. She raised her eyes and caught sight of herself in the mirror over Paulette's dresser. Was there the softest laugh hanging in the air? The glass flickered, glimmered, and then the face looking back was again, for an instant, not Molly's but Clementine's. When Molly blinked, the rosy-cheeked girl was gone.

Molly bit into another piece of toast, smiling through the crumbs. *At least I helped Paulette,* she thought with satisfaction. She had done what she could. This time she had not run away.

She finished her toast and curled sideways in the big chair, draping her long legs over one stuffed chair arm. She closed her eyes, exhausted but content, and listened to the rain starting up again, pelting the windowpanes. She might even have slept a moment or two.

And then, downstairs, the phone rang.

14

Molly struggled out of the chair. Seven, eight, nine—she counted the rings while flying down the back stairs. *Oh, please don't let Paulette have lost the baby!* Maybe it was Jared. But in the middle of the night?

She skidded around the kitchen table and grabbed the phone off the pantry wall, reaching for the light switch at the same time. "Hello?" she gasped into the receiver.

"I'm sorry to disturb you," said a woman's equally breathless voice, "but we may have an emergency on our hands."

"Who is this?" Someone from the hospital?

"Thelma Binder, over in Benson. Am I speaking to Molly Teague?"

"Yes, I'm Molly."

"We met today—well, yesterday—when you came to The Breakers," said the voice. "When you came to visit Abner Holloway."

Molly recalled the woman in the wheelchair. "What's wrong?" She glanced at the wall clock. It read 2:15.

"We're in a panic over here about Abner," the woman continued. "He's gone."

"Gone?"

"Disappeared, run off—kidnapped like that Clementine he keeps on about, who knows?"

"I—I don't understand," said Molly.

Thelma Binder grew more agitated. "After your visit Abner was in terrible turmoil. All about that cousin of his. At dinnertime he kept on moaning that he missed her, that he needed her, and so on. Sarah and I told him to stop acting ridiculous—we thought he was putting it on a bit, you know? But he got worse and worse. He said he was going to find her before he died. We all went to bed around nine-thirty or ten, I think. But when the night nurse checked the rooms an hour ago, he wasn't there. With all this rain, you know, we didn't even think to look outside. The staff searched the whole house and then woke people up asking if they'd seen him or knew anything. No one does, and he's just not here anywhere!"

"You should call the police, don't you think?" asked Molly, still dazed by lack of sleep. She noticed drops of water on the floor, saw the track of rainwater along the pantry wall. There was a leak in the ceiling, and the rain was falling hard.

"We just called the Benson and the Hibben police, and they're out looking for him. We're thinking, what with all his carrying on about Clementine today, what if he's trying to find her? Sarah remembers that she saw Abner at dinner reading the bulletin board out in the front hall. That's where the week's menus are posted. She didn't think anything about it at the time, of course. But, Molly, that bulletin board is also where the ferry schedules are posted! He could have gone out in this rain looking for his Clementine."

"But the ferries don't run at night," said Molly.

"The last ferry to Hibben leaves here at 11:00," said Thelma tersely. "And the last time anyone saw Abner was around ten when we went to bed. The police are checking the road. It's still closed to traffic, but Abner doesn't have a car, anyway. He may have tried to walk if he didn't catch a ferry. Oh, I'm worried. He's like a child sometimes. And you saw for yourself he's not strong at all."

Molly thought fast. "I'll look around outside and see if he's come up to the house," she said. "If he's not here, I can get Jared and we'll search all around Hibben."

"Bless your heart, dear girl. I'll call you back when I know something, or you call here. All right?"

"Right." Molly said good-bye and hung up. She reached for the flashlight on the top shelf next to the box labeled Camping. But when she pressed the button, it didn't work. She could hear her mother's voice in her head: *Typical Bill!*

She rummaged in a drawer under the counter and found an unopened pack of batteries. She fumbled in her haste to open it but at last had a working light. Rain slapped the windows as Molly walked through the kitchen and unlocked the back door.

The night was cool and windy. The sliver of moonlight that had illuminated the headland when the helicopter arrived had been snuffed out by dark clouds. Rain slashed the trees and flattened the long grass. Molly hesitated in the doorway, then grabbed a jacket off the coatrack beside the door. She stepped out into the rain.

Molly walked around the house. Her father's windbreaker was soaked in minutes. She shone the light around corners and across the headland, but there was no sign of Abner. She ached at the thought of the old man out in this wind and rain and darkness, confused and alone.

She felt like crying when she remembered the little boy's eager face as he begged Clementine to play. She remembered the lined face of the man she and Jared had met at The Breakers. The confusion in his eyes. He was the lone survivor of all the people Clementine's life had touched. That he had run off into the night, searching for something he could never find, Molly knew suddenly, was as much their fault as it was Clementine's. If she and Jared had not visited Abner and reminded him of the past, of his loss, he wouldn't be out there now. Somehow, they had to help him. The best thing to do, she decided, was to take the van and drive to Jared's campsite.

She went back inside and ran upstairs to shed the wet windbreaker and nightgown and put on jeans and a warm sweatshirt. She grabbed an umbrella from the stand in the front hall, hoping it would hold up to the wind. She left the house by the front door and locked it behind her, pocketing the key. She swung herself up into the van, worrying that she wouldn't be able to drive along the coast road even as far as Blueberry State Park, but there was nothing she could do now but try. If the road were blocked, she'd turn around and search without Jared's help.

There were no streetlights. The road was slick. She drove at a snail's pace for safety, all the while urging herself to hurry. *Abner might be anywhere,* she told herself. *He might be hurt.* She eased the big van around a fallen branch in the road, then turned gratefully into the Blueberry State Park campground.

The campground seemed nearly deserted. Only the most intrepid campers would stay in weather like this. Their tents were small, pointy shadows in the rain. She took the flashlight, put up her umbrella, and squelched in the darkness through the muddy pine needles. She crouched before the zippered entrance to Jared's tent. *No way to knock.* She hissed: "Jared! Wake up. It's me."

Rain was blowing under her umbrella. He couldn't hear her. She raised her voice, but he didn't respond. Finally she unzipped the flap and reached her hand inside. Jared was a hump in the darkness. She shook his sleeping bag–covered foot.

He sat up with a start. She could barely make out his features and flicked on her flashlight. He threw up his hands to cover his eyes. "What—?"

"It's me. It's Molly." She lowered the beam.

"Molly! I must be dreaming. I *was* dreaming— about you! God, I can't believe you've come in this weather. Get in here!" He reached for her with a grin, his dark hair tousled.

Pulling back, she nearly dropped the umbrella. "No, listen to me," she said. "Abner is missing. Thelma called me. She thinks he's come to Hibben, searching for Clementine. I want you to help me look for him." Her stomach felt hollow. How much was Clementine's guilt, how much her own?

"What the hell?" Jared started to struggle out of his sleeping bag, then stopped. "Look, I've got to get dressed. Do you have the van?"

"Yes. I'll wait there. Hurry up." She tried to tell herself as she waited that the shaky old man was down in Hibben, safe and warm. Probably he'd gone to his old friend, Grace Wilkins.

A few minutes later Jared climbed into the van next to Molly. "We have to stop meeting like this," he said as she started the engine.

In the light from the dashboard she could see his face, and he wasn't teasing. "I mean it," he continued. "We haven't had a moment's peace together since the day we met, do you realize that? Every time we get together, there's major trauma of some kind or another. I just want to be able to be, you know, *normal* with you. When I saw you just now, I was so glad to see you. I thought—well, never mind what I thought." He crossed his arms and stared, brooding, out at the rainswept night. "I just want this Clementine stuff to be over."

As they drove back to Hibben, Molly told Jared about what happened to Paulette.

"A helicopter—that's wild!" he said. "But is she all right?"

"I don't know yet. Everything is happening at once."

They headed down the hill, headlights cutting a path through the rain. "I hate to bother Grace Wilkins in the middle of the night, but there's a chance Abner went to her," Molly said. "So I think we should go to her house first. She told me she lives in the condos behind the church. Didn't she say number sixteen?"

"With a red door." Jared nodded. "At least it's a start. And even if he's not with her, she may know places where we can look."

Molly parked the van in the lot by the condominiums and they wandered up and down the paths until they located number sixteen. After ringing the doorbell again and again, and waiting almost five minutes, they were ready to give up and go away when they heard a shuffling sound and the outside light went on. Molly pressed the bell again. "Who is it?" inquired a sharp voice. "Don't you know it's the dead of night?"

"It's Molly Teague and Jared Bernstein, Miss Wilkins," called Molly through the door. "We're sorry to wake you up, but it's an emergency. Abner Holloway is missing, and we're trying to find him."

The door to the condominium flew open and Miss

Wilkins blinked at them. She was wearing a pink terry cloth robe and fuzzy slippers. "What's that again?" she asked, fumbling to push her glasses up on her nose. Her cloud of white hair stood on end and she looked confused. "The library doesn't open for hours yet."

"We're not here about books," Molly told her. "We're looking for Abner Holloway." She looked hopefully beyond Miss Wilkins. "Is he here, by any chance?"

"You may entertain your men friends at ungodly hours, my girl, but I do not."

"We met Mr. Holloway at the nursing home yesterday," Jared explained. "And just a while ago they called Molly to say he's missing."

The old woman adjusted her glasses and smiled suddenly up at Jared. "Oh, it's you!" she exclaimed. She opened the door wider. "You'd better come in and tell me about this."

They stepped inside the vestibule. Molly could see into a small, comfortably furnished living room. There were stacks of books on the coffee table and on the floor by the couch. Miss Wilkins took Jared's arm and led him into the room. Molly followed.

As Molly explained the situation, Miss Wilkins's expression grew less sleepy, less vague. "Oh my," she frowned. "This is terrible. Abner must be senile if he thinks he can find a girl who has been gone for more than eighty years. She's probably dead, anyway."

"We know that, of course," Jared told her. "But

if Abner thought she were alive, where would he search?"

"Try the harbor," Miss Wilkins said with certainty. "He told me she always took him to look at the boats. She also used to take him to play in the school yard on the swings, but of course the school isn't a school anymore. It's the antique shop. But it's worth a look."

They stood to go.

"Or try his house," Miss Wilkins added. "Molly's house. That's where he and Clementine spent most of their time together, after all. It was Clementine's job to look after all the children, remember. She must have played with them a lot up on the headland."

"We'll call you as soon as we find him," promised Jared.

"Nothing doing." The old woman shook her head and opened the tiny foyer closet. "I've known Abner all my life," she said firmly. "If he's in trouble now, he'll need all the friends he can get." She pulled out a pair of black rubber boots and reached for her beige trenchcoat and umbrella. "I'm coming with you."

Molly and Jared looked at her, then at each other. Miss Wilkins was so small and frail, and the night was so black and wet. *But the more people looking for Abner,* thought Molly, *the better chance we'll find him.*

Miss Wilkins led the way past the church and around to the back of the antique shop. "This was the school yard," she said. "But now look."

It was a parking lot, empty except for two

overflowing trash cans next to the street lamp. On the other side of the stone wall, Molly could make out the gentle humps of the gravestones in the churchyard. But no sign of Abner.

"I think the harbor's our best bet," said Jared. And they returned to the van and set off. Miss Wilkins sat up front next to Molly. Jared sat in back. Molly switched the wipers on high to help her see through the rain.

"This is just plain terrible," Miss Wilkins said sharply. "Running around in this weather—the very idea." She seemed angry rather than worried about Abner.

Molly and Jared left Miss Wilkins waiting in the van while they ran along the pier and investigated all the boats tied up at the moorings. They walked along the seawall. Then they walked up Main Street and down the other side, stopping to check in every doorway.

"Do you suppose he might have made it up to the headland while we were down here?" Molly was feeling discouraged and angry at the same time. "I can't stand thinking about what he must be going through. And it's all our fault!"

"It is not," said Jared staunchly. "It's Clementine's fault."

"I don't know why he liked Clementine so much, anyway," muttered Molly as they walked back to the van. "She didn't care about him or about any of those kids, really."

He unrolled his window a crack, and the salty wind and rain blew in.

Molly drove back up to the house and cut the engine. Through the rain she could see welcoming light spilling from the upstairs windows and from the downstairs windows of the hallway.

"Any normal person would wait on the porch," pronounced Miss Wilkins as Jared helped her climb out of the van into the wind and rain. "That is, if he were out at this time of night in this awful weather in the first place, which he wouldn't be, of course." She put up her umbrella and squelched across the driveway to the steps. "As you see, he is not here. Abner is not responsible. He's like an impulsive child." She pursed her lips disapprovingly.

"Let's circle the house," said Jared.

Miss Wilkins took his arm. "I'm sticking with you," she told him.

The two of them set off from the porch steps, moving around the house to the left. Molly went to the right. She shone her flashlight, as before, out over the lawn and against the house. Her hair was soaking, despite the umbrella, and her braid hung down her back like a heavy wet rope. Then, at the back stoop, her light flashed on something that made her gasp. The door to the kitchen was ajar.

She shivered in the wet wind as Jared and Miss Wilkins appeared from behind the conservatory. "Look at this," she said, beaming the light. "I came out this way when I searched earlier. I must have forgotten to close it properly."

"We'd better check," Jared said tersely, pushing open the door and stepping into the kitchen. "It's a chance to get out of the rain for a minute, at least."

309

Molly found herself trembling as she led them through the rooms of the house, flicking on lights as she went. She felt jumpy. The thought of the old man alone in the house made the back of her neck prickle. She was glad that the others were there with her.

All the sounds in the big house seemed magnified as they searched. The refrigerator hummed. The clock on the wall clicked. The back staircase creaked. Water dripped from the bathtub faucet upstairs where the sheets were soaking. Molly stood in the long upstairs hallway and shivered. She longed to run into her bedroom and strip off her wet clothes, climb into bed, and pull up the quilt. Walking through the house this way looking for Abner felt like walking down the hallway in her dream. She wanted to scream. She wished she were home with Jen.

It was nearly three-thirty in the morning and her whole body ached. She wrenched open the last door and stepped into a large empty bedroom. "This was the playroom," she said. Jared took her hand in his and a terrible sadness washed over Molly as they stood looking at the empty bookshelves and built-in toy cupboards. There was the window seat where little Abner had pretended to be a pirate sailing in a fine ship laden with treasure. Where was that little boy now?

"Nobody's here," Jared said.

But it wasn't quite true. Molly sensed they all were there—all the Holloways and Clementine, too—right there in the house. They played in the playroom and ran on the stairs. They ate in the dining room and read in the library. Aunt Ethel sighed in her bed, worn and wretched. Uncle Wallace smoked in his study, planning his children's lives for them.

"No telling where he's gone off to," said Miss Wilkins. "Can't be a mind reader with people like him."

Molly couldn't think of any more places to search for the old man. She led the way down the stairs to the front hall.

Behind Molly on the stairs, Jared tugged her wet braid. "You were in her head," he said. "So you should know all the places they liked to play."

"What's that?" Miss Wilkins grabbed his arm. "In whose head? What does that mean?"

Molly sighed. "I don't know how to tell this story, Jared. You can if you want."

As he and Miss Wilkins moved into the kitchen, Molly lingered in the hall, puzzled, gazing into an ornate mirror on the wall. The back of her neck prickled again.

Can't be a mind reader with people like him.

Her reflection flickered.

People like him. Like this man who thinks he's a little boy, who is trying to find his special cousin. People like him, who are lost in the past.

Quickly she closed her eyes and tried to get back into Clementine's head, into her memory. Where had she taken the children? They played up in the playroom. And there was a carriage house. But that had burned one summer. They played out on the headland, too. Hide-and-seek between the bed sheets Janie hung out on the wash line. Sometimes they went into the secret cave—

The secret cave.

But no one would go there now. It was too dangerous now that the shelf had crumbled over the years.

People like him.

Her heart started thumping as fast as the raindrops were pelting the windows. She tried to banish the thought. He'd *never* make it into the little cave now. He would have fallen over the cliff into the churning water of the cove.

The humming was in her ears again. *Lost and gone forever—!*

Jared came out of the kitchen looking for her. "Hey, what is it?"

She was staring into the mirror, and she didn't look quite like herself. Her cheeks were splotched red and her eyes were black pools. Surely her hair was darker.

"Come with me," she murmured.

"Where?"

As she raced out the back door, her flashlight gripped tightly, he followed. Grace Wilkins took time to grab her umbrella before following. Jared scanned the grassy headland as they tore through the grass. "Oh no, you're not thinking . . ."

She *was* thinking. She only wished she had thought of it sooner.

She knelt carefully at the edge of the cliff, Jared

next to her. Holding her breath, she shone her flashlight through the rain, down to where the rock shelf had been. With a groan of defeat she illuminated what was there on the narrow ledge six feet below: one black corduroy bedroom slipper.

"Oh my God," breathed Jared. Then he started shouting: "Abner! Abner Holloway, are you there?" over and over again.

The wind whipped his voice out into the cove. Molly joined him, lying on her stomach in the grass, her hands gripping the rocky edge of the cliff. "Mr. Holloway!" she screamed. "Abner!"

Miss Wilkins caught up to them, panting. She stood gripping her umbrella, her expression unreadable in the darkness. Then she moved forward and called out hoarsely: "I've had it with you, Abner Holloway. Get a grip on yourself, man!"

They were rewarded with a thin wail, and Molly, leaning over the edge, saw Abner's gray head poke out of the cave. When the wind dropped, they heard his feeble cry: "I can't climb up."

"Of course you can't, you old sea dog," shouted Miss Wilkins. "You must have been out of your head even to try to go down in the first place."

"Grace," he said, tipping his face, white in the beam of Molly's flashlight trained on him. "What are you doing out in this weather?"

"Having a lovely picnic, what do you think!" Miss Wilkins stepped indignantly away from the edge. "I'd better go back to the house and call the police. They can send someone to fetch him up."

"Hang on. I think I can get down there and boost him up," said Jared.

"Don't be crazy, Jared." Molly stared past the ledge, down into the roiling cove. "Look at that water. Let's get the police."

The old man, his thin body half inside the cave, half out, was resting his head on the rock ledge as if it were a pillow. "She found you," he moaned. "Clementine told me she'd get help, and now you've come . . ."—the waves crashed against the rocks below, drowning out the rest of his words—". . . so cold."

The rain had stopped, at least for the moment. Jared shook his dark, wet hair back and called down to Abner: "Hang on there, Mr. Holloway. I'm coming down."

"Don't," said Molly, putting a hand on his arm to restrain him.

"He's out of his head," said Jared. "I've got to try to get him." He inched backward over the cliff. Below him foam broke over sharp peaks as the surf pounded the rocks.

"Be careful!" Molly held her breath until Jared's feet safely touched the ledge six feet below.

Holding carefully on to the tufted grass in the rock, he knelt to peer inside the cave. Then he looked up at Molly. "Ready?"

She nodded, her mouth dry. Next to her, Grace Wilkins was holding her hands over her eyes, muttering, "I can't watch. I can't watch. Idiotic old sea dog."

Slowly, slowly, Jared helped Abner to his feet on the narrow ledge. Molly was afraid the shaking of the old man's limbs would be enough to knock both of them off into the rocky cove below, but Jared lifted him easily so Molly could reach over and grasp his hands. She dug her feet into the wet ground to brace herself as she pulled. Abner's grip was weak, and she tightened her fingers around his, pulling him up the cliff as Jared boosted him from below. The rain began to fall again in a steady drizzle. Abner scrambled for footholds on the slippery rock. Finally he lay at the top next to Molly on the grass.

She left him for Grace Wilkins to tend and leaned back over the edge where Jared still waited on the narrow rock shelf. Years ago when the ledge had been several feet wider, there was room for small-boned Clementine and little Abner to stand safely enough until they crawled into the secret cave. But now the ledge was crumbled and slick from the rain and waves, and Jared looked too big to be there. "Now you," she called down to him. "Get back up here." The rain began falling again in a fine drizzle.

"Wait a sec," he called up, tipping his face into her flashlight's beam. "There's something else coming up." He bent down and reached into the cave, then pulled out a large round box.

"The . . . hatbox?" Molly whispered.

"The hatbox!" Jared echoed, shouting up to her. "I can't believe it." He stood up carefully. "Can you catch this?"

He swung the big box back over his shoulder by

the string it was tied with and hurled it upward as high as he could. It sailed through the rain over Molly's head and landed near Abner's feet where he lay on the grass, eyes closed, sheltered by Grace Wilkins's umbrella. The sea crashed against the rocks below.

The force of the throw had unbalanced Jared. "Oh, be careful," whispered Molly as he steadied himself shakily by leaning back against the rock wall and pressing his hands flat on its surface. Then he grasped a handful of grass and started to pull himself up. But the plant pulled away from the rock in a shower of dirt and stone, and Jared slipped back down and landed half on the ledge, half off. He balanced precariously on the shelf, flat on his stomach with his legs dangling over the cliff.

Molly couldn't scream. She felt as if any little sound, any movement, anything at all might send him right over the edge.

"Heavens above!" shrieked Miss Wilkins.

"Molly, help me!" Jared's voice was as wispy as the dark clouds that parted now overhead, as thin as the sliver of moon.

Molly could hear the roar of the water in the cove and felt the rain pelt her head. Water, everywhere. She looked down at Jared. The flashlight wavered in her hands, Jared's upturned face white in its light. He shifted his body on the ledge, legs still swinging over the shelf, trying desperately to get a purchase with his knees. But the rock shelf was too narrow. He dangled there like a rag doll.

She *couldn't* go down there. There was water down there. She would fall into the cove and drown—they both would. Her body broke out in a sweat despite the cold night, and she drew back from the cliff's edge. She couldn't do it. She knew, she just *knew,* she would slip and fall on top of him, and they would both plunge down the rocks, dying together in the cove—again.

Molly peered down at him, her head throbbing with the crash of the waves. Jared's torso balanced on the shelf was all that kept him from death. He couldn't last long, she knew, hanging that way. In a minute or two his strong swimmer's arms would tire and he would have to let go. There was nothing she could do. Sickened, she looked away. She saw Grace Wilkins running back to the house for help. But help wouldn't come in time for Jared.

The roar of the surf seemed to call her name. And then she heard a moan behind her and turned her head. Abner was sitting up, trembling with cold. His eyes were open and wild, but his voice was encouraging. "You can do it," he said. "You can do it, Clementine."

For an instant Molly didn't know who she was anymore. If Abner belonged to both the past and the present, then she did, too. And with that thought, it all seemed so simple. Hob had died, but Jared was still alive. She must do what she could to make sure he stayed that way. It was the least she could do.

Hardly stopping to think, she climbed backward down the side of the steep, slippery rock. She felt for toeholds in the crevices and held tightly to the clumps of grass, praying the dirt would not give way. It seemed an age before her feet touched the ledge. She did not dare look over the side, down to the cove.

"That's it," panted Jared. "Just another step and you're here."

She crouched low, back pressed against the rock wall for support, and reached for Jared. Her fingers closed on his sweatshirt, and he cried out with relief, but she knew they were far from safe. If he tried to climb up onto the ledge now, he would pull her right over the side with him. She had nothing to brace herself with. "Wait," she gasped. "Please wait."

Holding fast, she inched her body toward the hole that was the cave. She slid inside and, with relief, found she could lie flat with her legs and body safely inside the shelter and her arms outstretched to hold Jared. She braced her feet against the dry rock inside and pulled steadily. Jared's weight dragged her forward, but the entrance to the cave gave her something to press on, and she blocked the opening with her body. She pulled hard, and Jared got one knee up onto the shelf. She braced herself again, scraping her cheek on the cave entrance, and pulled harder. This time Jared swung both legs onto the shelf and lay there, sobbing. After a moment he crawled in to lie next to her. They clutched each other in a wordless embrace, their hearts beating as one with the crashing water below. They didn't let go until they heard the shouts of the police above them on the cliff and saw a thick rope harness dangling in front of the cave.

15

They all sat around the kitchen table with the three police officers who had pulled Molly and Jared to safety and gave their reports of the night's emergencies. Molly made more mint tea. Abner looked at his cup distastefully and asked for a shot of whiskey instead. Molly obligingly rummaged in the pantry until she found some. The police officers looked longingly at the bottle, as if they would gladly follow suit were it not for the fact that they were still on duty.

Miss Wilkins poured an inch of whiskey into glasses and set them down in front of everyone. "Go ahead," she urged them all. "Drink up. After a night like tonight, we can just say it's medicine." She drained hers in a single gulp. The police and Jared did, too. Abner helped himself to a second shot, but it did nothing to calm his trembling. Molly sipped hers and the liquid in her throat felt like fire going down. But it warmed her.

The police phoned The Breakers to report that Abner was safe and secured permission from the head nurse for the old man to spend the night—or what was left of the night—at the house on the headland. After the police left there were hot baths to draw and warm, dry clothes to find. Once Abner was dressed in a pair of Bill's running pants and a sweatshirt, Molly helped him to bed in the master bedroom. She placed a hot water bottle at his feet and tucked the quilt around him in an effort to calm his trembling. Abner insisted the hatbox be set next to him on the bed. "It's mine," he said in a truculent child's voice when Molly reached for it. "She gave it to *me*."

The hatbox's pretty flowered pattern was all but rubbed off and stained dark with water. The lid was crumpled and wet from the rain. The blue satin ribbon was missing, and instead it was tied with string. It was the same box, though—Clementine's hatbox—and Molly longed to open it. But then Miss Wilkins came in to rummage through Paulette's clothes for something warm to wear, and Molly turned her back resolutely on the box. Maybe in the morning Abner would let her look inside. If not, she knew she would have to peek anyway.

She found a flannel nightgown for Miss Wilkins and led her down the hall to sleep in Molly's own bed. Molly changed into dry sweatpants and a sweatshirt, and brought down her father's bathrobe for Jared. They carried quilts to the study, and she bandaged his scraped and bleeding hands. Then he painstakingly combed out the tangles from her wet hair. They snuggled up on the couch together and slept.

It was nearly noon when they woke up. Molly smelled coffee. She opened her eyes. Jared's dark hair was an inkblot on the white pillow. He opened his eyes and blinked sleepily at her. "Tell me I dreamed everything," he said.

"What are we doing on this couch together, then?" She threw back the quilt and swung her legs off the couch. It had still been drizzling a few hours earlier when the phone rang, jolting her from sleep again. She had dragged herself from her cocoon to answer. Bill was calling to say that everything was under control and Paulette was all right. The doctors had been able to stop the bleeding before she lost the baby, and they prescribed bed rest for Paulette from now until the baby's birth. They would be coming home after lunch, Bill said, in an ambulance arranged by the hospital.

"That's wonderful, Dad," Molly had murmured, foggy with sleep. "That's great." She would wait till they returned to tell them what had happened after he and Paulette flew off in the helicopter. Was it possible so much had taken place in one night?

Now the rain was over. The fresh day sparkled. She left Jared on the couch and followed the smell of coffee to the kitchen, where she found Abner and Miss Wilkins sitting at the table drinking from Paulette's flowered china cups. They were eating eggs and toast.

"Good morning," said Miss Wilkins, "or afternoon, now. I hope you don't mind that I took the liberty. It didn't seem right to wake you, but Abner and I were ravenous. Would you like some breakfast?"

Molly smiled at them and rubbed her eyes. "Yes, please." She watched Miss Wilkins bustle competently around the big room. Abner slumped over the table. He still looked dazed, and she wondered whether the little boy were still with them. She sat next to him. "Are you feeling all right this morning, Mr. Holloway?"

"I'll do," he said gruffly, lifting his cup. His hand shook and coffee sloshed onto the table.

"What about your heart medicine? Don't you need it?" She accepted a cup of Miss Wilkins's bitter brew.

"Don't see why they can't just give me a double dose later on, if they want." He looked up and his eyes were clouded. "Where's Janie? She's the one who makes the breakfasts."

Oh, no. He's still half in the past.

Then Molly heard the front door open, heard her father's exclamation: "Jared? Isn't that my bathrobe?"

She hurried into the front hall to greet Bill and Paulette. Her stepmother looked small and haggard. Molly hugged her gingerly. Paulette's body felt so frail in her arms, too frail to be carrying the baby who clung precariously to life inside her. "I'm so glad you're okay," she said into her stepmother's soft hair. "You and the baby both."

Paulette hugged her back, then stood back with wide eyes as she saw Grace Wilkins coming out of the kitchen wearing her nightgown. "Hey, no fair having a slumber party without inviting us!"

Molly opened her mouth to explain but caught sight of the dark square of wallpaper at the foot of the stairs, where a mirror in an ornate frame had once hung. Once—long ago? Or when? She turned away, biting her lip, trying to remember. *Who's still half in the past?*

Miss Wilkins was trying to explain. Bill thanked the ambulance driver, who was standing out on the porch. After he left, Bill ushered Paulette into the study. "You need to lie down on the couch," he said. "And how nice that Molly has it already made up for you." He cocked an eyebrow at Molly as he pulled back the quilts and settled Paulette with the pillow beneath her head. "Now let's just move this slumber party in here."

A few minutes later they were assembled in the study, talking all at once, trying to relate all the events of the long night. Paulette settled on the couch, leaving room for Bill at her side. Abner sat in the armchair, sipping his coffee. Miss Wilkins and Jared and Molly all pulled chairs from the table over into a semicircle.

"So it was a busy night, was it?" asked Paulette brightly. "Here I thought I'd be the center of attention, carried off in a helicopter like that, but then I come home and find I haven't cornered the market on high drama after all!"

"Don't be jealous," said Jared, holding up his bandaged hands. "You can have it."

"Well, let's hope there's no more excitement for

you," said Bill, reaching over and ruffling Paulette's hair. "The doctors say it's got to be just about total bed rest if you're going to carry that little baby to term."

"I'm surprised you're out of the hospital so soon," said Molly. "But I'm glad."

"The doctors agreed I can rest just as well here at home," Paulette explained. "If not better." She grinned. "And I'll have you and Billy to wait on me. Better than any nurses in the world!"

"In my day," Grace Wilkins informed them, "women stayed quiet when they were carrying. It doesn't do to exert yourself. I hope you'll keep that in mind."

In your day, thought Molly, *women had too many babies and died young.* "Paulette will be a soap opera addict by Christmas," she predicted lightly.

"But I can't stand television," said Paulette. "The shows are ridiculous."

"We'll get a VCR and some good videos," promised Bill. "What about all the old musicals you like?"

"I'd rather have visions like Molly," said Paulette. "They seem to be a lot more interesting than anything I could watch on the tube."

Miss Wilkins spoke up. "I want to hear more about these visions. Jared revealed only the sketchiest details last night." She looked around at them all. "I think I'm the only one in the dark."

Jared put his bandaged hand on Molly's knee. "Your father and stepmother don't know all that's happened, either," he reminded her. "Go on. Tell them about Aunt Ethel. Tell about Hob and Clementine."

"Hob—my brother?" asked Miss Wilkins. "Now, how could he have anything to do with anything? He's been dead since 1912."

Molly didn't want to upset Abner further by telling her story. But his eyes were closed and he appeared to have drifted off into sleep, so she took a deep breath and began. She related how Aunt Ethel had died and how Clementine had run away with Hob. Jared chimed in with his memories of that night in the cove.

"What an amazing story," breathed Paulette when they had finished. "You guys must be about ready to crawl in a hole and hide—all these tragedies and near tragedies in both times. It's like you're leading double lives."

Tell me about it, thought Molly.

Paulette looked over at her. "I don't think I've even thanked you, Molly, for all your help last night. I was so scared—but you stayed calm as anything."

"It—it came over me sort of suddenly."

"You're quite the hero," said her father proudly. "All in one night—you helped Paulette, saved Abner's life, and Jared's, too."

"I haven't said thank you, either," said Jared. "You were fantastic, Molly. You were more than fantastic. What can I say?"

Molly shifted uncomfortably. "You know," she tried to explain, "in a way it wasn't me at all. I was just making up for what Clementine did—or didn't do."

"And you don't call that being brave?" asked Paulette.

The old man's eyes flew open. He sat up in the armchair, frowning. "Oh no," he said. "Clementine was the brave one."

"Gone clear off his rocker," snapped Miss Wilkins. "Old fool, running out in the rain."

"You stay out of this, Grace. No one said you had to come along for the adventure."

"But of course I had to," she muttered.

"You came asking questions about Clementine," he said, looking over at Molly. "I knew she must have sent you, after all these years. I got upset—"

"You call it 'upset,' Abner?" asked Miss Wilkins. "What I call it is 'crazy.' "

"Now I said keep out of this, Grace!" He lifted the coffee cup in his trembling hand and took a sip. His bony legs shook visibly through the cotton running pants he wore.

"I knew I had to go to her. Took me hours, walking up that steep road. But I knew there was only one place I'd find her. It was her special place." He set down his coffee cup and rubbed his hands together as if to warm them. "I remembered just where the cave was. Felt like yesterday I was last there. I almost fell going down. Conked my head crawling into the cave, I guess. Hard knock. But when I opened my eyes again, I knew it had all been worth it because there she was. Clementine was there."

Molly and Jared exchanged a worried look.

"Seems I lay there for hours. She kept telling me to go on home, but I couldn't get up. Sometimes she was with me, sometimes she wasn't. Finally she said she would have to get help. I waited and waited. But she told you to come, and you came. I would have died if you hadn't followed her back to the cave." He tilted his head back and closed his eyes.

"Clementine's ghost," murmured Bill, looking around at them all. "What did I tell you?"

There was a long silence, then Abner let out a gentle snore.

"But why would her ghost appear to Molly?" asked Grace Wilkins. "A girl down in Ohio? Now what would be the point?"

Paulette spoke up eagerly. "That's why my reincarnation theory makes more sense. It isn't just about Abner. Clementine and Hob had unfinished business."

Jared reached over and touched Molly's arm. "Well, I'm hoping we'll finish it for them, big time."

"Reincarnation's as hard to swallow as ghosts, if you ask me." Grace Wilkins frowned.

"Who'd want to be the reincarnation of Clementine Horn?" Molly scowled. "Pretty bad karma, if you ask me."

Paulette looked over at Molly. "You keep thinking Clementine was the bad guy, don't you?"

"She was the most selfish person I've ever met. She was singleminded and cruel."

"I think you're really being hard on her. All she

wanted was what all the girls I know today want for themselves—and expect they'll get."

When Molly looked at her with raised brows, Paulette nodded. "She wanted a good education, right? And work that paid a fair wage. That's not so much to ask for, is it? You want as much yourself."

"I see what you mean," said Bill thoughtfully. "She wanted an independent life."

"Like me," interjected Grace Wilkins. "Never married and never regretted it for a second." She glared fiercely over at Abner, whose eyes were still closed.

"That's right. But in Clementine's time those desires or needs or whatever were called unnatural. Her determination to get an education was called 'selfishness.' Sure, she stepped on people trying to get what she wanted. But how do we know we would be any different? We haven't been put to the test." Paulette's green eyes were serious. "When people are desperate, they do things they're not proud of. That's what I think happened with Clementine. Later she wished she had another chance."

"And saw that chance in me?" wondered Molly. "Or, you mean, I *am* her new chance?"

"Could be," answered Paulette.

"Damn," said Bill, picking up the empty coffeepot and heading for the kitchen. "I want a ghost for the inn!"

"Tell us about the hatbox," Molly begged Abner when the old man woke up. Bill returned with a new pot of coffee and refilled their cups.

"I'm keeping it to give back to her," said Abner in a querulous tone. "Found it a week after she vanished, washed up on the rocks down by the wharf. Knew it was a sign. She'll be back for her treasures."

Molly could scarcely breathe. "And her treasures—are they still inside?"

"Sure are." He looked at her suspiciously. "But Clementine only lets *me* see them. Not the others."

"She let me see them," Molly told him gently. "Or at least," she amended, "I know what was in the box the night Clementine ran away." His eyes challenged her, and she continued, "There was a gold locket with a snippet of baby hair inside."

Abner coughed sharply "*Eh?* Speak up, girl!" He fastened his eyes on Molly's face.

"The locket belonged to Clementine's mother, who was your own mother's sister. She died in a mine explosion in Pennsylvania with Clementine's father. There was a little doll in the box, too, with a rag body and a china head and yarn hair. It wore a blue dress. Clementine's Mollydolly. Molly—just like me." Abner's face crumpled into a frown. She lowered her voice. "And there's a scrap of red leather."

"*Eh?* What's that?" His arms and legs jerked.

"A scrap of red leather!"

Abner Holloway grew very still. After a long moment he spoke. "You are exactly right, my girl. To the very last detail."

"Oh, Mr. Holloway," breathed Molly. "May I please see the hatbox now?"

He nodded. "It's under the bed in the big bedroom."

Jared jumped up. "I'll bring it down."

Molly felt she was holding her breath. Abner Holloway sat rubbing his hands together. Paulette was smiling again. Bill's eyes were fixed on Molly, his expression unfathomable. Miss Wilkins was frowning, perplexed. Molly closed her eyes. The waiting seemed to take forever.

But then they all heard Jared's feet on the stairs, and Molly's heart hammered hard as he came into the room with the round box.

Abner held it on his bony knees. He looked up and met Molly's eyes with a grin of childish glee. "Ready?"

She nodded, leaning closer to see.

Abner removed the lid slowly.

It was like opening a grave. But a wide smile broke like sunlight across Molly's face when she saw the stained blue fabric of Mollydolly's dress. The painted china face was so faded the features were nearly gone. Most of the glue that held the yarn hair on had dissolved in the seawater, so the little doll was nearly bald. Molly reached out a hand, then drew back.

"No, go ahead." Abner Holloway placed the little doll in her arms. "And the locket, too." He fumbled with the clasp, then handed it over to her. She flicked it open. "Hair included," Abner added.

Molly stared down at the little curls of Clementine's baby hair. She shivered. Jared reached for the locket and she placed it in his palm. After examining it, he passed it on to Bill and Paulette.

Finally, Abner handed over the scrap of red leather. "The only treasure missing is Clementine's favorite book. It was her father's. When I used to beg, she'd show me the maps. Wonderful maps and pictures of far-off places. She'd tell me stories about them. Said she was going to go there someday, in a big ship or even in a plane. I made her promise to take me." His mouth quivered. "She said she would take me with her."

Just as Molly was afraid he would start crying, his eyes grew cunning and he reached over and placed the scrap of red leather on her knee. "Now that's a puzzle for you, girl. Since you know so much, can you tell me how that book washed out to sea, when everything else stayed inside?"

Molly rubbed the old leather between her fingers. "The book didn't fall out. It was burnt."

"What's that?"

"She said *burnt!*" Miss Wilkins told him.

Molly described how Uncle Wallace had thrown Clementine's book into the fire and how Clementine had, later, rescued only that single piece of red leather. "Look at the edges." She handed him the scrap. "See how blackened they are?"

"My father was a scoundrel!" Abner Holloway exclaimed, peering closely at the remnant. "A scoundrel, I say!" He looked alarmingly weak. "Oh, Clementine—my darlin'." He closed his eyes for a second, then opened them. "We used to sing that," he said. "Just to tease."

"Yes," said Molly. "I remember."

The doorbell rang. It was a nurse from The Breakers come to accompany Abner back to Benson. "And it's time for your medicine, Mr. Holloway," said the nurse, opening a brown bottle of pills. "When we get home, the doctor wants to see you. After such an adventure!"

"Oh, I'm fine, just fine," said Abner. He struggled to his feet.

"Just trying to keep us on our toes, is that it?" joked the nurse. She thanked everyone for their help and steered Abner toward the door.

He turned back to them, confusion clouding his face. "But where is Clementine? I need to give back her hatbox!"

There was total silence for a long moment. Molly ached to be able to do something to erase the loss from his eyes. And what did he need more than to know Clementine had not betrayed him?

She crossed to his side and put her hand on his arm. "When I was in Clementine's head," she began, speaking clearly and looking straight into his watery eyes, "I knew just what she was thinking and feeling. On the night she went out in the boat with Hob, she wasn't thinking straight. She realized she had been wrong to leave you. She knew her place was at home with you and the other children. Hob tried to turn back, but he couldn't."

Everyone was looking at her now. Molly trembled with the lie but had to continue. "When the boat sank, her last thoughts were of you, Abner. She was desperately sorry she had let you down and hoped you knew she always loved you best."

Molly held her breath, watching the old man struggle with this offering. A curious mixture of emotions raced across his lined face, and she thought for a moment she had succeeded in comforting him at last. But then he shook his head violently.

"But you didn't die!" he cried. "Because here you are." He reached for her hands. "Oh, Clemmy, you've come back to me."

Molly disengaged her hands and sighed, defeated. She looked helplessly at the others. The nurse patted Abner on the shoulder. "Now, now. Let's go on home, Mr. Holloway."

He pulled away, reaching for Molly. "Clemmy, your treasures!" He tried to give the box to Molly.

She put her hands behind her back. "Oh, no."

His wrinkled hands trembled as he held out the hatbox. "You have to, Clemmy. It's your doll and your locket. The atlas isn't there anymore, but you must want Mollydolly after all this time."

Molly backed away, hopeless tears springing into her eyes.

But then Paulette suddenly moved forward. She plucked the hatbox from Abner and pressed it into Molly's reluctant arms. She spoke briskly. "Thank you so much, Abner! Mollydolly was always so special, wasn't she? What a nice thing you did, hanging on to this box all these long years." She looked up at Molly. "And now, what do you say, Clementine? Aren't you going to thank Abner properly?"

And then Molly understood. She could almost feel the dark braids atop her head and the weight of the long gray skirt. She stepped up and smiled into

Abner's eager face. "Of course I'm delighted to have my hatbox and treasures back again," she said, reaching up to touch his lined cheek, then enfolding him in a quick hug. "You're my good, sweet, wonderful boy, and I can't ever thank you enough."

Abner stopped trembling. "All these years," he mumbled as the nurse helped him out the door, "I saved it for you, darlin' Clementine." Then he smiled, and it was the bright, carefree smile of a happy little boy.

. . . and gone forever

During the weeks that followed, Molly found herself stopping work and standing with wallpaper paste dripping from her brush, listening for the sounds of children. She would linger in the doorway to the study and sniff carefully, trying to detect a whiff of pipe tobacco beyond the scent of fresh paint. But there was nothing. The sudden hum of the refrigerator in the kitchen or the drone of bees over the blueberry bushes out on the headland made her shoulders tense with waiting for the song to begin—but the only music she heard had identifiable sources: the television or CD player or Paulette crooning a sentimental song to Bill. The dream had left her, too. She slept deeply each night and awoke refreshed. The only reflection in the mirror was her own.

Because Paulette was confined to the couch and Bill's ankle kept him off stepladders, Bill invited Jared to move in with them and help with renovations in return for free meals and a place to sleep. He happily agreed to come for the two weeks left before he had to return to Battleboro Heights to teach swimming at the rec center. He slept on the couch in the study at night, worked afternoons at Day's Catch, and spent the mornings with Molly, stripping the old and hanging the new wallpaper. Although Bill sometimes limped in to supervise their work, most of the time they were alone.

Molly and Jared worked companionably, mostly in silence, each keenly aware of the nearness of the other. As Molly measured patterned paper from the big rolls with a tape measure or stroked paste onto long strips of paper with her brush, she felt the band between them stretching all the way across the room to where Jared was pulling old paper off the opposite wall. They were links on the same chain, and when they stood close together to press new paper onto the wall, her whole body angled against his until they touched. The fear and hollow guilt had vanished completely that rainy night on the cliff ledge. Now her body wanted contact with Jared's in a way that Clementine's body had never cared about Hob's.

They finished painting the study walls on their last day together before Jared left for Ohio. As they were struggling to fold up the big drop cloths that protected the floor, Paulette walked slowly and carefully out of the study on her way to sit on the front porch. Molly didn't notice. She wrestled with the heavy cloth, then, annoyed, heaved it over to Jared. She loved the easy way Jared's muscled arms shook out the wrinkles, the heavy material fluttering high over their heads like a sail. She loved the way their fingers touched as they lined up the corners of the cloth and folded it together into a neat square. She loved the look on his face as she, walking toward him with the material still gathered in her hands, stepped right into his arms for a kiss.

Paulette leaned against the door frame and smiled at them. "I see you've got it right this time," she said.

After Jared left, Molly went with Grace Wilkins to flea markets in small towns along the coast. She read books from the library about the *Titanic* and played gin with her father. She even thought about going back to Benson to visit Abner in his nursing home but was afraid of upsetting him again. For her, the weirdness seemed to be over. There were no dreams, no visions. Whatever had been going on was finished.

At the end of July, Bill drove her to the airport in Bangor. He hugged Molly hard when they said good-bye at the gate. But as sorry as he was to see her go, she knew he wouldn't stay, as some people did, to watch the plane take off. Her father would be hurrying back to Paulette. Molly missed her stepmother already and planned to be hurrying back soon herself—at Christmastime when little Star was born. Or little Saint Nick.

The airplane lifted off with the afternoon sun glinting on the wings. Molly sat in a window seat with her nose pressed to the pane, watching the airport terminal grow smaller and smaller. She looked out the window to the east, where the line of sea was disappearing beneath the clouds. She reached down under the seat in front of her and pulled Mollydolly from the hatbox. As she held the little doll on her lap, the memory of cold dark water flowing into her lungs was for an instant as real as anything that had ever happened. But it didn't bring the sucking, lurching terror it once had. That fear was gone now along with the visions, settled somehow back into the past where it belonged.

She leaned her head against the headrest, smoothing Mollydolly's stained dress, and looked out at the sky and puffs of clouds like sea foam below. Then she closed her eyes, listening to the hum of the jet engines, and there was no hidden song, just tuneless humming. She had a sense of herself as a traveler, moving on and on—out of a wild, dangerous land into a new place where the roads were charted and the beasts had been tamed. There *were* more things in heaven and earth, she knew that now.

The second leg of the flight, from Boston back to Cleveland, passed quickly, and soon the plane was landing smoothly. Molly gathered her belongings and moved down the aisle. Jen was waiting at the gate, her smile wide and welcoming. Kathi stood uncertainly behind her and laughed with relief when Molly hugged her. They drove home in Jen's red car with classical music blaring, and Molly felt so normal again, it was almost as if she had never been away at all.

On the grass outside the pool at the Battleboro Heights recreation center, mothers and toddlers swarmed everywhere. Kids from the public high school and from West River Academy lay on towels, soaking up the sun. When Molly arrived with Jen, Derek saw them and cheered raucously from the far side of the pool. Kathi and Michael greeted Molly with hugs. Jen stayed outside chatting with them while Molly went into the locker room to change into the new suit she and her mother had picked out at the mall three days before.

The big room with the rows of metal lockers and long wooden benches was empty except for two little girls rinsing off in the showers. Then Molly heard a voice behind her and turned to see Coach Bascombe striding past the lockers. "Well, Molly Teague!"

Molly bit her lip.

"Here to sunbathe, are you?" Coach Bascombe's voice was teasing.

Molly took a deep breath. "No, actually I'm here for lessons." It was time to get out there and prove that the past—her own past and Clementine's—no longer held her prisoner.

"Well, good for you." The coach looked surprised but nodded approvingly and headed into the showers. "That's the way to do it," she called back over her shoulder in a jocular voice. "Just climb back in that saddle and head for the sunset!"

Molly reached into her canvas bag for her hair clip. Her fingers brushed Mollydolly's china head. She was carrying the little doll as a talisman.

Standing in front of the big wall mirror, Molly pinned her braid high on her head. She started walking out the door, then turned back and peered hard into the glass. Had the glass flickered? But the face looking back at her was her own, pale and calm.

She walked out of the dim locker room into the bright day. The squeals of the children and catcalls of boys leaping off the high dive reverberated in the air. She stopped at the edge of the pool and looked down. The blue surface rippled in the sun. She dipped in a toe, and the faces of Clementine and Hob flickered briefly in her memory. As she blinked them away, she knew quite suddenly and with absolute certainty that if she were to jump in and stretch out her arms and legs, the water would buoy her up. It would hold her just as it held harbor seals and sea gulls, fishing boats and swimmers everywhere.

Then she saw Jared standing alone. He was sporting the official green trunks of the swimming instructors, and he was waiting for her. She walked straight over and put her hand in his. The hubbub of the swimmers receded as he grinned down at her.

"Ready, darlin'?"

And the determined smile that had been Clementine's was now Molly's own. "Ready," she said.

About the Author

KATHRYN REISS is the author of a number of novels for young people, including the well-received *Time Windows*.

Ms. Reiss holds an M.F.A. in creative writing from the University of Michigan and currently teaches English at Mills College in Oakland, California.

Ms. Reiss lives in California with her husband, daughter, and two sons.